Slinky Jane

They walked together up the road out of the village. After some moments, Peter, unable to restrain his curiosity any longer, said, 'Well?'

Turning to him she thrust out her hands impulsively towards him, saying softly, 'Oh, Peter.'

His nerves were jangling. He held her hands tightly for a moment, then he lifted them and pressed the palms to his cheeks, so drawing her nearer to him, and when her face was beneath his, he said again gently, 'Well?'

Staring at him, she swallowed, then asked, 'Could you enter into a game for the next fortnight, Peter?' Her voice was small.

'A game?' His brows contracted slightly but he was still smiling. 'It would all depend upon what the game was.'

'Loving me.' It was an even smaller whisper.

SLINKY JANE

Catherine Cookson

A STAR BOOK

published by
the Paperback Division of
W. H. ALLEN & Co. PLC

A Star Book
First published in 1967 under the Tandem imprint
by Universal-Tandem Publishing Co. Ltd
Reprinted February and October 1971, June 1972,
January and August 1974, April 1975
Reprinted by Tandem Publishing Ltd, September 1975, 1976,
1977, 1978 (twice)

Reprinted in 1979 by the Paperback Division of
W. H. Allen & Co. PLC
44 Hill Street, London W1X 8LB
Reprinted 1980, 1981
This edition 1981
Reprinted 1983 (twice)
Reprinted 1985

First published in Great Britain by
Macdonald & Co. (Publishers) Ltd

Copyright © Catherine Cookson

Printed and bound in Great Britain by
Anchor Brendon Limited, Tiptree, Essex

ISBN 0426 16360 5

CHAPTER ONE

The village of Battenbun lies on a hillside in Northumberland. The village proper is shaped like a half moon, with its back closely wooded, and houses two-thirds of the population of a hundred and seventy-four; which number includes Tilly Boyle's son, Tony the half-wit, seven children of Mamie Spragg, each of whom just fails to qualify for the pseudonym of Tony Boyle, sixty women over fifty, fourteen men over sixty, eight over seventy, and one coming up to ninety.

The last mentioned, Grandpop Puddleton, lives and has lived since he was born in the central house of the village. This house forms the keystone of the village street, and from the outside it appears very picturesque, being built of stones filched from the Roman Wall and the dead quarries, and timber that had once been part of a boat that traded along the Tyne. Inside, it consists of seven rooms, each in its own way a death-trap, with ceilings so low as to brain you with their beams and floors so uneven as to whip your feet from under you. That all the Puddletons born during the past ninety years have survived is a tribute to their staying power.

From nine o'clock in the morning till the light fails, except for meals and the calls of nature, Grandpop Puddleton sits fully dressed and with his cap on before the front window, in his armchair on the raised dais which lifts him a foot above floor level, and watches the milling world of the village pass to and fro, and also what occasional traffic deems to make a detour from the main road three miles away which leads to Allendale.

Cuddled in the nest of the half-moon is the village green – without a pump in its middle, for in nineteen forty-four an

American lorry under the influence of drink, the driver at the inquiry having denied that he was, dispensed with it. And so now there is just a stretch of grass with a ring where the pump once stood, and the grass is divided in two by the feet that will persistently cross it in the same place. Beyond the green is the road, and beyond this Mrs Armstrong's house, which is also the Post Office and General Stores, interrupts one of the finest views across to the South Tyne. Although some miles from the actual river, the fells that run towards it, billowing with woods, heaths and lush green valleys seem but a cascading overture, spilling and tumbling, for ever tumbling, down to it.

At least that is how Grandpop Puddleton sees it, for when he takes his eyes from the interests of the street he is away once more, striding over the fells after his sheep, his dog at his heels, sometimes in the direction of Allendale, sometimes farther afield to Blanchland. Ah, Blanchland is a bonny place, as near as fine as Battenbun. Some say finer, but this is only because more folk see it, for out of the way as it is, it is easier to get at than Battenbun. But whichever way Grandpop goes in his mind, eventually he comes to the river, the bonny Tyne. Some folk madden him when they refer to the Tyne as mucky. They are the folk who never push their noses past Jarrow or Newcastle; they are the stay-at-hyems who don't even know that there is a North and a South Tyne and have never heard of Peel Fell or Cross Fell; they know nowt about their country's history, about its castles and abbeys, its Roman Wall, its patchwork of dry-stone walling, evidence of the art of forgotten men. They are 'pluddy numbskulls'.

When Grandpop brings his eyes back to the village he can see, to the left and without glasses, the far end of the crescent where the painted sign of the Grey Hart swings. And when he turns them right, to the other point of the village arc, he can see the garage, owned and run by his great-grandson Peter. Wherever Grandpop's eyes roam between these two points, to Miss Tallow's house-window drapery shop or Wilkins the baker on the garage side, to Bill Fountain's the butcher on the Hart side, or to the numerous grey stone houses that lean, bend over, or stand back independently from each other, invariably they come to rest on the garage.

It was nearly a year now since Grandpop had been to the garage. His legs one day refusing to obey his orders had deposited him quite suddenly on his buttocks opposite the Mackenzies' house, next door. And Grandpop had said, 'Blast 'em!' . . . if they had to give out why had they to do so on that particular spot and why had he to be helped to his feet by that upstart sharp-shooter of a Davy, who was out to get the better of their Peter at every turn. The Mackenzies were town upstarts, the whole lot of 'em. He'd said that twenty-five years ago when they first came here, and he still said it, and if their sickly-looking, psalm-singing, cow-faced daughter caught their Peter he'd give the whole family hell he would.

This reference of warmth to come was not promised to the Mackenzie family but to his own, composed of his son Joe, his grandson Harry, and Harry's family of three sons, the twins, seven years old, and Peter, twenty-eight – and of course, Rosie their mother, whom he hated, the main reason being her refusal to allow a dog in the house, not even to please Peter, and him the apple of her eye. . . .

Along the street, Peter came to the wide doorway of his garage and listened – over the years he had developed an ear for 'knockings'. He held his big, dark head to one side until a little anticipatory smile appeared on his face, bringing with it the glad thought that something was wrong there.

He could see nothing of the car yet, for just beyond the garage the road turned in a sharp curve, to become lost for miles on the fells before linking up with a main road again.

The knocking, accompanied by a loud rattling, came steadily nearer, but not wishing to appear too eager for what he hoped would be a job, he did not go to the end of the drive to meet the car.

When it did come into view he almost laughed aloud. No wonder she was rattling. In the past eight years he had seen some has-beens in cars, but this beat them all. She looked

7

older than anything that went into the Old Crocks' race, but without any of the spruceness that was the hallmark of such cars.

As the front wheels touched the gravel of the drive the car, with one final splutter, gave up and Peter, moving now hastily forward, looked through the windscreen at the owner before saying, 'In trouble, miss?'

He had hesitated between mam and miss. That the girl sitting at the wheel was a town type he could see, but whether she was old enough to be a mam or young enough to be a miss, he couldn't at such short notice make up his mind.

'Yes, she's given up. . . . Still, I got her here.'

The voice was warm and high, and, as he phrased it, a laughter-making voice, but he was quick to note that it was in strict contradiction to the owner's face. There was no laughter on her face, not even a vestige of a smile, and it was perhaps the whitest face he had ever seen . . . due, he had no doubt, to smart make-up. Yet why they wanted to look like that he didn't know.

He opened the door and she stepped out on to the drive, and again his mind was taken from the car and he thought, By! she's thin. But it was, he also noted, a smart thinness, accentuated by a grey woollen dress pulled in at the waist with a scarlet belt. She was wearing no stockings, only sandals, and his eyes lifted quickly from the matching scarlet of her toe-nails up to her shoulders, on which lay the ends of her long, straw-coloured hair. It looked damp, even wet, as if she had been sweating, and it lessened a little the effect of her over-all smartness.

'Has she been like this long?' He inclined his head to the car.

'About a mile back. I felt her hit something in the road.'

He nodded understandingly. The car was an Alvis, one of the early type, and likely had a low oil sump. 'I'll push her in and look her over.' As he spoke he went behind the car and with his back bent he slowly edged her up the drive and into the garage.

At the opening he turned and looked back to where the

8

girl was now standing in the middle of the drive. She was slowly and methodically wiping her hands on a handkerchief, and she raised her eyes and, looking towards him, said, 'It's a nice little village.'

He nodded. 'None better.'

'Battenbun . . . the name's intrigued me for days. I wanted to come and see what a place with a name like Battenbun could look like . . . it's pretty.' She turned her eyes and looked over the village green. 'And quaint,' she added.

'Aye, it's quaint all right.' He smiled as if she had paid him a personal compliment. 'Not a quainter or prettier village in Northumberland.'

'It's difficult to get at.'

'Well – aye, it is, but I suppose that's part of its attraction.'

She nodded understandingly. 'It hasn't been commercialised yet.'

'No. No, it hasn't.' But how I wish it was, he thought; then chided himself, No, you don't! You know you don't. No, he didn't want Battenbun commercialised, but what he did want was a bit more traffic through and a few more jobs like this one here might prove to be. It was twelve o'clock in the day and but for Honeysett's tractor he hadn't seen anything on wheels go past the garage. And it was a bonny day, a fine day, a day when cars should be whizzing about. They were whizzing about all right, but miles away on the main road.

'How long will it take you to find out what's wrong?'

'Well, I'll get down to it right away. Perhaps you'd like to have a meal. . . . Look, down yonder, at the far edge of the village there's the Hart. Mrs Booth does a good dinner.'

'Does she?'

'Aye, she does.' He smiled as he looked at her; then he took his eyes from her, for she was staring at him in a fixed kind of way. Her eyes, he had noted, were brown, large, like saucers in her white face, but tired, lifeless. Only her voice seemed to hold any animation.

As he looked away from her he happened to see his father running up the green from the direction of the Hart

9

and making for the house. This was so unusual that he lifted his head and his eyes narrowed in the sun. His father never left the Little Manor before ten to one, landing home dead on one for his dinner. And when he waved to him excitedly before entering the gate he was made to think, 'What's up? What's wrong?'

'Do you live here? I mean in the village?' The girl was speaking again.

'Yes.' He drew his eyes slowly back to her and repeated, 'Yes . . . dead centre. Our house is the black and white one.'

'Are all the houses old?'

'Not all – some. Ours is the oldest, goes back four hundred years. It's got the date on it. There's been Puddletons there for over two hundred years.'

'And your name's Puddleton?'

'Yes, I'm a Puddleton. My great-grandfather's alive, and he's near ninety . . . my grandfather is seventy-two.'

'You're all long-livers then here?'

'Yes, I suppose you could say we are. Plenty of fresh air, peace and quiet. Nothin' much ever happens here . . . you can time everything and everybody nearly every hour of the day.'

She was standing gazing at him, her hands hanging slack by her sides as she asked him, 'Do you like it that way?'

Now he became a trifle embarrassed. If he were to speak the truth half of him would say 'Aye . . . yes, I do. I don't want anything to change,' but the other half would say, 'I want a bit more business, and that means a bit more life.' But whichever way he would have answered her was forgotten, for at that moment his whole attention was brought to the village green again, for there in a huddle, and making their way towards him, were his father, his grandfather and his mother. Now what on earth was up!

So unusual was the sight of his family coming en masse to the garage that he had the desire to go and meet them but courtesy told him he had a customer, so all he did was to move a step or two on to the drive and await their coming.

His father, away ahead of his grandfather and mother, reached him first, and one thing about him was strikingly noticeable. His face was abeam. This was unusual, at mid-day anyway, without a drink . . . or a woman to chaff.

'What's up?' he asked. 'Won the sweep?'

'Sweep? No. What d'you think?'

'I don't know.'

'Road's goin' through!'

The effect of these words on Peter was electrifying. His six-foot-two long angular body stretched, his head reared up, and the beam that split his face outdid that on his father's.

'No! Who told you? How did you hear?'

'The major. He's just got back from Hexham. Saw his solicitor, Ludworth. Ludworth told him the road business is set. Of course, the major's furious . . . you know what he thinks about it.'

'This is news, eh, lad?' It was his grandfather speaking, and Peter answered, 'Yes, Old Pop, I should say.'

'We're set for life now.' The old man gazed around him from one to the other, until his eyes alighted on his daughter-in-law, and his look, so evidently full of the pints that future prosperity would bestow on him, wiped the bright gleam from Rosie Puddleton's face, and she said, tightly, 'Not so much of the we!'

'Now! now! Ma,' said Peter under his breath.

The 'Now! now!' was an entreaty, but Rosie would have none of it. Looking up at this great big son of hers, she spoke to him as if he were still in his teens. 'Never you mind, I know what I'm talking about.' She nodded at him, then at her father-in-law, then at her husband, and Harry Puddleton exclaimed, 'That's goin' to start now, is it?'

'It's never stopped as far as you're concerned,' said Rosie; 'you never wanted me to buy the garage for him.' She bounced her head towards Peter. 'It was a dry well you said, no good, money down the drain. Forgetting it wasn't your money that was going down the drain.'

Just as Harry, his face darkening, was about to turn on his wife, Peter put in soothingly, 'Now, now . . . look here, there's enough time for all that later. And anyway –' he threw his glance back to the girl standing in the opening of the garage, and his voice sank, 'Anyway, I'm busy.'

Harry, following the direction of Peter's eyes, stared for a moment at the girl, and the smile slowly returned to his face. Then remembering with a self-conscious blinking the presence of his wife, he turned his attention to the matter in hand again and exclaimed excitedly, 'You'll be busier still, lad. Just think!' He took a step back and his eyes swept over the garage, which had at one time been the blacksmith's shop, then on to the piece of spare ground to the side, and he murmured in something like awe, 'Only garage for miles, and only bit of spare land in village, for it's a known certainty that the major won't let them build on his ground.'

'There's Poynter's tree nursery,' said Rosie; 'he's got a good bit of land there.'

'And a good bit of income coming in from it. He's no fool, he won't sell that.'

'Well, there's the wood . . . don't forget that,' said Rosie, seeming bent on dampening her husband's enthusiasm.

'The wood!' It was Old Pop who turned on her. 'Who's goin' to build on that? The springs have it like a piece of wet yeast. The wood!' he said scornfully.

'They can drain,' snapped Rosie.

'You can't drain springs, woman. They would pop up all over the place, under the floors and everywhere. No, as Harry says, that bit of land –' he pointed towards the side of the garage – 'that bit of land is the only buildable bit for miles, at least where it's needed most, on the main road. The farms can't do nowt, theirs is agricultural land. No, you've no opposition, lad.'

As Old Pop was waving his hand about indicating the absence of opposition, his thoughts suddenly skipped away from garages and land and he, too, became aware of the girl. His grin widened and his eyes brightened, especially the one with the cast in it, and, touching the thin grey tufts of hair on the front of his bony forehead, he nodded brightly and called, 'Good-day, miss.'

The salutation brought all eyes round to the girl, reminding Peter that he had a job in hand, and he moved towards his client, saying apologetically, 'I'm sorry, miss, but we've had a bit of news we've been expecting for a long time.'

'Yes.' She looked from one to the other and smiled faintly; then added, 'I'll go down to the inn as you suggested. Will you let me know the trouble?'

'Aye, I'll come down as soon as I've looked her over.'

She moved away, and as she came abreast of the group on the drive, the cast in Harry's left eye, similar to that in his father's, twinkled and he said, 'Beautiful day, miss.'

'Yes. Yes, it is.'

Their eyes followed her, as if drawn by a magnet, and Peter, standing apart, also watched her go. Her walk reminded him somehow of her voice, lazy yet vital. He couldn't place her at all. She was an odd type, bit of all sorts, he thought. He noticed that she did not take the foot-worn path across the centre of the green but was walking in the grass, and this added to the slight sway at her hips.

It took just this movement alone to arouse the familiar 'Well!' in Rosie. She glanced quickly towards her husband. Like a vulture he looked, as did his father. They were all like vultures, the Puddletons, that is, all except Peter. She glanced towards her eldest son. He was of the same height and build as the other two, big-boned and dark, but not cross-eyed, thank God!

'Well, Dad, what did Grandpop have to say about it?'

This question of Peter's that touched on a still more poignant thorn in Rosie's flesh brought her swiftly from her critical comparison, to put in sharply, 'What he usually has to say, swearing and carrying on.'

Harry, ignoring his wife's remarks, answered Peter with a laugh, saying, 'Cursing his "pluddy" legs as usual, because they won't carry him no father than the back door. But he's game, he made an effort to come along wi' us, didn't he, Dad?'

Old Pop nodded and laughed as he remarked, 'Aye, he did an' all. Some spunk the old un's got.'

Spunk! thought Rosie, with a whirling of agitation in her stomach that she always had whenever this bane of her life was mentioned. I wish his spunk would bring on a fit and he'd die in it, I do, honest to God! Ninety a week come Saturday, and by the looks of him could go on for another ten years. She turned her back on the group and raised her eyes to Heaven in silent prayer, but quickly brought them to earth again as Harry remarked sharply, 'See there . . . there's Mackenzie.'

They all turned, and in silence looked to where a short, thick-set man was edging himself from a car outside the cottage below their own.

'I bet you what you like he's got wind of this, and not just the day either.' Harry turned and looked at his son. 'What made him come last week and ask you for a share, eh? That was funny, when you come to think of it. And after them always holding us up as nitwits for buying. Aye –'

A loud, sharp sniff cut off Harry's words, and brought his eyes to Rosie again as she said flatly, 'I'd like to remind you, Harry Puddleton, that us didn't buy it. Oh, you can come round now.' She waved her hand airily. 'Oh, I know. I also know that you've been on at me for the last six years for spending me dad's money on it.' And she ended, by saying flatly, 'This is Peter's and mine, and the money it makes will be ours . . . see!'

Harry Puddleton glared at his wife. Sometimes she aggravated him so much that he could murder her. He had to keep telling himself that she was a good mother. She was also a damn fine cook. Oh yes, he would always admit that. And their house was the most comfortable in the village – if only she would let you stay in it in peace! But as she got older she was getting worse. He knew that in his wife's eyes he was woman-mad. She had only to see him look at a woman and in her own mind he was already sleeping with her. All the Puddletons he had ever heard of had had an eye for a woman. It was their natural trait, that is – Harry paused in his thinking – all of them except Peter. He sometimes thought that Rosie had thwarted all natural desire in this strapping son of his, for never, to his knowledge, had he had what he himself would call an affair. He was nice enough with the lassies, but nothing seemed to get beyond

14

that. You couldn't call the business of Mavis Mackenzie an affair, although it had caused a stink in the house last night.

Then there was Miss Florrie. . . . But nobody was supposed to know about Miss Florrie, least of all Rosie. Rosie would have a fit if she thought that Peter had any ideas about the major's daughter. He was sure, in his own mind, that Peter hadn't. It was Miss Florrie who was doing the running there. She was a strong character was that young lady and, like her father, usually got what she wanted. But to get back to Rosie. One of these days, if she wasn't careful he'd walk out . . . he would that.

Mr Mackenzie having disappeared into his house, their attention was drawn once again to the girl now nearing the Hart, and to Bill Fountain, the butcher, who was standing outside his shop waving his hand to them while with his hips giving an exaggerated imitation of the girl's walk.

And there's another of them, thought Rosie. Another one that can't keep his eyes at home.

'Look at Bill wobbling his belly . . . mickying her, he is. Oh, he's a lad. Let's go down and tell him.' Harry turned to his father. 'Not that he'll be over-pleased either, for he's got the daft idea the road'll take some of his custom away. . . . Come on. See you later, lad, and then we'll talk.' Harry nodded to his son and, followed by his father, hurried from the drive on to the road, while Rosie, nodding after them, said, "And then we'll talk!" What have they got to talk about?'

'Now, mam.' Peter looked down on his mother. 'Don't go on.'

'They make me sick. What have they ever done to help? They've been at you for years about this place. Saying you couldn't give it away, and you should go on the buildings or some such . . . be another Mackenzie and try to own the village.

'Don't worry, I'll go me own way as usual.' He smiled gently at her. And when she answered his smile the hard lines went from her mouth and a softness came into her eyes, and, patting his arm, she said, 'If you're all right, lad, I'm all right.'

15

He nodded down at her. 'I know that, Mam.' It was a shy admission. And then he added, 'But don't go for Dad, he doesn't mean anything.'

Her head moved in small jerks from side to side. 'Doesn't mean anything! Oh, I know what I know. But there, I must get back and see to the dinner.'

'Be seeing you, Mam.'

He smiled once again at her before she hurried away, and he watched her compact body bustling over the green towards the house. Poor Mam. In spite of her iron will and dominant attitude, he always thought of her as 'Poor Mam.' But she should be better, he thought, when the road came through, for with it would come water, and this would mean a bathroom, one to outshine anything Mrs Mackenzie would have, of course. He smiled to himself. And why not? Why not, indeed! He himself wanted something to outshine the Mackenzies, especially Davy, the only fellow in this village or anywhere else who had ever been able to get his goat.

Honeysett's tractor came wobbling back up the village street, and he waited for it to wave an hello to George before turning finally into the garage to have a look at the job in hand.

Perhaps it was the rumble of the tractor that covered up the sound of the approaching horse, for he had just lifted the bonnet of the car when a voice from the doorway said abruptly, 'Hello, there,' and he turned with a definite look of apprehension on his face to confront a short, slim young woman in riding kit.

'Oh! hallo, Florrie.' His voice and everything about him showed his uneasiness and confusion, and as she slowly approached him he bent his head down towards the engine.

'Look at me!'

His head jerked up and he looked at her where she stood at the other side of the bonnet, and he almost spluttered as he said, 'Now, now, Florrie. Now see here!'

'Why did you do it?'

'Do what?' He had grabbed up a handful of tow and was rubbing his hands with it.

'You know what I mean. You took Mavis Mackenzie into Hexham on Saturday, didn't you?'

'Now, Florrie.'

'Didn't you? And out again on Sunday – didn't you?'

Florrie's voice was so tight that she seemed to be finding it a bit of a struggle to get it past her lips.

As if making an effort, Peter straightened his shoulders and, looking squarely down into Miss Florence Carrington-Barrett's face, said, 'Yes, I did. And what of it?'

'What of it! You are a fool. If I'd been here you wouldn't have had the nerve to do it, would you?'

Throwing the tow into the corner and taking up a fresh lump, Peter continued with his rubbing as he said, 'Look, Florrie, we had all this out last week. I told you it was no good . . . never could be. You'll only get yourself talked about.'

'Talked about!' She almost spat his words at him. 'What do I care about being talked about? It's you who are afraid of being talked about. You haven't the guts of a louse. You're petrified of your own shadow . . . and your mother.'

'Now, look here, Miss Florrie!'

It would seem that the mention of his mother had recalled to his mind the title by which the daughter of the manor was spoken of in the house, and it brought a minor explosion from the young lady. 'Oh, for God's sake! Peter, come off it, and stop the Miss Florrying. You know, I could laugh – if I wasn't so mad I could laugh – you're acting like one of last century's melodramas. Miss Florrie!'

'Well, it won't do. I've told you afore.'

'All right.' Florrie's voice was getting higher. 'Say it won't do, and say you've told me before. Was that any reason to take up with that nitwit after you had dodged her for years?'

'Mavis is all right.'

'Mavis is all right!'

'She's a good girl.'

'She's too damn good. Sanctimonious little hypocrite. She makes me sick. And you do, too!'

'Well, I'm sorry you feel like that, but as I said last week,

17

me mother would have a fit if she thought I was making up to you.'

'Let her, it's about time she realised you are grown-up. You know, when I look at Old Pop and Grandpop and your father, I can't believe you're a Puddleton. Why, they've got more of what it takes in their left eyes than you've got in your whole body.'

A pink hue crept up under the dark stubble of Peter's face; his head moved slowly from side to side; which other woman or man for that matter, of his acquaintance, would refer openly to the Puddleton morals and the family cast in one sentence? What could a fellow do? All he could think to say was, 'By! you are coarse, Florrie.'

'Coarse!' Florrie's scorn was vigorous: 'It wouldn't surprise me to know that you're an hermaphrodite!'

'Florrie!'

Although Peter wasn't sure in his own mind what an hermaphrodite was, he knew, by the way she had said it, it was bound to be something indecent.

'I'm going to tell you something.' Florrie was now stabbing her finger at him. 'If you hide from me behind Mavis Mackenzie you're in for fireworks. Once that little cat has her claws into you you won't be able to get them out, and now that the road's going through, as I suppose you know, her dear papa and brother, for business reasons alone, will see that she keeps them tightly fastened on you. They're not going to let the only garage for miles slip through their hands. They'll have it, with her help, and you. You'll see.'

'Will they, be damned!' Now there was no nervousness in Peter's voice or manner. 'Will they? That's where you're mistaken. There'll be no Mackenzie get a foot in here, not even over my dead body. The garage, as you know, belongs to me Mam and me, and she, like me, would sooner see it go up in smoke than the Mackenzies get it.'

'That's what I couldn't understand. I just couldn't understand –' Florrie was now staring up into Peter's tightly drawn face – 'you hating the Mackenzies like you do and then taking up with Mavis. I just couldn't understand it. Until the reason jumped at me. You hoped to put me off, by

18

doing it. That's the truth, isn't it? You thought I'd have too much dignity to come back at you. Daughter of the major and all that. . . . You don't know me.'

'No, now, see here, Florrie.' Peter's fiery countenance was abetting his guilt. 'I – I can't explain.'

'No, you can't explain, you haven't got the guts to. You'll dance at the hops with me, ride with me, but you won't walk with me. I'm too young.' She mimicked his voice. 'Ten years makes a lot of difference. You don't say you haven't got the spunk to face Mammy, or the village.'

In hopeless desperation Peter closed his eyes. But when he opened them his attitude immediately changed and with a quick gesture he turned his attention hastily to the engine again and whispered, 'Here's Miss Fowler coming.'

'Damn Miss Fowler!' Florrie's voice was low, but not low enough that Peter didn't hear her add, 'and you, too!'

Florrie and Miss Fowler passed each other at the entrance to the garage, and no one would have believed that Miss Carrington-Barrett had just been fighting for a place in the garage-owner's affections, for her voice was airy and not without a little condescension as she said, 'Good-morning, Miss Fowler. Lovely day, isn't it?'

'Yes, it is a lovely day,' replied Miss Fowler. 'But the lawns are parched, really parched, I wish we could have some rain.' Whereupon they parted with nods and smiles.

As Peter filled Miss Fowler's can with petrol he, too, nodded and smiled at her as she chattered, but his mind was not on the one concern of her life, namely, the job of keeping her lawn green, nor yet – although she both worried and scared him with her young, ardent and unmaidenly-like pursuit – on Florrie. But it was agitated, and very much so, by what she had insinuated about the Mackenzies. He knew he had been a blasted fool to take Mavis out, and Florrie had been right about his reason for doing so. He had thought it would put her off, for she was getting beyond a joke. The whole place would soon be talking about him making up to his dad's boss's daughter, and he didn't want that. Why, in fact, the way she had been going on lately, he could see himself waking up one morning in the Little

Manor house having to call the major 'Dad' and his old
battleaxe, 'Mum', and that scared him properly. Florrie was
young and spoilt, and up to now had had her own way in
everything. And if she were to yell loud enough the Major
and Mrs C.-B. might consent even to her latest whim. That
had made him desperate and he'd had to do something.
There being no one of his own age unattached in the village,
or nearabouts, he had, against all his better judgement and
in a moment, so he told himself, of great necessity, asked
Mavis out. The damn fool that he was.

In a sweating bother he tackled the car, and half an hour
later he knew all there was to know about it, and none of it
was good.

After applying more tow to his hands, straightening his
shirt, and trying to flatten down his wiry hair, he gave a
hitch to his belt and made his way through the village in
the direction of the Hart.

A few doors down below the garage, Wilkins, the baker,
was lowering full sacks from the loft, and he turned his
white-powdered face to Peter and called cheerily, 'Good
news, eh, Peter, lad? This'll set the ball rolling, eh?'

'It will that, Dan.' Peter's voice was equally cheery. Dan
was one of them who wanted the road to go through. 'It will
that.' He nodded total agreement. But when he came
opposite Miss Tallow's shop he could hear, through the
open doorway, her thin, piping voice bemoaning the fate of
her beautiful village. Miss Tallow was all for beauty – she
was a rustic poetess was Miss Tallow. Beauty, said Miss
Tallow, rose above everything. Even the Spraggs' cesspool,
brazenly fighting its own battle, could not convince her
otherwise. Beauty must be preserved with the help of Jeyes'
fluid. And she wasn't the only one who thought this way,
either. There were a whole number of them in Battenbun,
Peter knew only too well, who would rather see the village
die a long, lingering death than have one inch of its beauty
disturbed.

A shining yellow brake slowed up sufficiently to allow its
driver to thrust his head out of the window and with a
broad grin yell, 'Happy, Peter?'

'Hallo there, Brian. Aye – aye, I'm happy. Who wouldn't be?'

The car moved on, and Peter, with an inward glow, thought: I like Brian, he's all right. Now why can't Florrie see sense and marry him? He's nuts about her, and no social barrier to worry about there. Farm, money and name. The lot.

'Hello, Peter lad.' It was Bill Fountain, still not in his shop, but standing now across the road on the post office steps talking to Mrs Armstrong, the postmistress. 'Feeling like a millionaire?'

'Well, not exactly yet, Bill. I'll let them get started first.'

He nodded happily in their direction but noticed that Mrs Armstrong did not nod happily back. She was another one of them, for besides the post office she had the only grocery business in the place.

Bill's next shouted remark was lost in a bellow that filled the street, and Peter turned quickly to confront his great-grandfather where he sat in the window of the cottage, the living origin of the cast, hook nose and big mouth; all, in fact, that went to make up the questionable handsomeness of the Puddletons.

'What's pluddy well goin' on? Whole place gone mad and me not hearin' a word. Come here a minute, can't ya!'

'Now look, old 'un.' Peter went through the gate and across the narrow strip of garden to the window. 'I can't stop now, I've got a job in. You would see it coming in.'

'Aye, I saw it, I'm not blind. But I don't want to know about no pluddy car, what about road? Harry's goin' runnin' round as if he'd suddenly found God or summat and Joe, as usual, has made himself scarce. Always was a dab hand at that, he. As for your mother, you try to get her to shut that mouth of hers when she's got nowt to say, but when there's summat to talk about the ornery bitch goes mute.'

Peter smiled tolerantly down on the old man. 'Well, old 'un, you know as much as me. I hear it's going through, and that's all I know.'

The old man's attitude underwent a lightning change; a

21

softness came into his face and his big, bony hand clutched at Peter's arm, and shaking it gently, he said, 'Lad, you're on to summat now. You're set for life . . . you're made . . . thousands and thousands you'll make out o' that garage. I'm tellin' you' – he raised a finger and wagged it in his great-grandson's face – 'that'll be a gold mine, a real gold mine. But mind –' his attitude changed quickly back to its former truculence, and in what he thought was a low tone, but in a voice that would have carried to the neighbours in question, he added, 'But mind you, lad, you look out for them lot.' He thumbed in the direction of the Mackenzies' house. 'They'll be after you like flies in a midden, you're on to a good thing, and anybody that's on to a good thing has the Mackenzies in their way. What do you think?' His voice did drop a shade lower now. 'Joe tells me this mornin' that old Mackenzie's bought shares in the mill – took them by way of payment for repairs. Just like him, ain't it. And Cuthbert's in Allendale is selling their contracting business, and he's after that an' all. I tell you, lad, look out for yersel'.'

'Don't you worry, old 'un, I'll look out for meself where the Mackenzies are concerned.' Although Peter's voice was a whisper it held strong emphasis, and Grandpop nodded and said, 'Ay, ay, you do . . . but lad. . . . Here a minute.' With a backward jerk of his head he beckoned Peter even closer, and his deep-set misty eyes fastened on his face and his voice was thick and rumbling in his throat as he demanded, 'Not true what I'm hearin', is it, you takin' up with their dry cow?'

Peter's eyes dropped, his shoulders drooped, and he sighed, and Grandpop, his voice returning to normal, cried, 'Well, lad, you must be up the pole. Dodged her for years you have. Laughin' stock she's made of hersel', trailin' after you. What's come over you? My God! do you expect to bundle with that 'un? I'm tellin' you you're in for a dis-appointment, for if ever I saw a dry –'

'Now look her, old 'un.'

'Ah! don't you start arguefying with me about she, no arguefying in the world'll put any blood into that 'un.'

Peter straightened up and was about to turn away, knowing the uselessness of argument, when old Grandpop, giving the final stamp to his displeasure, whirled his old lips round and spat towards the bunch of phlox at the gate. Perhaps because of his disturbed state of mind his aim was not so good today and he missed. A suppressed squeal coming from behind him on the pavement gave Peter the desire to duck and dive round to the back of the house.

'You dirty old man!'

The indignant words were almost spat back at Grandpop, and Peter, his expression a mixture of sheepishness and dismay, turned and looked, not without sympathy, at Miss Collins, the vicar's sister. Grandpop's ammunition had not hit her, but that had been only a matter of luck.

Miss Collins's tight-lipped, narrow, sagging face was pink-hued as, trying to ignore the old man who would not be ignored, she addressed herself to Peter. 'Something should be done . . . one can't walk the street. At least, this particular section of it. It's a disgrace!'

'Yes, miss. I'll speak to him.' Peter's voice was very low.

'Speak to him! He should be –'

What Miss Collins would have liked to do to Grandpop seemed too big to get past her gullet, for her neck, after jerking up and down a number of times, only allowed her to swallow hard, and she walked away, her body twitching.

'Pity it didn't hit she. Who does she think she is? Like to run village, she. Pluddy Bridget!'

'Now, old 'un, you'll do that once too often. What's going to happen when me mam hears?'

'Never mind yer mam. She's another of 'em. All women should be smothered.' Grandpop blinked rapidly, champed his lips, then demanded, 'You on your way to Hart?'

'Aye.'

'Bring me a wet, I'm near parched.'

'I can't now, old 'un, I'm going to see a client about the car.'

Peter walked out of the gate and the old man's voice, now low and wheedling, followed him. 'Ah, Peter lad, bring me a wet. Go on, man.'

Peter smiled to himself as he walked on. By! the old 'un

was a tartar. But there'd be the devil to pay as usual when his mam found out, as she would from Miss Collins, about the spitting.

Before he got to the Hart he was hailed a number of times, and he thought, By! the place is like London the day. Never had he known such bustle before, and on a Monday, too. Saturday might see the village street a bit busy like, but the rest of the week it could be dead.

He went into the bar of the inn and Mrs Booth, from behind the counter, asked without any preliminaries, 'You come to see her?'

'Yes, Mrs Booth.'

'She's in the livin' room, havin' a bite. Here –' she leaned across the counter and whispered confidentially – 'what d'you make of her, eh? Some piece that. What d'you say?' She poked at him with her finger. 'I bet you what you like she's just come out of jail. That skin of hers looks like it hasn't seen daylight for months. She looks a type, doesn't she? And what do you think about the road, eh?'

Peter blinked. He'd never had much time for Mrs Booth, never got on with her somehow. Perhaps that was because his mother couldn't stand her. Some talk of her making up to his dad at one time. So without commenting upon her observations of either the girl or the road he said, 'Can I go in?'

'Aye, go on.' Mrs Booth swept the counter clean with her ox-like arm, and he went along the passage towards the 'private' room.

When he reached the open doorway he could see the girl sitting at the end of the table, and she lifted her eyes from her plate and looked at him for a moment before drawling, 'Oh, hallo. You've been quick.'

'Well –' he moved uneasily and gave a little laugh – 'I haven't done anything to her yet.' He went slowly into the room and stood looking across the table towards her. It was as Mrs Booth had said, her skin didn't look as if it had seen much daylight lately and it wasn't the usual pallor associated with blondes either, yet jail! Trust Mrs Booth to jump

24

to the worst conclusion. Likely, as he'd thought earlier, it was just smart make-up.

'Sit down, won't you?'

Peter glanced back towards the door. Mrs Booth was of a funny temper; you never knew how you had her, and him in his dirty clothes. This one here was as easy in her manner and invitations as if she had a share in the place. He smiled to himself and sat gingerly on the edge of the chair before beginning, 'Well, I'd better tell you what I think. You see I could fix her up but it would cost you a tidy bit, so my advice is for you to get another secondhand one. But mind –' he gave a short laugh – 'I haven't got one for sale; I'm not trying to sell you one or anything.'

She was leaning back in her chair, and she looked and sounded very tired as she asked, 'How much would it cost to repair her?'

He bit on his lip as he stared at her, then said hesitantly, 'It's difficult to say at the moment. The big ends are gone. They'll have to be rebored. She'll have to be stripped and reassembled. And the engine's on its last legs. You see, it's hard to say to the shilling what she'll cost. About sixteen pounds, I should think. Perhaps a bit more.'

She stared at him, her dark brown eyes, in sharp contrast to her hair, looking almost black. And then she stood up, and turning her back to him she walked to the window.

He, too, rose to his feet and added haltingly. 'And I'm afraid it'll take some time to get the big ends done an' all.'

'How long?' She spoke without turning round.

'A fortnight. Perhaps three weeks. They have to be sent to a depot. As I said, I think you'd better call her a bad debt and get another. But, of course, it's up to you.'

When she did not answer he thought, you're a blasted fool, doing yourself out of a job. What's up with you? Not a thing in for a week and turning this down. He shook his head at himself and looked at her back and commented privately again. By! she's thin.

As he continued to look at her he saw over her shoulder running from the green towards the bar the twins, with Tony Boyle jangling after them, and Penelope the tame duck, as always, endeavouring to catch them up.

Tony's garbled words came through the open window, crying, 'Le' me Jimmy! . . . Jimmy! . . . Johnnie, le' me! . . . Petter . . . Tell Petter.'

'It's beautiful country here.'

His eyebrows moved up a trifle. They had been talking of cars, but he smiled and said, 'Aye, it is fine . . . Yes, there isn't better. At least, that's what I think. It's wonderful country. Once you've lived here you can't settle nowhere else.'

'I'll stay till she's ready.'

Her abruptness slightly nonplussed him.

She still had her back to him, and he said with a kind of naive surprise, 'Here? . . . But the car, it'll be a fortnight, even three weeks, as I said. It could even be longer, you never know.'

She turned now and looked at him, and her face seemed wiped of all expression, telling him nothing. And when she made no effort to speak he went on, lamely, 'But if time doesn't matter – he didn't add 'and money' – 'it's up to you.'

Her eyes held his in an odd way until he became uneasy, and there came back to him Mrs Booth's comment regarding time, to be thrust aside quickly, and he heard himself asking, 'Are you on holiday?'

'Yes. Yes, I am sort of.' She walked to the table again and sat down. 'They take boarders here?' She was looking intently down on her half-eaten dinner.

'Yes, they can take two. There's nobody staying at present.'

'Then I'll stay until you put the car right.'

She smiled up at him, and he was quick to notice again that there was no brightness in her eyes, the smile just touched her lips.

'It's up to you.'

'Yes, it's up to me.'

Like the look in her eyes, there was an odd quality about her reply, and he stood awkwardly confronting her. She was the most unusual customer he had come across for a long time. In fact he couldn't remember having met anyone quite like her. And her voice . . . He found he wanted to listen to her speaking. 'You American?' he asked with a grin.

'No.'

When she did not enlarge on this, he said lamely, 'Oh.'

'Psst! Peter! Peter, man!'

He turned sharply to the window, and there, just above the low sill, were the faces of his brothers, and high above theirs the wide, flat, gaping countenance of Tony Boyle.

'Here!' They gesticulated wildly to him.

He frowned at them and said sharply, 'Get away now. I'll be out in a minute.'

The girl had turned in her chair, and from the three faces she looked back enquiringly to him. And he grinned again and said with something of embarrassment, 'Me brothers.' Then added hastily, 'Not the top one, He's Tony. He's – he's just a trifle odd.' Trifle, he thought, was putting it mildly, but people were scared of the word mental.

'We've got sumthin' to tell yer, Peter . . . aw! Peter man.'

The two small heads were thrust well into the room now and Peter, looking distinctly uncomfortable, commanded 'Get away! Get yourselves off. Now! This minute!'

They stared at him in some surprise; then instead of doing as he had ordered they transferred their cheeky glances from him to the girl.

Hastily now he made for the door, from where he turned and asked, 'Will I bring your cases?'

'It would be very kind of you.' Her lips were smiling again. The situation with the bairns seemed to have amused her.

Without further ado he went along the passage and out of the side door, for he did not want to encounter Mrs Booth. Somehow he didn't quite know what attitude Mrs Booth would take on knowing the girl was to be a guest, but one thing was certain, Mrs Booth would be glad to have someone in, for trade at the Hart most of the week was almost on a par with that of the garage.

As he came out into the sunshine the twins came pelting round the corner with Tony behind them, and he greeted

27

them with a sharp 'Now, look! Quiet a minute! And you listen to me.' He held out his finger and stabbed it at them. 'When I'm talking to anybody you keep your tongues still and keep away, or I'll pay your backsides for you, the pair of you. And you too, Tony.' He looked at the creature who was almost as tall as himself.

'Me, Petter? Me, I found –'

'You shut yer mouth! I'm goner tell him. It's a fish, Peter, like an eel, only bigger. It's in the little lake,' said Johnny in an excited whisper. 'Come and see.'

'A fish?' The sternness slid from Peter's face.

'Aye. A great, long big 'un, a whopper.'

With a smile now forcing its way from the depths of his eyes, Peter looked down on the twins and said, 'A whopper, eh? How big? Like that?' With his large hand he measured about six inches, and the twins cried in chorus, 'No man, no!'

'It's as big as Tony, it is. It's as long as him!' Johnny nodded towards their gangling playmate, and Jimmy added, 'Aye, it is. It's as big as Tony, honest!'

'Big, like me, Petter. Big!'

The smile was hidden behind Peter's narrowed lids now as he said, 'You're having me on. You know there's no eels in the lake, nor fish bigger than me hand.'

'I'm tellin' you, Peter man. Come and see, man, for yersel. It's lying below the bank in the clearing.' Jimmy took on a dignity that doubled his seven years.

Peter, more puzzled now, surveyed them in silence. He knew what type of fish there were in the little lake, but he also knew that there must be something unusual there for the twins were no fools where fish were concerned. They had been bitten with the bug from the time they could toddle. All the Puddleton men were crazy about fish. And so the lure of this enormous one was too much for Peter. For the moment he forgot about his client, her car, and her cases, and in a whisper he said, 'Well, look, we'll have to be slippy, 'cos I'm busy. You, Jimmy, run down and tell your Grandpop to keep an eye on garage. Then come up Wilkins' cut and you'll be there as quick as us. Go on now.'

Hardly had the words left his lips before Jimmy was away, and together with Johnny and Tony, and Penelope quacking her disgust at having to start another trek, he hurriedly went into the road, skirted the wall of the inn yard, and getting under a broken fence ran across the field, and within a minute was in the wood. Another two minutes of running and they were all scrambling in single file through a narrow opening in a high wall of bramble and on to the only firm piece of bank bordering the lake.

Throwing himself down on to the edge of the bank, Johnny pointed into the water, saying, 'It was just here.'

Peter's eyes followed his small brother's fingers, but there was no sign of a fish of any kind. He knew the elusive ripple of the carp, the squiggle of the roach, and the dash of the salmon, but there was nothing here, only a little family of tiddlers sporting in a splash of sunshine.

'It was here.' There was a keen note of disappointment in Johnny's voice. And when Jimmy came pelting through the hedge crying, 'Have you seen it?' he spoke dolefully down into the water, 'No, it's gone.'

'Was it an eel? You know what an eel's like,' said Peter, looking from one to the other.

'No, it wasn't an eel,' said Johnny. 'We know an eel, man. This was big. It was like an eel, but longer, yards longer.'

At this moment the quack-quack of Penelope came from behind the undergrowth, and Peter, nodding in the direction of the duck, said, 'You're not having me for a Penelope, are you?'

It was a family joke.

'No, honest Peter, am I, Johnny?'

Johnny shook his head gravely.

Suddenly there came a spluttering yell from Tony. 'There! . . . there! Petter . . . fish . . . fish.'

'Where? Steady man, where?'

'There! Petter.'

Peter's eyes searched the expanse of water indicated by Tony's great flapping arms. And then he saw it, and he silenced them all with a lift of his hand. He watched it slithering about in a shallow, its long body gleaming like silver against the mud, and he lowered himself slowly down on to the bank and gasped, open-mouthed, scarcely believing what he saw. The length of it! The length of it! Four foot, if an inch. What would it weigh? Ten, twelve pounds, perhaps more. It was the biggest eel he had ever seen – or thought to see. He was actually shivering with excitement. Never had he seen an eel of any size in this lake; in the rivers, aye, in both of the North and South Tynes. He had seen one about two foot long once, slithering past at Featherston's Bridge, but this one here was beyond even a fisherman's nightmare! She must be ten inches round.

The eel slid forward, the light on her turning her to mother-of-pearl; she was like a floating stream within a stream. She moved nearer, and did she look at him? Everything now was wiped from Peter's mind – garage, road, women, and cars to repair. She was a beauty. By, lad! she was – a wonder. Oh! if his dad could only see her. He wouldn't believe it unless he saw her with his own eyes. But they must be careful who they let on to about her, for if the village got wind of her every man jack would be after her. He gave a gasp as she flashed out and away, but his eyes tight on her he managed to follow her to where she went into deeper water against the sunlit bank and became still on the mud.

Their heads were all close together now, their eyes concurring to the one point, and Peter, letting out an excited hiss of breath through his teeth, said softly, 'Mind, all of you, don't breathe this to a soul, except Dad. Do you hear? And you, Tony?'

'Aye, Peter.'

'Aye Peter.'

'Not me, Petter.'

'Are you fishing?'

Not having heard the approach of anyone with whom the voice that asked this question could be associated, they almost overbalanced into the water, and Peter, swinging up to his feet, turned to face the guest of the Hart. And his colour rose just the slightest when he thought, Lord! her cases.

'I was passing and I heard you.' Again she asked, 'Are you fishing?'

'No, no, not just at the moment.' He scratched his head, then by way of explanation gave a short laugh and said, 'The lads here told me of something I couldn't believe. It sounded like a Lambton worm story, but it's true all right.'

'What have you found, a ten-pound salmon?' Her voice was slightly mocking.

'No, there's no salmon in this water, but there's something here that I never expected to see.' His eyes narrowed at her. 'And I bet you've never seen anything like it.'

'What is it?' She moved forward, and he, pushing the twins to one side, knelt down on the bank and beckoned her to him. And when she was kneeling by his side he pointed along the bank and down into the water. 'See that, down there?' He felt as well as heard the gasp she gave, and her thrill of excitement went through them all as she exclaimed, 'Why! it's an eel.'

'You've seen one afore?' There was a trace of disappointment in Peter's voice. She didn't look the type who would know anything about fish, let alone eels.

'Dozens.'

'Dozens?' There was open disbelief in his tone, and she turned her face to his as she repeated firmly, 'Yes, dozens.'

'Where did you see them?'

'I was born in Norfolk. I lived by the river for years.'

Well, didn't that cap all! And he had thought she was an American.

She was looking at the eel again, and he looked at the back of her head, not more than a foot away from him, and unconsciously he sniffed. She had a nice smell about her, different from the scent that Florrie wore. But then Florrie only wore scent at a hop, and then it couldn't cover up the smell of the horses. And Mavis's scent. . . . He cut off his thoughts abruptly.

'Oh, she's a beauty! Has she been here long?'

'I shouldn't think so. I come here pretty often and I haven't seen her afore. I've never seen an eel of any kind in this lake. Too far from the rivers. I'm wondering how long she'll stay.'

'Not for long, I shouldn't think. She's full grown, ready to go back.' She moved her head in admiration, and her drawl was more defined as she added, 'She's a real Slinky Jane.'

They all looked at her, and Jimmy gave a giggle of a laugh, and hung his head as she turned her eyes towards him and asked, 'Well, what do you call them?'

'Nowt, miss, 'cept eels.' He looked up at her under his brows and smiled, and she returned his smile and said, 'We always called them Slinky Janes.'

Jimmy giggled again. Then Johnny joined him, and Tony, not to be outdone, let out a high, hysterical yell, which brought the girl's eyes sharply to him. She stared at him prancing like a dervish, until Peter cried, sharply, 'That's enough, Tony!'

'He's perfectly harmless.' He spoke reassuringly under his breath, his face turned towards the water.

'I'm sure he is, I'm not afraid.' She moved casually around and looked in the direction of the eel again.

Her hair fell forward on to her face and caused him to comment privately that she looked better like that . . . younger. Yet he knew now she was no young lass, not with that air and that walk she wasn't. And a young lass couldn't possess that something which lay in the depth of her eyes, like age or –

He stood up abruptly, saying, 'I'd better be getting back. I'm sorry, miss, about your cases. I'll bring them down right away. The trouble with me is I can never resist a fish.'

'No?' She turned her head, and for the third time in their short acquaintance she looked steadily at him, and her scrutiny made him feel as gangly as Tony, as if he were all arms and legs, so it was in a very self-conscious tone that he said, 'There's just a favour I'd ask of you, miss. We're not going to let on about it.' He nodded towards the water, 'Except to me dad. If the men of the village knew there was one of her size here, there'd be open competition to net her.'

'Oh, no!' She was on her feet now, all her casualness

gone. 'Oh, no! I wouldn't like to see them do that . . . she's making for home – the Sargasso Sea to breed – she must have a chance.'

His eyebrows moved the slightest. She even knew that. 'Aye,' he nodded, 'that's where she'll be bound for. So you won't say anything, miss, down at the Hart?'

'No, no, of course not.'

'Thanks. I'll get those cases down right away for you. Come on, you lot.'

He marshalled his brothers and Tony and the quacking Penelope through the opening, and just as he was about to follow she said, 'I have nothing better to do, I could sit here and ward off intruders.'

He didn't know whether she was laughing at him or not, but he answered, 'Aye, you could do that, there's worse things than sitting by the lake.' And just for a moment he returned the concentrated look in her eyes before swinging about and following the boys.

CHAPTER TWO

By six o'clock that evening not even its owner would have recognised the Alvis. From the bits of her that lay strewn about the garage one could be forgiven for thinking that she had been shot to pieces. Peter had decided to give her a 'fair do.' If the girl was determined to put her back on the road, well, she would be as good as he could make her, although he realised that, in this particular case, that wasn't saying much, for he was no miracle worker.

The afternoon had been exceptionally hot, and now feeling both tired and hungry he decided to pack up for the day and go home. Towards this end he straightened his back, wiped the sweat from his forehead with his forearm and inhaled a deep breath, and was about to go into the office to get the key to lock up when a low, red M.G., coming to a skidding stop almost an inch from his pumps, caused him to turn on it a countenance that was so full of fury as to make him almost unrecognisable. Gone was the loose-limbed, easy-going and, at this moment, tired individual; in his place was a dark, taut, glowering mass of anger. And without any preamble he barked in a voice that almost outdid Grandpop's, 'Now! Davy Mackenzie, I've warned you about that trick afore!'

'Aw! man, be quiet.' The slight, dapper young man eased himself out of the car and came into the garage. 'You're frightened of the death you'll never die, and your pumps an' all. Look, they're still standin'.' He pointed. 'Calm down, can't you?' He stood surveying Peter's convulsed face with a grin that drew up one corner of his thin, clean-shaven lip. Then his eyes slowly, almost insolently, dropping away, he walked round the stripped Alvis, his raised eyebrows clearly showing his opinion of it, and coming to a stop outside the office, he kicked at the upturned beer box which was old Pop's seat. Then from this he turned sharply about, stretched his chin out of his collar and began, in a tone which sounded in direct variance to the one of incitement he had just used, 'Now look, Peter, I'll come straight to the point, I'm after something.'

'You're telling me!'

'All right! all right! don't bawl. I'm telling you. Didn't I say I was? Well, here it is. Dad's bought up Cuthbert's haulage business, and I won't deny we're stuck for a place to park the lorries. I offered you four hundred pounds for a share. Now I'll go further, we'll give you nine hundred pounds for the lot. There, we can't be fairer. And you know me, I don't shilly-shally. It's a darn good offer, let me tell you, for as a garage it's a dry well and you know it.'

When disturbed in any way, Peter's hands became restless, and he was now rubbing them with tow as if they were made of cast iron. And he kept his attention on the process for some moments until he could force himself to say, with a semblance of calmness, 'And you're offering me nine hundred pounds for a dry well, nine hundred pounds just for

34

a place to stick your lorries in! It's not because the road business is settled, is it?' Without raising his head he raised his eyes and looked at Davy, and Davy, blinking rapidly now, had the grace to look sheepish, and he blustered, 'Why man, that's been in the air for years, it's only another rumour.'

'It isn't in the air any longer, and you know it. It's no rumour. I can see you offering me nine hundred pounds for a place you said a few days ago wasn't worth five hundred altogether; I can see you jumping four hundred overnight for a piece of land to stick your lorries on.'

'Well,' Davy wagged his head, 'All right, say it's as you say. What if the road is going through? It's a fair enough offer. And when it goes through, where are you going to get the money from to expand? I ask you that. You might raise what this is worth,' with a disparaging gesture he waved his hand about the garage, 'but I'm telling you money's tight these days and you'd want at least three thousand to build any kind of a show here. Of course, there's always the other side to this.'

'Aye, I know,' Peter put in quickly 'partnership. I think I've heard something of that afore an' all. Now look, once and for all Im not selling, and I wouldn't have you, Davy, for a partner and you know it, at least you should if you weren't so bloomin' thick-skinned.'

This statement, which left nothing to doubt, did not apparently hurt Davy's feelings for he replied, even soothingly, 'All right, all right, don't lose your rag. Huh! I've never met a bloke like you, Peter – like a lamb with everybody else in the place except me. It's funny, I've never been able to understand it.'

Peter looked at Davy scornfully. Davy Mackenzie would suck up to a cobra if he thought he'd get a share of its venom. Then his scorn gave place to a leaping anger, as Davy in a soft, sly undertone said 'And there's our side to this you know, Peter, for if you're thinking of coming into our family I don't suppose you'll be above taking anything that comes our Mavis's way, will you?'

For a moment Peter found himself unable to speak, but

when he did it was like a spluttering explosion, as he roared
'Well, I'm not coming into your damn family, so don't you
worry.'

They stared at each other in silence until Davy said, 'Oh!
so you're not, eh?' There was no sign of amusement on his
face now, nor laughter in his voice. Whereas the refusal of
his offer for the garage had not, seemingly, touched him,
this second refusal brought a tautness to his whole body
which showed that he was not only surprised but, in his
turn, angry.

'No, I'm not. And what I do is my business! Get that.'

'But there you are mistaken, lad. It isn't just your business, she's me sister and you're not going to play fast and
loose with her.'

'Now look – get out!' Peter's attitude again left nothing
to doubt, but Davy stood his ground and the two men
glanced angrily at each other, as they had done at intervals
since their school days.

As always, Davy was the first to recover, and he did so
on this occasion quicker than usual, saying, 'Aw! Peter man,
we're fools. What's between you and Mavis is your business,
as you say.' He stared a moment longer at Peter, waiting for
a retort; and when all he got was the continued fiery glare
from Peter's eyes, he gave a laughing 'Huh!' before turning
away, saying, 'I'll look in the morrow.'

'You can save your feet.'

The car roared round the garage drive and away along
the village, and Peter, pelting the tow into a corner, cried,
'Damn!' and then again, 'Damn!' Why did he let that
fellow get under his skin? There wasn't another person in
the whole world who reacted on him as Davy Mackenzie
did. And him suggesting that because he had been out twice
with Mavis he was thinking of moving into their family.
My God! Florrie had been right.

He strode into the office, grabbed up the key, and made
for the door, there to be confronted by the subject of his
thought in the flesh, Mavis herself.

That Peter was astounded by the sight of Mavis was
plain to be seen. It would almost seem as if Davy had willed

36

her out of the air and dropped her here to further both his and her own cause.

'Hello.' Mavis's slightly bulging blue eyes blinked up at him while her lips made a vain but refined effort to meet over her slightly protruding teeth. Everything about Mavis was refined. From her too small shoes to her neatly permed hair there was a tight, prim compact refinement about her. And it had thoroughly soaked itself into her voice, for Mavis did not speak 'North Country' except for a few revealing words. But she spoke a twang of her own, which she considered very refined-like.

'I thought I'd look in and see you . . . I got off early.'

Peter did not speak, he only stared.

'Oh, it's been hot in the office today, sweltering.'

Still Peter said nothing.

Mavis looked up at him through slightly narrowed lids now; then she smoothed down her gently heaving bosom with one hand and, lowering her lids, said, 'Oh, I got annoyed today. That Mr Pringle was on again . . . pawing. Really, I think I'll have to leave there.'

Peter's greasy hands ran through his hair. Why in the name of heaven had he let himself in for this. He had known on Saturday night that he couldn't stand her, yet he had to go and ask her again for Sunday. He must have been barmy, clean barmy. Even Florrie didn't warrant his putting up with Mavis Mackenzie for two nights, and one more night of her would drive him round the bend. She had always got on his nerve, which was why he had constantly striven to keep her at a distance. And then he had let himself in for . . .

'Are you going anywhere tonight?'

The sweat ran down from his tousled hair, and he pulled a lump of tow from his back pocket, muttering as he did so, 'I've got a big job in.' He nodded back to the dismembered car.

Mavis putting her head to one side, looked at the skeleton frame of the Alvis and an understanding, even a maternal gleam came into her eye. For Peter she would even babysit to a car. 'I'll come along after tea and keep you company,' she said.

Her eyelids were drooping again and her lips straining to meet, when Peter's voice, with a distinct note of panic, brought them all wide.

'No! no! you'll not, thank you very much. I've got me hands full. I can't stand anybody – I mean –' What he did mean he couldn't bring himself to say, and he turned from her muttering something about shutting up, and with a great deal of 'to do' brought the garage doors together and locked them.

'What's up with you?' Mavis's voice was slightly off its refined key now, and he answered her over his shoulder, 'Nowt's up with me.'

'I thought we –'

He clipped the lock into place with a loud bang, saying 'You shouldn't think; people take too much for granted by thinking.'

'Well!'

He was compelled now to turn and face her, and he nodded at her and said, 'Aye . . . well?'

'I want an explanation.' Her head was up and her lips had almost accomplished the impossible.

He forced himself to throw out his chest. 'And I want me tea and a wash . . . I'm tired.'

As he marched away another swelling 'Well!' hit his back, and he thought again, Aye, well, you can go and tell your menfolk that. They would have to think again if they were going to try and hook him through her.

But although he was thinking in these strong and firm terms he was feeling anything but strong and firm. As Florrie said, Mavis would take some shaking off; it would take more than a little incident like this to get her off his track.

He was still agitated and was sweating visibly when he entered the house, and he hadn't got his hands under the tap when his mother, from the kitchen door, demanded, 'Who's Slinky Jane – do you know?'

He turned quickly. 'Why?'

'Listen to them.' She lifted her head to the ceiling, and he

38

put his head to one side in an effort to make out what the lads were singing.

Rosie's face split into a grin as she said, 'It's a song of some kind they've made up about somebody in the village, listen.'

'Slinky Jane's a girl with style.
For Slinky Jane I'd walk a mile,
Through a dark wood and over a stile,
All for Slinky Jane.'

'It's a nice tune, catchy. Never heard it afore, have you?'

'No.' He grinned back at her, then turned to the sink again. The lads had never made that up. Likely it was the girl. And his mother thinking it was somebody in the village. Funny that.

There followed a short silence before Rosie, her tone now completely altered, put in abruptly, 'Your dad's not in yet. If he's gone to the Hart again the night afore coming home there'll be summat to do here, I can tell you.'

Ignoring now the nice tune which was still going on, Rosie banged the cups on to the tin tray and Peter screwed up his eyes against the soap and her voice, as she gave him a sample of what she would say to Harry when he did come in.

O, Lord! He gave a quiet moan. That was one thing he couldn't bear to listen to – his mother going for his dad, even if she was in the right. The security that the house offered from Mavis tonight would, he saw, have to be waived. Yet as he finished drying himself he realised that he had left it too late for even the bus into Allendale, and also that the danger consequent on a walk was not to be considered, so there would be nothing for it but the Hart. The Hart was one place into where Mavis wouldn't follow him; they were all teetotallers, the Mackenzies, too damn mean to be anything else . . .

He had washed and changed and eaten his meal so quickly that Rosie, suspicion gathering on her brow, demanded, 'Going some place the night?'

'The Hart.'

She had warned him about the Hart in the past, saying 'You don't want to get like him,' 'him' being his father, but

39

now there was a look of undisguised relief on her face. Far rather the Hart than that Mavis Mackenzie, and she smiled at him and there was no sting in her words as she said, 'I'll soon have to take all the meals down there.'

'Aye, you might an' all. That'll be the day.'

They both laughed together now at the improbability of such a happening.

As he let himself out of the front door Grandpop's voice, endeavouring to be hushed, came to him heavy with warning saying, 'Watch yerself, lad. One after t'other's been at the window. On the look-out for somebody I should say. You didn't say to meet her the night, not by her face as she passed here, you didn't, and they're puzzling their pluddy heads as to where you might be off to.'

Peter did not reply, only cast a warning glance in his great-grandfather's direction. Nothing escaped the old 'un. You'd think he'd be past taking an interest in the goings-on, but not he. Although he had a tongue that would clip clouts, he was generally right in all he said. And he was right again this time, for as he went out of the gate he detected a watcher behind the Mackenzies' fancy-curtained windows. This fact lent wings to his heels, and he was within a few yards of the Hart when he heard the unmistakable click of the Mackenzies' gate. He did not turn to ascertain who might have come through it, but it took all his control not to sprint the last few yards to the inn.

Once safely in the bar parlour he glanced through the window to see if his assumption had been right, and yes, there she was crossing the road away from the contamination of the wicked place. He heaved a sigh that released a grin to his face, then he answered the remarks being thrown at him from the regulars, as one after the other they called:

'Goin' to stand us one for the road, Peter?'

'Peter Puddleton, made millionaire through being only one in village with bit spare land and garage.'

'Guess of all the lot of us you're the one who's going to gain by this, Peter.'

'Well, it serves you right,' he threw back at them. 'Old Parkinson was trying to sell that place for years, and you laughed at him. You see, them that laughs last laughs longest.'

'What's yours, Peter?' Mr Booth's flat voice asked of him.

'Oh.' Peter turned back to the counter. 'A burton please, Stan . . . small. . . . Dad been in?'

'In, and still is.'

'Where?' Peter looked around.

'Darts with the lady.'

Slowly Peter's eyes moved along the room, but they couldn't go round the corner to where the dartboard was. What they did take in, however, was the fact that nearly all the customers were seated in positions which enabled them to take in – the corner.

Nonchalantly taking up his glass, he walked to a point from where he, too, could have a view of the proceedings, and he was just in time to see the girl poised to throw a dart. He watched her thin body give a slight twist, then jerk forward. For one brief second the chatter and laughter ceased, then one voice after another cried, as if to proclaim the achievement for the first time in history, 'Double twenty! double twenty!'

'Double twenty! Lordy, lordy. Why, miss . . . not first time you've seen dartboard.'

'Why, I be jiggered! What's she got?'

'Double twenty.'

'Double twenty? No! That's the second time she's done it.'

Peter smiled to himself and turned away. It was evident that his client had caught on.

The dart players were moving from the board now and coming towards the bar proper. The girl was walking with his father on one side and Bill Fountain on the other, and Peter kept his head turned away, but his ears were wide to his father's voice as he said, 'What's it to be this time, miss? Now come on, make it something stronger than grapefruit.'

'Hallo there, lad.' Harry addressed Peter's back, and Peter, turning as if in surprise, said, 'Oh, hallo there,' before adding under his breath, 'been home yet?'

Harry's beam didn't actually fade, but he looked sharply

at his son while saying quite pleasantly, 'No, not yet, lad.'
Then turning to Mr Booth he added, 'Two bitters and a
grapefruit, Stan.'

'Hallo, Peter.'

'Hallo, Bill.'

Bill Fountain looked like an outsize Billy Bunter who had
just brought off a scoop of some kind, the kind in this case
being not far to seek. Really, thought Peter, both his dad
and Bill looked like a couple of old roosters in the spring.

And now it was the girl who said, 'Hello.'

'Oh, hallo there, miss.' It was as if he had only just
become aware of her presence, and although he smiled his
voice was slightly offhand.

The girl's gaze was full on him as it had been earlier in the
day. It seemed an odd trick of hers to look you dead in the
eye, and for all his outward seeming casualness it disturbed
him, made him sort of uneasy. He didn't know whether he
liked her or not, but he felt sure that if he didn't he was the
only one in the bar who had come to such a decision. In
spite of this feeling he couldn't help but notice things about
her, for instance her eyes. Behind their directness they
looked tired, very tired: yet in their depths did he detect a
hint of laughter? This suspicion made him turn away from
her, but determining not to be outdone by his sire, in small
talk at least, he leaned his elbows on the bar counter and
asked lightly, but under his breath, 'And how's Slinky
Jane?'

The girl reached out for her glass of grapefruit and took
a sip from it, then looked away from him across the counter
to a row of bottles on a high shelf, before answering with
equal lightness, 'Very well. Thank you very much.'

He had the desire to laugh at the way she said this, and
strangely now he began to feel excited, as if they were
discussing in code something of great import.

'When did you see her last?' he asked, still under his
breath.

'About an hour ago. Are you going to have a look at her
before it gets dark?'

Peter finished his beer in one long drink before commit-

42

ting himself – Mavis was still lurking in the back of his mind. Even so he heard himself say, 'Yes, I think I'll have a dander down and see her.'

No sooner had he said it than he knew he had done a damn silly thing, and he almost twitched the glass off the counter when her voice came softly to him, saying, 'I think I'll have another peep at her, too.'

He turned his head sharply and looked down at her. His mouth was slightly open in an attempt at a protest, then he looked quickly away again, straight ahead and into the mirror, and to his consternation he saw that there was hardly a man in the room who wasn't looking in their direction. If he walked out of here with her the village would be set alight, and if they were seen in the wood together . . .! Frequenters of the wood were the odd fishers going to the lake, the few children of the village, and courting couples. And at present there were only three couples courting strongly enough to warrant their retirement to the wood.

The pink hue was glowing under the dark stubble of his face when she said very softly, and with an unmistakable gurgle in her voice, 'I'll get my coat and dander across.' She stressed his word dander. Then she turned from him to Harry, saying, 'Thanks for the game.'

Immediately Harry broke off his conversation with Bill and gave her all his attention. 'You're very welcome, miss . . . it's been a pleasure. I'll be happy to play you any time, win or lose.'

'That goes for me an' all.' Bill was swelling visibly with this anticipatory pleasure.

As she smiled from one to the other of the older men and Harry bent towards her beaming his broadest, Peter wondered what it was about his dad that made him get on with women. Apparently they didn't seem to notice he had a cast in his eye, yet it wasn't a thing that could escape anybody's notice. Perhaps it was his unselfconsciousness – and nerve. He wished he had inherited a bit more of both himself.

As the girl walked out amid a chorus of 'Good night,

mam' and 'Good night, miss', Mrs Booth came in from the saloon, and having given her list of orders to her husband, she turned and faced the three men, saying, 'Enjoying yourselves, gentlemen?'

'Now, now, there,' said Harry. 'What'd you mean by that?'

'What do I mean? There's no fools like old 'uns.'

'What do you think of that, Bill?' Harry turned his straight eye, full of assumed indignation, on his pal, and as Bill's stomach rumbled with his laughter preparatory to a juicy retort Peter moved away from the counter. He was in no frame of mind to listen to further gallantries, either from Bill or from his father, though they were directed this time towards Mrs Booth. Moreover, he told himself, he couldn't risk staying here in case the girl took it into her head to look in the bar again on her way out. 'Twixt her and Mavis he saw himself now between the devil and the deep sea.

As he reached the open doorway leading to the porch, Harry called, 'You off, lad?' and without turning round he threw over his shoulder a terse, 'Aye.'

Mrs Booth's eyes were on him as he left the bar, and when they noted that he did not turn towards home she went swiftly into the passage and towards the back of the house, and Bill, turning quickly to Harry, said, 'Say, Harry, your Peter know her afore she come here?'

'You mean?' Harry jerked his head upwards indicating the guest room.

'Aye.'

'No, he never seen her afore the day.'

'Fact?'

'Fact. Why?'

'Well' – Bill scratched his chin and gave a deep-bellied chuckle, which managed to convey a complimentary note – 'he's a Puddleton all right, and miles ahead of you, Harry, though I'd never have believed that possible.'

'What you mean, Bill?' Harry's face was straight.

'Well, didn't you hear 'em, man? Christian names it was, and all very intimate like. Sylvia Jane he called her. 'And

44

how's my Sylvia Jane?' he said. Just like that. S'fact. You not hear him?'

Harry had just lit his pipe, and the first full draw went scutting down his gullet like the shot from a gun, bringing him doubled up and choking.

'Steady on, man,' said Bill. 'Gone the wrong way?'

'That's your lies choking you,' said Mrs Booth, now behind the counter again. Then apropos of nothing to do with choking as Harry, red in the face, continued to cough, she said, 'I've just ascertained –' she liked a long word, an educated word, did Mrs Booth – 'I've just ascertained that our guest has gone for a walk in the wood, and it near on dusk. And she's not the only one what's decided to take the same road.'

With a significant nod of her head Mrs Booth departed with a full tray, and Harry, still coughing and dabbing his mouth, said, 'It's as you say, Bill, he takes after me.' With one long drink he finished his beer, then stated, 'Well, I'd better be off an' all. Missus'll be after me else. So long, you old potbelly.' Harry aimed a sham blow at the protrusion, then went out laughing, and Bill laughing in return, leaned his back against the counter and sipped at his beer. By! Harry was a lad, wasn't he?

His thoughts on Harry, it gradually dawned on him that he hadn't yet seen him pass the window on his way homewards. He must be still in the yard. Or was he? Slowly Bill scratched his head.

After having finished his glass of beer and having joined in sundry bits of conversation without taking his eyes off the window, and still not having seen Harry pass, Bill went out into the yard, but could see no sign of his mate. What prompted him to look over the neat hedge of the Booths' garden down to the fence at the bottom and the field beyond would not have been clear to anyone else but himself. There was a gate in that fence, and it was only a hare's leap, so to speak, from there to the wood. 'Harry,' said Bill half aloud, 'you didn't oughter do it.'

Bill looked about him. There wasn't a soul in sight and twilight was deepening. Nobody could accuse him of any-

thing for walking down the bar garden, could they now? –
he was a keen gardener himself – and once through that
gate. . . .

It is astonishing how fast fat people can move when
necessary. Bill certainly moved swiftly down the garden
path, and Mrs Booth moved back more swiftly from the
yard door into the bar and to her husband, who, behind the
cover of a china rum barrel, was measuring whisky into a
wet glass.

Putting her head close to his, although the din did not
occasion her whispering, she gasped, 'What do you think?
Fountain . . . he's gone sneaking up the garden into the
woods after her.'

Mr Booth turned his long horse-face towards his wife,
but no change appeared in his expression. 'Fountain? That
makes two of 'em. Guess young Peter went.'

'Three, if I know anything. Harry Puddleton an' all.'
Mrs Booth looked angry and sounded incensed, but the
only alteration in Mr Booth's face was that it seemed to
stretch to even longer proportions as he commented briefly,
'Safety in numbers.'

'Safety in numbers! I'm not putting up with it.'

'Shut tha mouth.' It was an order. 'The likes of her bring
custom. You'll see, the morrow night we'll be packed out.
Keep your tongue quiet. Say what you like to them but
nothing to her. As for Harry Puddleton . . .' Mr Booth left
the statement unfinished and turned away, and after a lift
of her chin and a prolonged stare in her husband's direction,
Mrs Booth flounced about and into the saloon again.

It was evident that Mr Booth, if not quite master in his
own house and of its mistress, was in absolute control of the
bar and its proceedings.

As nonchalantly as his long legs would allow him Peter had
attempted to saunter through the wood. Should he by
chance be seen, he was out for a stroll; or he could be going
fishing. Without a line, and it on dusk? No, that one
wouldn't do. Anyway, whose business was it what he did?
His shoulders went back and his head went up, but its

position was uneasy. What if Mavis should ... To the devil with Mavis! And Florrie as well, for that matter.

This way of thinking was indeed daring, and his native cautiousness questioned it and asked tentatively: but wouldn't it be awkward for him if he were seen at this time of the evening in the wood with the boarder from the Hart? As quickly again he defended himself. She wasn't the reason for his coming here – ten-to-one he wouldn't come across her anyway – he was going to the pond for a minute to see the eel, and then he was going straight home to his supper and an early night. Aye, that was all very well, put like that, but he'd have a job to talk himself out of it if he were seen with her, wouldn't he? This cautious pricking was too much for him, and abruptly he left the main path and made his way over the soggy ground and through under-growth that was almost shoulder high, and somewhat dishevelled in his appearance and disturbed in his mind he came at length to the path along which earlier in the day he had led the twins, and so to the lake.

There it lay before him, dark-shadowed, beautiful, yet eerie. But there was no sylph-like figure bending over its water. Slowly he walked to the bank. It was funny she wasn't here. He looked across the water to where a small shoal of rudd was feeding, snapping up at the black gnats, which through weariness or fly bravado were skimming the surface. Perhaps she'd lost her way – you could you know. Well, she had found her way here twice already the day. ... Aye, but now it was dusk.

From the far bank a moor-hen skidded into the water, followed by her mate, leaving double rows of light catching thin froth in their wake. They swam towards the great dead oak that lay half submerged, its head almost reaching the middle of the lake. He brought his eyes from them to the darkening water below his feet, searching for the silver line that would betray the eel. But there was no movement except that of the little bleak dizzying about. She had, he surmised, taken refuge out in the middle of the lake, or at the other side where it was deeper; it wasn't likely that she had gone yet. He'd come again in the morning, earlyish, but now he'd better go and see where she was, she, this time, being his client. If she had wandered off the path and into the sog she might get a bit of a fright, and it on dark an' all.

He was in the act of turning about to leave the clearing when her voice came to him. It startled him and at the same time brought his brows together, for she was saying in her soft gurgle, 'That's a real fishy story, Mr Puddleton.'

'No, it's a fact, miss, true as I stand here.'

That was his dad, and not gone home yet. Well really, it was a bit thick. No wonder his mam went on. He felt a sudden unusual anger against his father, and turning quickly to the bank again he knelt down and concentrated his gaze upon the water.

'Well, I'm damned! You beat us to it, lad.'

Peter cast his glance sideways for an instant but did not speak, and the girl, moving quickly across the grass to his side, said eagerly, 'Is she here?'

It was odd but he found it impossible to give her an answer, so shook his head; and when she knelt down beside him with her coat-sleeve touching his arm, he thought, she's as bad as him. It amuses the likes of her to encourage an old fellow. Yet in calmer moments he would be the first to admit that his father carried his age even a little too well, for he could pass for fortyish any day. To his added annoyance he again became conscious that she smelled nice.

'She can't have gone,' said Harry; 'ground's like powder. And there'll be no dew the night either. Look' – he went down on to his hunkers at her side and drew her attention as he pointed to some bubbles on the surface of the water – 'there goes an old stager. I've always wanted to catch she . . . an old carp. Ever seen a carp, miss?'

'Yes. Oh, yes.'

Always wanted to catch she! Peter jerked himself to his feet. His father was always wanting to catch something, even if it was only a smile from a mere stranger like the girl here. Was it any wonder that the Puddleton men had a name in the village. And not only in the village. Oh, give over, he chided himself. What was up with him? He knew his father's

48

ways, and there was no use in getting ratty. But he was ratty.

'I'm off,' he said.

'Here, wait a minute, hold your hand!' Harry turned sharply, almost overbalancing himself, then stood up. And as he looked at his son his face sobered for an instant and something came from his eyes that could have been an appeal, an appeal for understanding of a nature that refused to recognise age. And something of it did come over in his words as he buttoned up his coat and said, 'I'm getting back home, lad, your mother'll be waiting. I'm well over me time the night, but I never could resist a fish, you know that.' He paused, and smiled, then nodding to the girl where she was still kneeling on the bank as if deaf to the conversation that was going on over her head, he said, 'I'll say good evenin', miss.'

'Oh! Good evening.' She turned towards him now. 'And thank you for your company.' She stressed this with a little inclining movement of her head.

'Thank you, miss. It's been a pleasure. So long.' He nodded to Peter, then went through the gap.

The girl remained kneeling, her back to Peter. He did not move from where he was, and with silence hanging between them they gazed over the pond. So quiet did they remain that the night sounds became loud; a rabbit scurrying through the undergrowth, a vole gliding into the water that he was used to, but was she? Yet none of them he noted had had the usual effect. She had not exclaimed at the sight of the rat, or jumped as the bat swooped above her head, which was odd for a town person.

He watched her now slowly rise to her feet. Then as she dusted down the front of her coat, she said, 'I don't think we'll see her tonight, do you? Not in this light.'

'No.' He smiled quietly at her, for the moment all embarrassment gone.

'We'd better be getting back then.' Her eyes were high up under her lids, looking at him.

'Yes.'

Why couldn't he say something besides yes and no? He

managed more than that with Florrie, or even Mavis.

He had turned and was about to lead the way out when the sound of steps breaking harshly through the undergrowth checked him. And then came the sound of a voice, which he recognised instantly as Bill Fountain's, and although it was hushed and held a cautionary note, and was full of Bill's deep rumbling laughter, his sharp ears caught the words clearly as Bill said, 'Aw! you can't hoodwink me man Harry, but you didn't oughter do it.'

'Don't be so bloody soft, Bill.' His father's voice was muffled, yet loud. 'I tell you it was an eel.'

Peter threw a quick glance towards the girl, then away again.

'Ooh! Oh, Harry!'

'Look, you great lumbering, fat fool, come back here a minute.'

As Peter heard their feet scrambling nearer, he chewed on his lip for a moment; then somewhat sheepishly he sauntered back to the edge of the bank. But the girl didn't move, she was standing with her head bowed, and he had the uneasy feeling that she was laughing at him. And then her next words startled him, bringing the colour up to his hair. 'We'd better prove the point, hadn't we?'

He shot a swift glance at her, and she made a little face at him.

'What point?'

Without answering she came with unhurried steps to his side, and, deliberately kneeling down again, she leaned over the bank and gazed into the darkening water.

He stood looking down at her. By! she was a cool customer ... experienced. He wondered how often she'd had to prove the point. And in the moment before his father and Bill Fountain made their appearance a number of questions raced through his mind. Where was she from? Where was she going? What had she done? Who was she, anyway, with her pale skin and that tired look on her face, which robbed it of what he thought to be her natural youth? Yet she wasn't young, her ways weren't young. Where had she learnt to be so smart on the uptake, on this particular kind

50

of uptake, anyway? With men. Aye, with men. Perhaps in pubs – she threw a dart like a man. Yet she didn't really look or sound like a brash pub-type. And she knew about eels. . . .

Harry was not wearing his usual grin when he made his reappearance, closely followed by Bill, but before he could give any explanation the girl turned from the bank and, with slightly feigned surprise, said, 'Oh, hello. You've come back again.' Then to Bill, 'Hello, there.'

It appeared all of a sudden as if Bill's weight was becoming burdensome to him, for he threw it from side to side. As for Harry, his jaws champed a number of times before he managed to bring out, 'I wanted to show him where we saw the eel, miss.'

'Oh, the eel. Well, it was just about there.' As she pointed Bill moved to the edge of the bank and peered down into the water; then glancing at her, he asked, 'Fact, miss? An eel here?'

'Yes . . . fact. And a real beauty, too.'

'No – can't believe it.' Bill shook his head. 'We're miles from the river. Up above it an' all. Who found her?'

'The twins,' said Harry butting in. 'And it's like this here, Bill: if Mackenzie or Crabb hear of it, it's so-long to the eel.'

'Aye, I see.' Then as Bill looked at Harry his expression became puzzled. 'You not going to catch it yersel', Harry?'

After moving his head impatiently, Harry's eyes steadily avoided those of his son and the girl, and concentrating his gaze on his mate as if Bill were a backward youth who had to be instructed in the rudimentary habits of eels, he said, 'She's on her way back to the sea. She's likely had a tough enough time getting here. I believe in giving any fish a sporting chance.'

'You do, Harry?' This charitable characteristic of his friend where fish were concerned was evidently a new one on Bill.

'Yes, I do.' Harry's head bounced once. 'And for your information her name's Slinky Jane.' He laid some emphasis on the Slinky, making it distinct from Sylvia.

51

'Slinky . . . Jane!' Bill's lower lip was hanging in an astonished gape.

'Yes, the lady here christened her.' Harry indicated the lady without looking at her.

'Well, I'll be damned! Slinky Jane.' Bill's round, bright eyes rolled in their nests of fat. They went from Peter to the girl, then on to Harry, then back again to the girl. And he chuckled, 'Good name, miss, for an eel. Never heard one like that afore for 'em.'

'No?' The amusement came over in her voice. 'We always called them that when we were children. What name do you give them here?'

Whatever answer Bill would have given to this was checked by the bark of a dog, and from quite near, and the bark caused Harry to jerk his head up. 'God above! that's Felix, and where he is the Major's not far behind. I don't want to have to go over all this again, come on.' He nodded to Bill, and Bill, somewhat reluctantly, said, 'Aye, yes;' then touching his forehead in salute, he added, 'Be seeing you, miss – and,' he chortled, 'Slinky Jane.'

Peter's one desire at the moment was to follow on the heels of his father and Bill, the last thing in the world he wanted was to explain about the eel to the major. The major wouldn't believe a word of it. Unless he saw it he would be harder to convince than his father had been this afternoon. And the major would talk. He would talk about the eel not being here, of the impossibility of an eel ever reaching this water; and he would, as likely as not, cap every remark with a quotation, for the major had a known weakness for quotations. What was more, if he found him alone here with the girl, he wouldn't be above putting two and two together and making it a topic of conversation at breakfast tomorrow morning. Peter had a swift mental picture of Florrie descending on him again.

'Come on, let's get out of here.'

In his eagerness to be gone he forgot for the moment to whom he was talking.

'Why the hurry?'

He threw a glance back at her, and then said, 'I'll explain later. Come on.'

When they were out of the clearing he found that he had to make a quick decision. If he went back the usual way he would like as not run into the major, so there was nothing for it but to go down the beech drive which would bring them out by the church.

'We'll go this way,' he said, turning sharply to the right. 'We'll have to go in single file for a bit. You'd better keep close behind.'

They had gone quite some distance before he spoke again, and then it was just to throw over his shoulder the evident fact that it was, 'Almost dark now.'

Her voice sounded very small, as she answered, 'Yes,' and he realised that she was some little way behind, and so he called, 'You'll have to keep up and watch where you're going here.'

He slowed his pace a little but she still seemed to keep her distance, saying nothing. Once he heard her stop, and he turned. He could just make out that she was loosening a bramble from her coat. He knew his father would have sprung back to her assistance, but all he could make himself say was, 'You all right?'

'Yes.'

Somewhat reluctantly, he moved on again, until he came to where the path broadened into the beech drive. Here it was darker still, and he stopped and waited for her to come up, and when she did they walked on, now side by side, but in silence.

All about them was a quietness. There was no wind, there were no night noises here, no rustlings, only the sound of their feet on the leaves. He looked up into the thick, dark mat of the beeches. It was like the roof of night, for he could see no light through them. He cast his eyes sideways at her and wondered if she were afraid, and thought how odd it was to be walking in a dark wood and with her, when only a few hours ago he had never set eyes on her. He found himself wishing she would speak, just say something – anything. But instead she made a noise which sounded like a

strangled cough, and he felt rather than saw her grope for
her handkerchief. A little farther on she made the noise
again. They were nearing the end of the beech wood now
and it was getting somewhat lighter, and when they came
to where the oaks took over he saw the moon coming up –
she was heavy and gold-laden, and almost full. It was, he
thought, as if her rising had stilled the wind and silenced
the wood. He liked the moon. He could never really describe
the feeling the moon had on him; he only knew that he liked
her hanging over his village, draping the mountains and
washing the valley bottoms with a light that did things to a
man and transferred his life momentarily to a dream place,
where the secrets of his inner world were no longer secrets
but took over with a naturalness that made his days seem
false.

Peter had moments when the deep poetry of the hills took
hold of him, and this was one of them. His natural shyness
and slight gaucheness were sliding away, leaving him with
words with which to break the silence. And he did break it,
to quote of all things, Wordsworth. Softly the words slipped
out as he gazed up at his inspiration:

> 'She was a phantom of delight
> When first she gleamed upon my sight:
> A lovely apparition, sent
> To be a moment's ornament.'

So beguiled was he in this moment that he saw no double
meaning in the oration, but he was abruptly brought from
his moon-dream to a dead-stop, and was suffused from head
to toe in a hot, prickling glow. In a lather of embarrassment
he jerked his head stiffly to the side and peered at the girl.
She had stopped, and with her handkerchief pressed over
her mouth she was struggling to suppress her mirth. She was
standing in a patch of moonlight, and he could see her face
plainly. And now she gasped, 'D-don't look like that. Oh . . .!
I'm – I'm sorry.' She seemed in pain with her laughter.

'Go on – laugh,' he said, 'it does you good to laugh.' His
voice was cold and had an edge to it. She had one hand
round her waist and was holding herself closely, and her

head dropped forward as she said, 'I've – I've got to – to – to laugh. I must – I must. Let me laugh.'

His face was dead straight. 'There's nobody stopping you.'

Once more she looked up at him; then turning swiftly to the solid trunk of the oak she leant against it, and to his actual amazement laughter burst from her afresh and mounted, peal on top of peal, and so ringing was it that he had the idea that it stirred the trees, for at that moment the top branches swayed and the leaves rustled, building up a wave of gentle sound to pass over the wood. But her laughter outdid the rustle, and in real panic now he thought, They'll hear her in the village. What was she laughing at, anyway? Just because he had said that bit of poetry? Surely it couldn't have tickled her that much. It wasn't ordinary laughter; it sounded a bit hysterical to him. He went close to her, saying, 'Ssh! Ssh!'

'Oh dear! oh dear!' Her laughter took on a cackling quality, and in spite of himself he was forced to smile, although he looked about him apprehensively as he did so as if expecting the entire village to appear.

He was cautioning her again when he remembered with something akin to horror that it was Monday and the minister would be holding his weekly educational meeting in the church hall, which lay not more than fifty yards to the right of them. This knowledge forced him to entreat her now, 'Look . . . look, steady up . . . be quiet now, you see we are near the church and they'll . . .'

'Oh dear! oh dear! . . . What? What did you say?' She was drying her eyes but he did not repeat what he had said, only waited for her to quieten down further.

Slowly now she moved from the tree and stood with her head bowed for a moment as if trying to regain her composure before starting to walk along the path again. But although her mirth had lessened, apparently she could not gain control over it altogether, and when they came to the stile that led into the road she stopped and said apologetically between gasps, 'I – I must wait. It will pass . . . in a minute. Oh, I'm sorry.'

He stood looking at her, with the bar of the stile between them. The moon was full on her now, showing her face as it had perhaps once been, pink and rose-tinted. The laughter had made her eyes bright and dark; her lips were wide and very red. He watched the moisture gleaming on them as they moved without framing words.

'Why did you laugh like that?' he asked soberly.

She seemed to think a moment before replying, and then she said, still between little gasps, 'It was a bit of everything. It's been such an odd day. Finding the eel; then meeting your father in the wood; and Mr Fountain thinking . . .' She did not elucidate further on this point and explain what she thought Bill had been thinking, but went on, 'And us all scampering from the major. Then – then Wordsworth – in the wood.'

The heat rose again and he rubbed his hand tightly across his mouth.

'Please –' although she was still smiling, there was a sincere note of pleading in her voice – 'please don't be vexed.'

'I'm not vexed.'

'Yes – yes, you are.' She dabbed at her eyes and added, 'Oh, if I'm not careful I'll start again, and I mustn't. Oh, I'm sorry.'

'Be quiet a minute.' His tone compelled her silence, and she was quiet, but only with the aid of her handkerchief held tightly to her mouth.

'There's somebody coming.'

Her eyes widened and they seemed to say silently, 'Well, why worry?'

There were more than one pair of footsteps, and if Peter had wanted to retreat it would have been impossible now, for stepping off the grass verge on to the road came four people: the Reverend Mr Collins, Miss Bridget Collins, Mrs Armstrong, the postmistress, and Mavis Mackenzie. They were all silent. They all hesitated, and they all looked towards the stile. Then they all, without exception, gaped at the couple behind it. And it was evident from their varying expressions that the source of the unseemly laughter was being revealed to them. Peter Puddleton had been in the wood with a woman, was in the wood with a woman. Had it been Harry Puddleton or even Old Pop, three of the onlookers would have said 'Well, what do you expect?' But when it was Peter who was supposed to have none of the Puddleton ways, it would just show you, wouldn't it? Blood would out! For here he was, before their eyes larking boisterously in the wood in the moonlight with a woman. And such a woman! Long, blonde hair and painted!

It was unfortunate that Mavis should have been standing nearest the stile, for she was being given a first-class view of the depraved pair, and her eyes seemed to leap from her aggrieved countenance and take in all that she could see of the girl. Then they were switched to Peter, and, her voice expressing their fury, she exclaimed, 'Well!'

Never had a word said so much.

Peter's reaction should have been a desire to sink through the ground, but, strangely enough, he wished to do no such thing. In this incident, which was the culmination of a strange evening, he saw a ready-made loophole for his escape from Mavis and the implications resulting from his having been a damned fool. So, in a tone quite unlike his own, for it held a ring of cockiness, he called out to her, as if she were at the end of the road, 'Evening, Mavis.'

Mavis, after one sizzling glare, gave voice to another pointed exclamation. 'You!' she cried, before marching off after the rest of the company, with nothing now of her genteel, mincing nature evident in her back view.

'Oh, dear!' This was not the prelude to more laughter but a definite expression of sorrow. The girl's face showed deep concern as she looked in the direction Mavis had taken, and after emitting another drawled out 'O . . . oh!' she turned quickly to Peter, saying, 'What have I done? I'm sorry. It was such a stupid thing to do, to laugh like that. I must explain to her and put things right.'

'No! No! You'll not.' Hastily, Peter put up his hand to emphasise his words. 'No, don't explain anything – please.'

'Are you sure?' She gazed up at him, her brows puckered,

'Yes. Oh, yes, I'm sure all right.' Slowly his body relaxed. a grin spread over his face, and from under his breath he said, 'I might as well tell you, you've done me a favour. And,' he added, 'you've wiped the slate clean for having taken the mickey out of me.'

'Yes?' It was a question.

'Yes, honest. You couldn't have done it better. I should thank you. The truth is –' He took his eyes from her face and, looking down at his feet, kicked gently at the stile support, 'I'm an easy-going type, I always take the line of least resistance. She, Mavis, was the line, in this instance.' He raised his eyes now to hers, and the twinkle in them was deep as he concluded, 'She's aiming to tie me up with it.'

Their gaze held, their eyes laughed into each others; their teeth nibbled at their lips, then like two errant children they clapped their hands over their faces to suppress their laughter, and above the horizon of their hands they stared at each other. And it would seem that the testing period of friendship, without the aid of time, was accomplished, and in the first knowledge of it their laughter died in them, and there came on them a silence, and in the silence the girl turned away and leant on the stile and looked on to the road, while Peter turned and looked up at the moon. He had a 'don't care a damn' feeling, and for no accountable reason that he could see he felt bubbly happy, as if he had caught a fish, perhaps an eel four feet long.

'It's odd, but today has been like a short lifetime.'

'What did you say?' He turned quickly towards her, but she continued to look down on to the road as she repeated, 'I said today has been like a lifetime, a short lifetime.' She lifted her head and looked away over the low hedge on the other side of the road, across the moon-capped fells down to the valley. Her voice held no laughter now but a deep sadness, as she added, 'Nothing ever happens in life as you expect it. Do you know that when I came into this village today I thought I would never laugh again, and I didn't care.' Her voice trailed away, and he moved with a soft step to her side, and his gaze like hers looking away into the moon-flooded night he waited, with a feeling strong in him that he was being taken into her confidence.

And the waiting held no embarrassment. Then she went

58

on, as if she were thinking aloud, 'There was nothing left to laugh about, only things to cry over and questions to ask, and silence for answers – and fighting and probing and longing.'

She turned her gaze from the road now and found his eyes on her, narrowed and puzzled. For a moment she remained very still, returning his scrutiny, then with a little smile touching her lips she asked softly, 'Can I call you Peter? If I'm to be here for two weeks, or more, I cannot Mr Puddleton you all the time, can I?'

Still he gave her no direct answer. Her eyes were filled with moonlight – its soft shadowings had lent to her face a flush – she was beautiful . . . she was the most beautiful thing he had ever seen in his life. 'What's your name?' he asked.

'Call me Leo . . . Leo Carter.'

'Leo?'

'Yes, Leo, short for Le-o-line.'

'Strange name.' His voice was deep in his throat.

'Yes, it is.'

Suddenly she shivered and pulled her coat closer around her. 'I'll go back now.' She put out her hand, palm front-wards, in a small protesting movement. 'Don't come.' There was a pause before she added, 'Goodnight, Pee-ter.' She split his name. 'I'll see you tomorrow.'

'Goodnight.' His voice was gruff.

She had her foot on the stile as she turned and prompted him, saying, 'Leo.'

He leaned forward and took her hand and helped her over; then repeated, 'Goodnight, Leo.'

She smiled at him once again, but now it was a small, somewhat sad smile. It was the smile that she had worn earlier in the day which just touched her lips, there was no trace of her laughter left. He watched her walk away, and when he could no longer see or hear her footsteps he turned and retraced his own to the beech wood again.

It was queer, but he no longer felt bubbly happy, no longer did he have that don't-care-a-damn feeling, but the feeling that was in him now he would not recognise, he would not say that he was afraid. Would his father have been afraid? Or yet, in their time, his grandfather, or great-grandfather? No, they would have known how to deal with her and all her strange facets. They certainly wouldn't have let her walk off without an effort to stop her – and the night so young.

But there were two weeks ahead, and there was one thing he was now certain sure of . . . there was something coming about between him and her – an affair. Aye! an affair. He paused and looked up at the moon and became lost in it.

CHAPTER THREE

As he dressed Peter whistled softly under his breath, but before opening his bedroom door he abruptly cut off this expression of his feelings and went quietly out on to the landing. His intention was to make himself a cup of tea and slip out without waking any of them, but, on creeping downstairs and entering the kitchen, who should he see sitting at the table, a pot of tea between them, but the old 'uns.

'Hello, what's up with you two?' he asked.

'Oh, hallo there, lad,' they answered him, almost together. Then Old Pop, sucking at his tea, added, 'Couldn't sleep. Never do when moon's full.'

Although he had heard it before, this remark, for some reason, annoyed Peter, and he exclaimed, 'Don't talk daft, Old Pop.'

'Daft? Nothin' daft about it.' Old Pop sounded huffy. 'Affects old 'un an' all, even at his time, don't it?'

'Aye, it does that.' Grandpop wagged his head, then raised his bleared eyes to Peter. 'And your dad, it does – oh, aye, your dad. Ah well –' he gave a throaty laugh – 'them days are gone for half'n us, any road. What d'you say, lad?'

Peter, looking towards Grandpop's thin, bony, multi-coloured legs, where they stuck out of his nightshirt, remarked, 'You know what'll happen if me mam finds you out here like that, don't you?'

This threat brought forth no nervous murmurings from Grandpop; instead it released a mixed torrent of resentment and warning. 'Blast yer ma!' he said. 'And all women. And you'll get caught – aye, you'll see me lad, with one or t'other. And not in till ten past twelve. Aye, I heard you. Moon's got him an' all, I said. Aye, I did. Never been late like that afore. Were with that buck-teeth after all, weren't you? You wasn't with t'other one, for close on dark she went galloping along street as if devil was after her. Waved to me, she did. Aye, she's all right, but too young and silly. Not for you, lad, not for you. But that other one . . . God above!' Grandpop's eyes roved around the ceiling as if searching for the Deity, and Peter, knowing that any comment whatever would only succeed in getting him more deeply involved in this conversation, made his escape to the scullery, where he washed hastily, made himself a cup of tea and slipped out of the back door.

And that was the beginning of a very odd morning.

At nine o'clock he had a visit from an agent. The man had breezed in, said his name was Funnel and offered him two hundred and fifty pounds for the spare bit of land. And he was hardly gone before old Mr Mackenzie himself put in an appearance. Like oil he was – he had come to warn him about the agent. He stayed half an hour doing this, and Peter went through three handfuls of tow.

Then from ten o'clock onwards he had visits from his neighbours. Their sociability he laid down to curiosity about his intentions regarding the future of the garage; yet funnily enough most of them never mentioned the garage, they just stood about watching him tearing at the car, and laughed and joked, as far as he could see, about nowt.

It had also been a good morning for petrol. If he'd had nothing to occupy him he wouldn't have sold a gallon, but he had been from his knees to the pumps on and off all the morning.

But most important of all was the fact that the twins had visited him twice to report that the eel was still there, but that they hadn't seen 'the Miss'. And he himself hadn't seen 'the Miss', and it was now eleven-thirty. You would have thought, after what had taken place last night, that she would have dandered down towards the garage, wouldn't you? He asked this of himself during one of the quiet spells, and when by twelve o'clock he still hadn't seen her he began to ask himself further questions, such as had he been daft to imagine what he had done last night? Had his father and Bill Fountain jumped to similar conclusions because she had smiled at them? Had they thought, I'm on an affair? When he came to think about it he must have been a little cuckoo. And not only a little . . . plum barmy, he would say. And then to keep on wandering about in the woods till twelve o'clock on his own! Perhaps the old 'uns weren't so far wrong after all about the moon.

When another three cars in close succession drew up for petrol, he began to ask himself if the road had already gone through and he hadn't noticed it.

The last one was unusually big and bright. It was a deep blue outside and deep red inside, and it had lent a little of its flamboyancy to its owner who was wearing a fawn coloured suit, a blue check shirt, and light tan sandals, and although, apparently, only in his forties he claimed parentity over Peter straight away in addressing him, 'Fill her up, son, and tell me where the hell I am supposed to be!'

'Battenbun,' said Peter briefly.

'There, I told you, I said it was Battenbun.' It was the other occupant of the car speaking, and Peter, looking through the window at the lady, summed these two up as 'jaunters'. The fellow, likely, had a wife and family some-where, and the present female was what was left over from a week-end. The garage business created the faculty of tabulating types, and these two were not new.

'I want to get Durham way.'

'Straight through the village, turn right at the crossroads. You can't miss.'

It was after Peter had switched off the last gallon that he

noticed that the man had got out of the car and was now walking towards the garage door. He had his back towards him and he didn't turn around when he spoke. 'Here, a minute,' he said. And when Peter got to his side he didn't say what he wanted but walked with exaggerated casualness right into the garage and, of all places, to the back of the office, and there his casualness vanished.

'Where did you get that plate?' he demanded, pointing back to the number plate of the Alvis lying against the garage door.

Peter did not reply immediately but stared at the man, and the man, shaking his head with a nervous movement which did not tie up with his bizarre manner, said, 'Look, I know that number, and the car, an Alvis. Where is it?'

Slowly, and without taking his eyes off the man, Peter nodded towards the jumble of pieces lying at the back of the garage, and the man, after following his direction, jerked round again and exclaimed, 'You bought her! Who off?'

'I didn't buy her.'

'No?'

'No, she's in for repair.'

This statement had an odd effect on the man. He glanced back at the pieces which had comprised the Alvis, then in the direction of his own car, then again quickly to Peter.

'The owner, where is she?' His voice was a low rumble.

Peter's eyes had never left the man, and now there was a stiffness about his jaw that made his words slow of utterance. 'At the Hart,' he said.

'Here?' The man's nervousness increased.

'Along the street.'

The man wetted his lips as he asked, 'She waiting till the job's done?'

'Yes.'

'What's wrong? At least –' he gave a shaky laugh – 'it would be easier to tell me what wasn't wrong with that.'

'Big ends.'

'Oh.' He pulled at his tie; then licking his forefinger and thumb in his mouth, he rubbed them together, before carefully following the knife-crease down the front of his trousers.

If for no other reason, this action alone would have aroused Peter's dislike.

'Well, thanks.' He turned to go, then stopped, and with his eyes on the jumble of the Alvis pieces he said under his breath, 'I happen to know the owner, Miss Carter, isn't it?'

'Yes, it's a Miss Carter.' Peter went to the cash box in the office and took out some change, and when he handed it over the man said, 'That's all right.' Then straightening his shoulders and adopting again his jaunty air, he made for the opening of the garage, saying loudly and clearly now, 'Well, thanks for the information.'

Peter jerked his head in acknowledgement, but did not thank him for the tip, for never had he felt so reluctant to accept a tip from anyone. He stood some way inside the garage and watched the man get into the car, and heard his snappy rejoinder to the woman's enquiry as to what had kept him. Then, to his surprise, he saw the car swing round the drive and leap away, not through the village and past the Hart towards the road that led to Durham, but back the way from which it had come.

So he knew her, did he? Well, and what of it? He'd had folks draw up here because they'd recognised the number plate of a standing car as being from some town in the South or in Scotland or as far off as Wales. The fact that someone knew her should make her less of a mystery for apart from her name, the number plate which indicated Essex and the fact that she had lived in Norfolk was the sum total of his knowledge of her. Yet if it hadn't sounded so daft he would have argued that he had always known her, that she hadn't descended on this village at twelve o'clock yesterday but had been here from the time his memory first started to register. This quaint knowledge was not pleasant to him, for it brought with it a disturbed feeling as if there was something here he just couldn't fathom.

He went on to the drive and looked down the street, and his eyes, skipping over the usual people doing the usual things, came to rest on the Hart. Should he go and tell her about the fellow? The fact that she was acquainted with such a type did nothing to enhance her; and yet hadn't he already agreed that she was well acquainted with all types? She hadn't learned to play darts like she did in Sunday school, nor yet cope with men, in the same place. And she could cope with men. She'd had a lot to do with men, he could tell that. His arm went up in an impatient wave to Grandpop at the open window, and almost instantly the old fellow's voice could be heard bellowing, 'You, Jo . . . oe?'

When Old Pop, very short of breath, came hurrying to the garage, he asked, 'What's up now?'

'Nothing very much, I just want you to stay a minute. I've got to go to the Hart and see the owner ' He nodded back into the garage

'That all?' Old Pop wiped his forehead. 'I wish you'd get up some signal, lad, when I've got to rush and when I ain't.'

Peter gave his grandfather a wry smile. 'Wouldn't be much use as far as I can see. It's the old 'un's voice you want to alter.'

'Aye, lad, you're right there. Wouldn't surprise me if he weren't to blast them all out of the graveyard when he gets in it. But it's a sure thing there'll be a helluva bellowing that day.'

This comment on Grandpop's future activities brought a short laugh from Peter, and as he went down the street and past the garden he waved to the old man. And Grandpop returned his greeting; then yelled after him, 'You dry, lad? S'm I, begod! mouth like an ash pit. Could do with one an' all . . . a long 'un.'

Peter's answer to this was merely a backward jerk to his head.

At the Hart he went into the main bar. It was empty but for Mrs Booth, and she did not as usual greet him with a 'Hallo, there,' but went on with her occupation of arranging some flowers in a vase in the deep bay window.

'Morning. Nice day again.'

'Oh! Good morning.' Mrs Booth had half-turned as if in

surprise; then she turned her whole attention to the flowers again.

'I'll have half a pint, please.'

As if reluctant to leave her artistic occupation Mrs Booth stood back and surveyed her handiwork, and Peter watched her. There was something amiss here – she was on her high horse. He knew the signs all right.

'Half a pint you said?'

'Yes, please.'

Mrs Booth sailed slowly round the counter and drew the half pint, and Peter, putting his money down, said, 'I'll take a bottle for Grandpop.' He looked around the empty bar, listened for a moment to the sounds from the cellar where Mr Booth was busy, and then asked as casually as he could, 'Miss Carter in? I'd like a word with her.'

Now the nature of the high horse was immediately brought into the open, for with her hand covering the top of the bottle Mrs Booth became still, and very slowly through pursed lips, she said, 'Yes, Miss Carter is in. Very much in, if you ask me. It's now twelve o'clock and Her Ladyship has just decided to get up. Asked if she could have tea and toast in bed, if you please!'

At this point Mrs Booth breathed deeply before going on. 'I said people didn't usually stay in bed here until twelve o'clock, and if they didn't come down for their breakfast they went without. And she's gone without, she has!' Her hand grabbed up the money from the counter with such force that the muscles rippled up her brawny arm. 'I've never known the likes of it! Coming in here after we were all locked up last night and then expecting to have her breakfast taken up to her.' She glared at Peter, and he, flushing in spite of all his efforts not to, said, 'Well, it's got nothing to do with me – it's none of my business, is it?'

'Oh!' Mrs Booth drew her chin in, 'Isn't it?'

'No, Mrs Booth, it isn't.'

Her next words brought his mouth open. 'There were two people drunk and roaring in the wood last night – I'm mentioning no names – and if My Ladyship wasn't lit up

66

when she came in at midnight then her eyes belied her and my eyes deceived me.'

'Hello.'

Peter swung round towards the doorway.

To say that he felt uncomfortable was very much of an understatement. His mind was grappling with a number of things at once! Where had she spent her time from when she left him last night? And did Mrs Booth mean she was drunk when she came in? And she'd had no breakfast. And old Ma Booth was a real swine; but the thought which burst the surface of his mind was: That fellow could be her husband.

'It's a beautiful morning.' She was looking directly at him.

'Yes. Yes, it is.'

The girl having ignored Mrs Booth completely, turned away and walked along the passage, while he picked up the bottle, dropped it into his pocket and followed her out.

She had stopped just under the roof porch. Her head was back and she was looking up at the sky, and as he came to her side, her eyes swept over the green and along the street, and she repeated, 'It is a beautiful morning.'

'Yes. Yes, it is.'

They had both said the same thing before.

As he stood uneasily by her side he was conscious that somewhere behind them Mrs Booth was both watching and listening, and that if he wanted to talk to the girl he would have to move away from here. What he would have liked to say to her was, 'Come on down to our house and have a bite,' but he could see his mother's face if he dared to walk into the house with her.

He glanced at her. She was all in red, a soft red dress, sandals, and toe-nails, and the colour made her face look whiter, if that were possible, and her hair more straw-coloured.

In the lowest whisper he could manage, he said, 'Would you step along here a minute? I've got something to say to you.'

She glanced quickly at him, then without further words she walked with him to the far wall of the inn yard, her sandals making a loud clip-clop, clip-clop on the stones.

And when he stopped she looked up at him with a smile similar to that of yesterday just touching her lips and said, 'Don't tell me that the vicar has issued an ultimatum that I leave in twenty-four hours.'

He laughed; then stopping abruptly, he said, 'A man called in for petrol this morning. He recognised your number plate. He said he knew you.'

For some moments her expression did not change, and she continued to look at him as if what he'd said had not registered. Then blinking her eyes rapidly she murmured, 'Knew me? Did he say who he was?'

'No. He had a big car, an Austin Princess, blue body.'

From her profile he could see that the description meant nothing to her, but as he went on, saying, 'He was about forty-five, I should say, tall, black hair . . . curly,' he saw her teeth drop sharply into her lower lip, and she remained perfectly still for a moment. Then she looked along the length of the village before bringing her eyes up to him. 'It's a small world,' she said.

'That's what they say.' But instead of this inanity he had wanted to ask abruptly, 'Who is he, your husband?'

'Did you tell him I was here?'

'Yes. I couldn't do anything else.'

'No, of course not. Did he say he'd be back?'

'No.'

He watched her open her bag and take out a handkerchief and dab at her mouth with it. He watched her replace the handkerchief then click the bag closed, and he was waiting for her look as it came to his. But he was both surprised and piqued when all she said was, 'Is there any place where I could get a cup of coffee in the village?'

He seemed to think a moment, although it wasn't necessary, but her changing the subject like that had flummoxed him a little. Then he said, 'Yes, Miss Tallow does coffee on occasions.'

'The little drapery shop?'

'Yes.'

'Well, I'll take a walk down there. Are you coming this way?'

He swallowed before saying, 'Aye – yes, I'm on me way back.'

Together they walked through the village, side by side but not too close. No, he saw to that . . . there'd be enough chipping and chaffing because he was walking with her. He had walked with other strangers through the village, but she was different somehow. She was like nobody that had ever been in this village before, she was one of those people who had only to sneeze to cause an epidemic.

They had an over-hearty wave from Bill Fountain; they had an interesting peer from Mrs Armstrong through the post office window; they had a long following glare from Mrs Mackenzie; they had a loud hail from Grandpop; so it was not without relief that Peter left with just a nod at Miss Tallow's door.

She was a cool customer, he'd say that for her – nothing appeared to ruffle her. Yet when he had first mentioned the bloke she had been startled. But it was only for a second or so, she was a dab hand at covering up.

When we reached the garage, all Old Pop said was, 'Aye, aye!' and Peter, in an unusually sharp tone, asked, 'And now what do you mean by that?'

'Nowt, nowt, lad,' said Old Pop as he walked away, 'just aye, aye!'

It was three o'clock and Peter was standing in the middle of the road trying to carry on a conversation with Josh Turnbull above the rattle of his tractor, when out of the corner of his eye he saw his mother rampaging over the green. Immediately his mind registered trouble, for her walk was such as he had witnessed only when she was on the war-path, going from room to room in the house after a to-do with his dad. This was Tuesday afternoon and Women's Institute. He patted the vibrating machine and yelled, 'All right, Josh, I'll pop over in the morning and have a look at her. 'Bye.'

As Josh raised his hand in farewell and set the tractor moving Rosie came on to the drive. She didn't look at Peter but made straight for the garage, which augured bad, for he knew that his mother liked to fight her wars in private. When he followed her in Rosie was already in the office, the doorknob still in her hand.

'What's up, Mam?' he asked.

'Come in here.'

He went in, and Rosie with some manoeuvring closed the door behind him, which left about two feet of space between them.

'What's the matter? Is it Dad?'

Rosie's bosom took an upward tilt, her nostrils narrowed and she said, 'We'll come to that. Where were you last night?'

So that was it. He commanded his expression to give nothing away. He knew his mother. If he were to speak the truth and say, 'At the lake with the girl from the Hart,' she would not only jump to conclusions but be miles ahead of anyone else in the village, at least where he was concerned.

'Now look, Mam,' he said soothingly, 'I don't have to keep a diary of where I go, now do I?'

'Don't try to sidetrack me, Peter. Do you know what they're saying?'

'They're always saying something, you should know that by now. There's a saying that goes, "They say, let them say . . ." '

'I don't want to hear any sayings,' said Rosie tartly; 'I hear enough. I know full well about sayings, I've had a bellyful of them in this village. And when they're the truth you've got to put up with them, but this is lies. You weren't drunk last night, were you?'

'Me, drunk!' His eyes widened. 'No, of course not. Not on two half-pints I wasn't.'

'There!' Rosie's breath escaped in a faint hiss of relief. 'That bitch!'

'Who? Mrs Booth?'

'No, Miss Collins.'

'Miss Collins?'

In spite of his determination to give nothing away Peter moved uneasily, and he turned his attention to the petrol-stained ledger lying open on the desk, and this guilty and evasive action sent Rosie's relief fleeing away and she demanded, 'Look here. Were you in the wood last night with her – the woman – the owner of the car?'

'Now, Mam. Look, I can explain.'

Rosie, suddenly covering her eyes with her hand, said, 'I don't want no lies. I've had enough of lies all me life . . . don't you start. You were there and that's all there is about it.'

'There's no need for me to lie, Mam. I just went to the lake to look at –' he salved his conscience in giving the presence of the eel away by saying, 'a fish.'

'A fish?' The unlikelihood of this excuse aroused Rosie's anger again and had a drying effect on her tears. 'A fish?' she cried. 'Huh! I'll say she's a fish, and men's her bait. Did you know your Dad was looking for fish an' all – and Bill Fountain?'

'Aye,' said Peter now, with a wry smile. 'We were all together.'

'You were all to –!' Rosie's mouth sagged.

'Yes, we were all together.'

Peter was beginning to enjoy her discomfort.

After looking blankly at him for a moment, she asked in a very subdued tone, 'What kind of fish is it?'

Peter moved his feet and he rubbed his hand up over his face, and after some slight hesitation he brought out, 'Look, Mam, it's an eel, the biggest we've seen, and if it gets about Mackenzie or Crabb, or one or other in the village will have her.'

'An eel! But why not?' asked Rosie puzzled. 'Your dad an' you've always been on about the eels pinching your bait and spoiling the fishing.'

'Yes, I know, but this one's such a size and we feel she should have a chance to get home.'

'Home?' Rosie's face slowly screwed up, and Peter giving a patient sigh, went on to explain as briefly as possible where the eel was going – that's if it got there – also who had first seen it and how the girl had come into the picture. 'Well,' he said, drawing his breath in, 'now you know.'

71

'Yes,' said Rosie. But after a moment's thought she was back to where she had come in. 'Then what made them think it was you who was drunk and carrying on?'

'We weren't carrying on. She – Miss Carter –' Peter stopped. If he were to explain, even if he could, what had tickled Miss Carter it would blow the lid off again, so with a little bit of quick thinking he said, 'She was tickled about the twins. It was her who made up that song about the eel.'

'Oh!' Over Rosie's face spread a slow beam. That's where they got it then. Well!' For a moment she looked a little foolish, then again remembering the full text of what Miss Collins had made sure she should overhear, she reverted to her starting point. 'But what made you yell out to Mavis Mackenzie?'

'Yell out? I didn't yell.'

'Well if you didn't, why did you call to her at all?'

Peter's head now swung on his shoulders. There seemed no escape, so he said somewhat grimly, 'Well, this should please you, you've been on about her enough, I did it to shoo her off. We were coming back; we'd got as far as the stile – Miss Carter was laughing – then that lot came past and I saw in the situation an opportunity I'd been, I suppose, looking for. As I said, Miss Carter was laughing, we were by the stile, the moon was shining and the whole set up was something I couldn't have manufactured or put over with my tongue, not in a life time. I might as well tell you I knew I'd been a blasted fool over Mavis, even when I took her out the first time, but when I went and did it again, well, it looked as if I'd jumped in with both feet and I couldn't see how I was going to pull out. And then – well . . .'

There was no need for Peter to go on, the beam was flowing like oil now over Rosie's whole body and she was slumping with relief. 'I knew you'd have sense, lad,' she said softly.

Again Peter's feet moved, and so much breath left his body that he felt his ribs cave in. 'Well, now that's cleared up,' he said briefly, 'I'll get back to work.' He squeezed towards the door, but before opening it he turned to her saying, 'But mind, you won't say anything about the eel, will you, Mam? Don't even let on to Dad that you know – or the lads.'

She nodded her head in small jerks and laughed as she said, 'And that explains that, an' all.'

'What?' he said.

'The twins hammering a couple of the Spraggs and chasing them out of the wood. About ten minutes afore I went to the meeting I had Daisy Spragg at the door asking if we were joint owners of the village along with the Mackenzies, and what she was going to do if I didn't do something with the lads. Well' – she smiled at her son – 'I'll send you some tea along.'

The air was clear again. He smiled back at her and nodded and watched her go out, then returned to his work. But he hadn't been at it more than ten minutes when Florrie's voice, coming from just behind him, startled him, causing the spanner to squeeze out of his hold like paste from a tube.

'Ah! guilty conscience. . . . Be sure your sins will find you out!'

'What –' he swivelled round on his knees, then got clumsily to his feet – 'what are you talking about now?'

'What am I talking about now!' She smiled at him with a funny little smile that deceived him into thinking that perhaps she wasn't on the warpath this time.

'So you took my advice, did you?'

He returned her crooked smile with a grin, and said, 'You mean Mavis? Aye . . .'

'No, I don't mean Mavis.'

'You don't?' His brows puckered.

'How long is this going to take?' She kicked at the mudguard of the Alvis none too gently.

'I don't know.' He turned and grabbed up a handful of tow and began to rub his hands vigorously.

'That's a pity.' Florrie was holding him with a straight stare and there was a quirk on her lips, as she went on, 'You might find yourself with a maintenance order if you don't hurry up and get rid of it – and her.'

Like a thermometer plunged into boiling water, Peter's mercurial colour shot up, and with it his anger, startling both himself and Florrie; as did his words when he barked, 'That's enough of that! If you want to make such comments, then do so, but keep them for your social set at the Hunt Ball or any other place where it fits, but don't direct them at me.' He threw the tow against the wall.

Florrie's quirk was no longer in evidence, but the look she now bestowed on him sustained his anger and caused him to surprise himself further when he faced her squarely and said, 'I've had just about enough of this business all round, and I'll thank you to leave me and my affairs alone, Florrie, and do your hunting in the proper quarters.'

After this unchivalrous delivery his anger died quickly away, too quickly, for it left him sapped and thinking, 'That was a nice thing to say; you needn't have gone that far.'

The insult, however, did not seem to worry Florrie unduly, for she remarked, with a maddening casualness that she could adopt at will, 'It's a free country. And that, too, is what I said when I heard you were drunk and disorderly in the wood last night.'

'I was neither drunk nor disorderly.' His colour deepened.

Florrie, straddling her legs a little, pursed her lips. 'But you were in the wood with a certain lady of questionable aspect, weren't you?'

Slowly Peter's eyes screwed up, and he peered at her as if bringing her into focus as he repeated in a tone from which all the heat of his anger had died, leaving it cold, 'Questionable aspect?'

'Well, I understand she's a type – blonde, trailing hair –' Florrie's hand demonstrated just how trailing – 'dead white face, skin-fit frock – the lot that one usually associates with that type.'

On Peter's face now was an expression Florrie had not seen there before, and in his tone a quality that annoyed her as he said, 'Have you seen Miss Carter?'

Florrie's chin jerked. 'No, I haven't seen Miss Carter, and I have no wish to.'

'That's as may be. Miss Carter is no more of a piece than – than you are. Not so much if the truth were told.'

Florrie stared at him in open amazement. That the lazy, indolent Peter Puddleton should take a stand like this for a woman – she did not class the owner of the car as a girl – whom he had known but a few hours added significance to the conclusion that was forcing itself on her. Something, almost with lightning speed, had changed him, and it certainly wasn't Mavis. And, with equal certainty, she knew it wasn't herself. This last admission was humiliating to say the least, but being fundamentally her mother's daughter, she drew herself up and for the first time in their acquaintance she put on an air, and the air was prominent in her tone as she said, 'Indeed? you must have been busy to find out so much in so short a time.'

'Now look here.' The hauteur of her manner must have escaped him, for he actually took a step towards her. And if she needed anything further to convince her that something drastic had happened to him it was this – this mild form of attack coming from him constituted a revolution. But after the step, her stare held him and checked what further defence he would have made, for at this moment she was looking an exact replica of her mother, and with much of her mother's manner and her flair for carrying off the honours of battle, whether as victor or vanquished, she now turned from him and without a word of any kind left the garage.

'Damn and blast!' He stamped into the office. What was the matter with everybody the day? He had never known people behave like it, not all at once he hadn't. Could he have done otherwise than defend himself against such an assumption? He went hot under the collar. What if the others thought the same. But no, nobody would think things like that, except Florrie. She was as racy as – He would not give a definition of her raciness, but said to himself: If it's got as far as the Manor the whole place must be yapping about me – and her, and the lass not in the place five minutes.

'Where are you?' Old Pop came stumbling into the

75

garage. Ah, there you are. Tea's here. What's up with your ma? Saw her come dashing up here like a retired greyhound. Owt wrong?'

'No, nothing.'

'Ah! you can't tell me there's nothin', she don't leave the wives inferno for nowt. Ah! you can't tell me. Tale going around you were blind drunk last night. You weren't lad, were you?'

'No, I wasn't.'

The bawl caused Old Pop to put his hand up and scratch the sparse hairs behind his ears. Then he commented, 'No, I thought you wasn't would have heard you else. We none of us were ever quiet when we was bottled. Not the first time of being bottled, we wasn't. No, by gum.' He grinned at Peter and handed him the mug of tea he had poured from the steaming jug. Then pouring out one for himself, he went to the box and sat down. After taking a long drink he wiped his mouth and remarked, apropos of nothing that had so far been mentioned, 'She's nice lass that, that miss at the Hart. She is an' all. What she don't know about eels ain't worth learnin'.'

Peter's mouth fell into a straight line, and he said, with a frankness he rarely used towards his grandfather, 'You like to nose, don't you?'

'Me? I wasn't nosin', Peter. Just taking a dander in the wood, and there she was with the young 'uns. The lads made me swear not to say a word, and it's all right with me. That's not saying I'd not like to catch she . . . the eel. There's some flesh on her and there's nothing tastier than a bit of eel. Though I have a fancy for them a bit younger, more tender then. And you know summat? The young lady knows every step of her road back – Saggassen Sea she makin' for, so she says.' He cocked his squint eye at Peter's stiff profile. 'She comes from Fenlands way, she says. Not the eel, her I mean. Says she used to fish the river with her grandda, and the young eels used to pinch the bait. Knows all the different flies, an' all. Never met no woman what didn't look like a sack an' talk fish like she. Started from scratch, so to speak, she did. Used to dig worms for her grandda. Fish he did, rain, hail or shine, she said. Had a big umbrella and a lot of paraphenalia. From morn till night they'd stay on the banks. Told me all about it, she did. Any more tea to spare there?' He handed his mug to Peter, who took it, filled it and handed it back to him without a word. And Old Pop, staring down into it, gave a chuckle and remarked, 'Remember like yesterday first time I got real sozzled. 'Twas right here at the Hart. Late summer 'twas, hay smellin' and moon shinin'. At least I remember the moon shinin' and standin' on Green singing at top of me voice. Fine voice I had an' all in those days. But be damned, I can't remember to this day how I reached Layman's Farm, and it three miles on, though when I woke in the morning and saw where I was I sprinted down the drainpipe and away across the fields as if the bull was after me. Young Miss Phyllis got married two months later and off she went to foreign parts.'

'You finished?'

Old Pop, purposely misunderstanding his grandson, said, 'Aye,' and handed him the empty mug. Then rising from the box he added, 'Some bloke at the Hart's enquiring for the young lady. Booth himself came through the wood to tell her. Seemed in no hurry to go back, neither, he didn't. Talked like I never heard him afore. . . . Well, you had enough?'

'Yes,' said Peter with some stress, 'I've had enough.'

Old Pop gathered up the things and, placing them in the basket, gave his grandson a cheerful leer. Then going to the doorway he turned and delivered his advice without any diplomatic coating. 'Remember, lad, time's flyin'. There's no time like the present. You leave your fling much longer and you'll lose the taste. An' I'm tellin' you.' He nodded solemnly before adding, 'Me, I could look back at summat at your age, I'll say. Though I don't blame you for steering clear of the Mackenzies' cow and Miss Florrie. One's as dry as the Methodist Chapel; as for t'other – she'd be another Bill Fountain's doe. Pregnant forty-seven times a year.' After which exaggeration of nature's bounty Old Pop departed, leaving Peter bursting, but speechless.

In the past, it had always been a source of satisfaction to

Peter when his old Austin was out on hire, but tonight he was deeply regretting its absence. If it had been on hand he would have got her out and gone off somewhere.

He walked up the street, in the opposite direction from the Hart, past Miss Tallow's and past his own garage, which to him now looked somewhat unreal and not a little dilapidated. The closed doors seemed to make his name stand out starkly from the board nailed above them: PETER PUDDLETON, Garage Proprietor. He gave a disparaging 'Huh!' as he glanced at it. It was a daft-sounding name if ever there was one. Why with a name like Puddleton had his mother to call him Peter? Arthur, Bill, John, even Harry – but Peter! His life, he felt, had taken the cue from his name . . . there was no sense in it. He hadn't even the sense he was born with. For years now he had been content to slide along thinking that one day things would work out, which meant that one day he would find a lass to suit him and he would marry her. Then last night, because a woman, a strange woman, had laughed at him in the moonlight, he had been mad enough to imagine he was on to something.

He jumped the fence and, skirting the trees, took to the fields. Going by little-known paths and leaping gates and walls as if he had a grudge against them, he came to the lake. There was no one looking into the water tonight; they would, he thought wryly, all be in the Hart, laying bets with each other no doubt as to what relation the flashy fellow was to her. Yet when you thought of it there was hardly any scope for betting, the relationship was pretty obvious.

The lake was still; the after-glow from the sun lay on it like patches of translucent paint. He stood at the edge of the bank but did not trouble to search the water for a sight of the eel, for in this light nothing could be seen but the reflection of the sky which seemed to have drowned itself in the lake. Soon the quietude and the colour had their effect upon him and he felt somewhat soothed and sat down with his knees up and his hands hanging slackly between them.

'You all on your own, lad?'

The voice of his grandfather seeming to come out of the air, for there was no sight of the old man, jerked Peter out

78

of his reverie and brought him from the bank like a shot.

'I'm in here, lad. Thought you was somebody else when I heard you comin' . . . dashed for cover.' The brambles parted and Old Pop, pulling himself clear, stood before Peter with head downcast, meticulously picking the burrs from his clothes.

With an indrawn breath of exasperation Peter demanded, 'What are you doing here?'

'Just out for a walk, lad.'

'Out for a walk!' Peter's mouth squared itself, and Old Pop, cocking his good eye at his grandson, repeated, 'Just that lad, out for a walk.' Then nodding towards the water he added, excitedly, 'I've seen her.'

Peter, making absolutely sure to which 'her' the old man was referring, said stiffly, 'The eel?'

'Aye, half an hour gone by. She made me fingers itch. What say, lad, we have a shot at her?' Old Pop thrust his head forward. 'I could scoot back for line . . . or rig a few worms on some worsted.'

'You'll do no such thing. You leave her alone. Now mind, I'm telling you.'

Old Pop walked slowly to the water's edge and looked down. 'Pity . . . she'd be something to brag about the rest of your life, lad.'

'Maybe.'

'Heard young lady telling a bloke about 'un, little while gone.' Old Pop did not turn but kept his interest concentrated on the water.

'Where?' Peter was looking at his grandfather's back.

'In the wood here, with the bloke what came to the Hart for her. Said some funny things, both on 'em did, and not all about eels neither.'

'You didn't have to listen, did you?' Peter now sauntered the few steps back to the bank, and he too looked down into the water.

'Couldn't get out of it, lad.' Old Pop threw an amused look upwards at his grandson. 'Was answering urgent call behind bushes when they stopped close by. Was in a pickle, sure enough! But knew 'twould be they would get biggest shock did they see me. So just kept doggo.' He turned his face, now full of merriment, on Peter, but when it met no answering gleam he turned it away again and concentrated his gaze once more on the water. Then, after some moments, he commented, 'Nice girl, she – but fancy she's been in trouble.'

'What makes you think that?'

'Oh, just something what was said, you know.' Old Pop, with unbearable contrariness, now settled himself down on the edge of the bank and completely turned the course of his reminiscence. 'When I looks at this pond sometimes,' he said, 'I get creeps. Like now . . . look at the red in it – like blood. The old 'un, he never liked it neither. Ever notice that he never come here when he could get around?'

Peter did not answer this, but waited. He knew it was worse than useless trying to force his grandfather to divulge anything except in his own time. He also knew the old fellow was playing him as he would a fish.

'No, he never did.' Old Pop jerked his head. 'Saw something here when he was around fourteen that put him off lake. It was the day of the riot, you know. That Sunday when the women of the village all went mad, parson's wife an' all. I know you've heard some of it afore, but not all . . . no, not all.' Old Pop moved his tongue over his lips. 'And you don't hear many speak of it now . . . men a bit ashamed of their dads being locked up in church like and kept there at the point of shot-guns . . . want to forget it.'

Peter still remained mute, and presently Old Pop went on: 'Connie Fitzpatrick was an Irish maid in two senses when she came over, but she didn't remain either of 'em long.' He sniggered in his throat, 'No, she didn't by jove, if all tales be true. When she suddenly came into money she had that cottage built, nicely tucked away in the grove. Hard to get at it was then, and still is. Now had she remained like her cottage, hard to get at, she could have carried on for years. But she wasn't one for making flesh of one and fish of t'other. Connie's motto, by all accounts, was "Come all ye faithful" and they came, including the minister. That last did it! They dragged her, the women did, shriekin' and screamin' through the wood here to the lake and threw her in, and when she tried to get out they pushed her back. Bet you wouldn't believe it, lad, but Ma Armstrong's mother was one . . . Grannie Andrews. A bit lass she was at the time. Did you ever hear that afore?'

Before Peter could answer Old Pop forestalled him by saying, 'But there's something I'm gonna tell you now that I bet you never have heard afore. See over there,' he pointed across the water, 'It was from there that the old 'un watched 'em. Like wild animals he said they were, howling and yelling. He watched Connie swim the lake to yon side. She was more dead than alive, and when she crawled into the undergrowth she fell almost on top of him, and he petrified. Can't imagine the old 'un petrified.' Old Pop laughed. 'And what did he do?' Again he turned an enquiring eye on Peter, but gave him no chance to comment before going on, 'He covered her up under shrub, and then ran out on to the back path making a hullaballoo. And when they came pelting round the lake he led them a wild goose chase, supposedly after her. That was smart, wasn't it? Later he came back and found her almost finished. He got her to shelter in the sheep hut on the far fell. And then, would you believe it, he went at her bidding to the cottage and brought back a deed box which she had hidden under the floor of a summerhouse. She had her head screwed on, had Connie, and she paid the old 'un in more ways than one, she did an' all.' Old Pop turned and faced Peter now. 'You never heard that bit afore, did you?'

'No,' said Peter flatly, 'I haven't. But it's the tallest one yet.'

'Nowt tall about it.' Old Pop seemed a trifle annoyed now. 'You ever wonder how we came to own our house, lad, and we only farmhands at eighteen bob a week, eh? Just ask yersel that one, all our folks had lived in cottage but it was Squire's. It was Connie who gave the old 'un the cash for services rendered and some et ceteras, which was nobody's business but the old 'un's and hers an' he bought it. But he's always steered clear of this bit water, and always hated the guts of the village women, so much so that he picked me mother from as far away as North Shields.'

This knowledge of how they had come to be living in their own property was indeed a surprise to Peter, for he had always been under the impression that the house was bought with money left to his great-grandmother; he had got that information from his mother. 'Does me dad know this?' he asked.

'Aye, he does.'

'And me Mam?'

'Rosie? No, begod!'

'Then I wouldn't ever tell her.' Peter's voice was stiff.

'What, me?' Old Pop threw his head up. 'Not me! Think I'm barmy lad? Like as not she'd walk out. Very respectable is your mother. Look at the fizzle she's caused the day in meetin'. All over the village it is. Raised stink in hall 'cos somebody hinted you was drunk in the wood and havin' a bit of a lark.'

'I wasn't drunk. Nor having a lark. I've told you.'

'All right, lad, don't sound so testy. But if you was, there was nothin' for her to get shirty about, was there? I wish they could still say it of me, I wouldn't have been past a bit lark with she. Which reminds me, I was telling you, wasn't I? Funny how I went off about the old 'un. She sort of put it in me head, the Miss, I mean. Don't know why. Well, there I was behind the bushes when they stopped –' Old Pop picked up the main trend of his discourse as if he had never let it drop – 'and I heard them. "Anna", he said, that's what he called her.'

'Anna?' Peter put in sharply, his brows drawn together.

'Aye, Anna. That's what he called her, that's her name. "Anna," he said, "I tell you you've got to believe me on this one point. You could have knocked me down when they said you had gone three days afore". That's what he said, and she kept saying, "It doesn't matter." And he kept saying it did, and then he said, "You think me a rat, don't you?" and she said, "I don't even think about you, you don't matter any more. You'll never believe that, but you don't." And I stood there with me pants half up, almost seeing his face, cos he didn't speak. And then she said, "I'll be here for another week or so and all I ask of you is to leave me alone." And then he went on jabbering, said a lot and so fast I couldn't get it. But then I heard him say, "What about money?" Sharply, like that, he said it, and she said, "It's too late for that an' all, I have all I need.' "Well, what do you intend to do?" he said then, and she said, "That's entirely me own affair." "You can't go on in the old Alvis," "let me leave you the Austin." It was at that she walked off saying she didn't want the Austin or anything else. The last I heard her say was, "The Alvis is mine. I started with her and I'll finish with her." What do you make of it, lad?' The old man now looked soberly and enquiringly at Peter.

What did he make of it? Mrs Booth's comment was surging through his mind, and Old Pop sharpened this particular suspicion further by saying, 'This coming out business that the bloke talked about sounds as if she'd been in somewhere, along the lines perhaps.'

'Nonsense.'

'Well, it may be. I wouldn't think none the worse of her for that for she's a nice Miss. Take as you find, I say. Still, if you'd heard them 'twould have sounded to you as if there was something fishy. Then later I came along on, strolling like, an' I heard them in here. He was at her again, saying, "You can't stay in this dump" – dump he called the village, mind – "What you going to do with yourself?" An' d'you know what she said?'

Peter waited.

' "I can sit and watch an eel", she said. Yes, she did. "And imagine I'm young again." What d'you make of it, eh? And her just a young lass when all's said and done. What d'you make of it?'

To this repeated question Peter said slowly and quietly, 'It's none of our business.' Then he turned away and went out of the clearing, in case his feelings should reveal themselves to the all-seeing eyes of his grandfather. But Old Pop was quickly on his heels, and on coming to the main path he walked abreast of him, but had the sense to keep his tongue quiet until they reached the main road. And then he asked, 'You comin' along for a glass?'

Half an hour earlier he would have given a definite 'No' to this invitation but now he answered flatly, 'I may as well.'

The Hart was packed, both bar and saloon, for a coach had come in, and after having stood his grandfather a drink they parted company, Old Pop joining his cronies while Peter stood near the counter, as if waiting.

He saw his father and Bill in their corners, and all the regulars, but there was no sign of her, or the fellow. Some of the villagers craned their necks and threw greetings at him, and one bolder than the rest called, 'You on your own the night, Peter?'

He made no answer to this, and the smile that had been on his face slid away and he turned to the counter to be confronted by Mrs Booth. But she, looking over his head, answered the man by saying, 'He's been given the go-by. Anyway, he's one of the nightshift lot.'

A muffled cry from Mrs Booth which indicated her having received a kick on the shins from her husband, who was standing with his back to the counter, did nothing to soothe Peter's feelings. His face had now assumed almost a purple tinge. He had a strong desire to go for Mrs Booth, and he might have done so at that but Mr Booth, turning to him at that moment, asked in a level tone, 'Well, what is it to be tonight, Peter?'

'Give me a whisky. Double.'

Mr Booth showed not a flicker of surprise. Peter Puddleton's drink was beer, and not much of that either; this was the first spirit he had asked for in this house. The only Puddleton whose drink was whisky was the old 'un, and Mr Booth remembered unhappily the results on certain occasions on the old man of an overdose of the delectable fire. But hadn't he said last night that she would bring custom. Her type always did, one way or another.

'And a pint.'

'And a pint.'

The pint and the whisky gone, Peter did cause a slight ripple to pass over Mr Booth's poker face as he demanded, 'The same again.'

'The same again,' said Mr Booth. And when Mrs Booth stopped in her transit to the saloon and watched Peter give a mighty shiver after depositing the second whisky, she remarked under her breath, 'What did I tell you!' and Mr Booth, addressing a miniature keg of cider, replied, 'Get on with it!'

Catching sight of Mrs Booth's fixed stare upon him Peter now had a great desire to spit in her eye or to produce the equivalent effect in words, and these words presented themselves to him with such force that, for safety's sake, he was urged to put some distance between himself and the mistress of the inn. And this he did, much to the disappointment of Mr Booth.

Outside once more, he stood for a moment looking about him. The night was young: it was barely nine o'clock, too light to go to bed, too light even to go home, for his mother would still be about and she'd likely start on one thing or another, and he couldn't stand that the night.

To save passing the house or going back through the village he returned up the road along which he had come earlier with Old Pop. The whisky was now glowing soothingly inside him; he felt in some measure comforted and took on himself not a little of the blame for being so edgy. Folks were all right. He had always got on all right with everybody; that was all except Davy Mac. The name in his mind coming at the same time as he caught sight of Mavis checked his step and made him gulp. He had reached an opening to the wood where once had been a gate, and standing almost hidden behind one of the old oak supports was Mavis.

He'd had no intention of going into the wood, and with Mavis about he would have shied like a hare from it but now, for some unexplained reason, he made straight for the gap, and when he came abreast of her he stopped, for if he hadn't she would undoubtedly have brought him to a halt in some way.

Mavis, from the shelter of the gate-post looked at him hard, very hard, and her eyes on this occasion did not appear doll-like and her tone was not just one of enquiry, as she asked sarcastically, 'Off some place?'

'Aye,' Peter replied slowly, softly, and very definitely. 'Aye. Yes, I'm off some place, Mavis.'

The reply and the manner in which it was said was certainly not what Mavis had expected. But her good sense coming quickly to her aid told her she must change her tactics as he had so obviously changed his, and so she assumed an expression of having just been struck . . . her face crumpled, her lips strained to meet, and into her eyes came the look of a woman betrayed, and she whimpered, 'How could you, Peter!'

Peter, the Peter warmed with two double whiskies and two pints was on top. 'How could I what?' he grinned at her.

The whimper turned into a sob and she said, 'You've changed. Why – why did you ask me out last week?'

'God knows!' This answer, by its boldness, tickled him, it also checked Mavis's tears. Her eyes narrowed now, their pale blue turned to steely grey; she moved a step nearer to him, and after staring up into his face for a moment she exclaimed in horror, 'You're drunk!' then added, 'again.'

This accusation brought no denial from Peter. Strangely, he had no desire to get mad and deny his supposed previous lapse, and what he was led to do next made him laugh loudly inside, for he opened his mouth wide, breathed hard on her, and uttered one word, 'Whisky!'

This flippant action together with the strong aroma of spirit caused Mavis to react naturally, and she cried, 'You!' and it was the same kind of 'You!' she had thrown over the stile at him last night. Then again she delivered it, but followed it now with a spluttered, 'Don't – don't you think you'll get off with it, I'm not as soft as you think I am. As for your tart –' Peter's eyebrows shot up, he hadn't known she had even a nodding acquaintance with the word – 'do you want to know where she is? She's in there!' With a thrust of her arm Mavis indicated the depths of the wood. 'Lying full length on the grass. And who with? The major. Yes, the major. I saw them with my own eyes . . . they couldn't get closer. The things I saw and heard! Quoting

86

poetry to each other . . . love poetry! The major at his age!
You were always a fool and she's made a bigger one of you.
You're the laughing stock of the village. Everybody's
sniggering at you. You know what they're calling her?
Slinky Jane. And you let yourself be taken in, you big
galloot!'

'You finished?'

'Oh, you can appear cool and pretend you haven't been
taken for a ride, but you're not taking me for a ride. You
haven't heard the last of this, Peter Puddleton. You're not
going to make a fool out of me. You wait, I'll have me own
back, you'll see.'

After one bounce of her head that should have ricked her
neck, Mavis turned and flounced away, and not until the
heels of her shoes tapping out her indignation on the road
could no longer be heard did he move on into the wood.

This was getting beyond a joke. Eel or no eel . . . things
would have to be made clear. Damn the eel! No eel was
worth her losing her name for – the eel must be brought into
the open. Aye. Aye, it must. Its presence must be proclaimed
to the entire population of the village and its name an' all.
Damn silly name anyway. Why had she to go and give it a
name like that? And Major lying on the grass with her!
Bloody silly thing to do, lie on the grass. You should never
lie on the grass with a woman, even he knew better than
that. By! if this got about it would take some explaining.
He knew why they were lying on the grass; the eel must have
been on the move, tucked itself away under the bank
perhaps. The major had likely gone into the clearing and
she had told him about it, and only seeing was believing
with the major. But lying on the grass together, and Mavis
to spot them. What if it had been him? On this thought he
stopped abruptly, not brought to a standstill by his thinking
but by the sight of Leo at the other end of the beech walk.
She was coming towards him, and alone.

He moved on again, slowly, almost casually now, and as
the distance between them lessened his thoughts toppled
over themselves. She looked whiter than ever. Had she done
time? Who was the fellow? If Mavis spread the rumour that

she was lying on the grass with the major there'd be the devil's own dance in the village about her, and there wasn't much doubt but that Mavis would. She was beautiful, but she wasn't good looking, not really. But she was beautiful. And the way she walked, not throwing her feet about as if they didn't belong to her. Who could the fellow be?

'Hullo.' It was he who spoke first.

'Hello.' She sounded tired and did not smile.

He looked steadily at her for a moment, and then remarked, 'You look tired. Walked too far?'

'Yes, I do feel a little tired.' With the faintest of smiles now she added, 'But not with walking, it's all the hard work I do. That eel takes some watching. I've just seen her. Your major was there. He got very excited, he couldn't believe his eyes. He's a nice old fellow, don't you think?'

'Yes, the major's all right.' He stood smiling blandly down at her and blinking.

With a sharp, amused glance she asked, 'Have you been celebrating?'

His grin stretched. 'Well, not exactly celebrating, but I went off me usual. Can you tell?'

The smile came to her lips again, wider now, and she said, 'A little.' Then with a movement of her head to each side she tossed her hair back from her face, and looking about her, asked, 'Do you mind if we sit down?'

Sit down! This was going to be the major over again. What if Mavis should decide to come back? Damn Mavis!

Pointing to a tree with a fallen branch lying at its base, he said, 'There's a seat over there.'

As she left the path he moved ahead towards the log and snapped off some of the side branches, with their dead foliage still clinging to them, to make a seat for her. She watched him for a moment, then sat down on the part he had cleared. Slowly she leaned her back against the trunk, and after drawing in a number of deep breaths she sighed and then she asked him a very odd question. 'When did I come here?' she said.

He looked at her as he laughed. 'You need me to tell you? Dinner-time yesterday.'

88

'Dinner-time yesterday. If you had said dinner-time ten years ago I should have said it was even longer than that. Yesterday I liked this place, I had made purposely for it. I was fascinated by the name, I had heard it somewhere years ago. And then recently I heard it again and felt I must come here. Yesterday I wanted to stay – the car seemed a good excuse – now I don't know.' She remained quite still but her eyes moved swiftly about, seeming to encompass the whole of the wood and the village beyond, and she finished, 'I feel I must go.'

The warmth of the whisky left his bowels and he said 'I thought you were going to stay put until the car was finished.'

'I thought I was, but I can always come back for it.'

When he made no reply to this she looked up at him and said, 'You're a very nice person, Peter. Why you're at large I don't know, somebody should have snapped you up. Come and sit down –' she tapped the trunk – 'you look too big standing there, like one of the trees. And you must be tired after working all day.'

He did not do as she ordered, and again, not a little to his own surprise, he heard himself saying, 'Don't talk like me mother.'

Suddenly she laughed, not the loud, free laugh of last night, but a soft, gentle laugh of amusement. 'All right, I'll drop the maternal role. Nevertheless, come and sit down.' She chuckled now. 'You know, that sounded funny coming from you . . . "Don't talk like me mother." You must go off your usual more often. Have you got a cigarette?'

As he pulled out his cigarettes he said, 'I've never seen you smoke.'

'No. I gave it up some time ago, but I feel the need of one now.'

She put the cigarette to her mouth, and he struck a match and cupped the flame for her.

'Do sit down.' It was now a request, and slowly he took a seat beside her, but not close.

'Where's your father?' she asked.

'In the Hart.'

'And Bill?'

'Yes.'

'They're a nice pair . . . refreshing.'

'Do you think so?'

'Yes. Don't you?' She blew the smoke gently upwards.

'They're all right.' He would not commit himself.

'Have you ever thought of leaving here, Peter?' The question brought his eyes to her face. They seemed to press on it, so hard was his stare.

'No – not really.'

'Then don't. Stay here until you're old, like your grandfather.'

'Now, you are talking like me mother again.' He said this not as he had done before, but quietly, almost under his breath. Then bending forward, with his hands between his knees and his eyes straight ahead, he asked, 'How old are you?'

'What a pertinent question!' She was laughing gently at him now. 'You'll be sorry for all these questions in the morning and you'll chide yourself for having dropped your guard, that's if you remember.'

With his hands still between his knees, he turned his head towards her. 'I'll remember . . . and look, I'm not drunk, not really. I've had two whiskies and two pints. You don't get drunk on that.'

'No,' she cast her eyes sideways at him, 'only curious.'

'Yes,' he repeated boldly, 'only curious.'

She did not pick this up but asked, 'Do most visitors to the Hart arouse the entire interest of the village?'

'Not usually. But then they're mostly very ordinary.'

She smiled a little at the covered compliment, and her head fell back against the tree. Then she blew the cigarette smoke upwards into the leaves, and remarked in a polite tone which dissociated itself from the content of her words, 'Mrs Booth is what is commonly known as a bloody bitch, isn't she?'

Now it was his laugh that rang through the woods, and he was past caring who heard it.

'You've said it there; we're agreed on that point anyway.' He straightened his back and brought his shoulders into a line with hers, and she turned her face full to his as she said, 'If I were to know you long, I should insist that you had two whiskies and two pints every night, and then everything I did or said wouldn't shock you.'

His brow gathered, 'What makes you think you shock me?'

'I know I do. Last night you thought I was much too free with the men, didn't you?'

The silence hung between them for a moment before he said, 'You know too much. But I wasn't shocked as you call it, just puzzled and –' he became bold – 'set wondering where you'd learnt all you know.'

She did not answer immediately; then she said off-handedly, 'You pay very questionable compliments, Peter. But I learnt what I know as you call it in America and repertory – and in a garage.'

Ignoring the first two he exclaimed in open amazement. 'In a garage!'

'I used to help sell cars.'

'You did?'

'Yes. What's so very surprising about that?'

'In America?'

'No, here, in England. I was evacuated as a child to America, to the south. Hence the touch of accent. I came back when I was seventeen.'

'But cars, how did you get into that business?'

Her lids dropped and her lips fell together, and she stretched her arm forward and tapped the ash from the end of her cigarette. 'That's a long, long story.'

'The fellow today – was he part of that story?'

She looked slowly back at him again. 'Yes, he was.'

Peter ran one dry lip over the other. 'Is he your husband?'

Again the silence came, longer this time. 'No, he's not my husband.'

Did he detect regret in the admission . . . longing. His mouth was still dry as he asked, 'Who is he then?'

'Someone I know.'

'In the car business?'

'Yes, in the car business.'

She turned her face away and it looked to him almost transparent now, standing out like chiselled alabaster from the tree and the deepening shadows of the wood. And as he stared at it there leapt into his body an urgent longing to hold her. He wanted to pull her towards him and bury himself in the whiteness of her. It was no gentle urge but a fierce demand that sought to wrestle with something that was embodied in the pale thinness of her. Almost imperceptibly he moved a fraction along the log; then after a short lapse, during which neither of them spoke, he moved again. It was at the third move that her voice, quiet and with her drawl more pronounced, said, 'Don't come any nearer, Peter.'

Nothing she could have done or said could have had a more douching effect. His boldness, created by the whisky, deserted him, and with it fled the last vestige of stimulation the drink had afforded. Her quiet command knocked him sober.

The manner in which she had exposed his urge, which some delicacy told him should never have been made plain with words, shook him, and for the moment he had the uncomfortable feeling of being stark naked . . . and added to this the very strong feeling of having stepped out of his place. Even Florrie had never made him feel like this.

He got to his feet, humiliated and angry. Not for him the stalling tactics of 'What do you mean? Who's doing anything?' Nor yet the charm his father might have used. In this moment he was as he imagined himself to be, gauche. His face was scarlet; his hands were searching for tow; his long legs refused to be still, yet would not carry him away. So much, his lacerated vanity told him, for the affair he'd dreamed of last night. He was no more capable of handling such an affair than would be any village idiot.

When she, too, rose to her feet with a swift movement that was not in keeping with her lazy attitude, and stood so close to him that the tiny beads of moisture on her brow below her hair line were visible to him in the fading light, he became rigidly still, and it wasn't of the smallest consolation to him to note that it was now she who was disturbed.

'Peter –' she touched his sleeve – 'I'm sorry I said that, but–' She paused and her head moved downwards in a troubled, bewildered fashion. 'This is mad, utterly, utterly mad. Twenty-four hours. It's crazy and it can't happen, even in fun.' She pulled her eyes upwards towards him now, and fixed them on him, and with her drawl hardly evident she said rapidly, 'Peter, you're nice, and a little fun with you would be nice, too. There was a time when I would have enjoyed it, then driven on, but not now. And don't think I can explain why – I can't. I'm not snubbing you when I won't let you start anything, believe me. I like you, Peter. I liked you the moment I set eyes on you. I like to be near you – you make me want to laugh, and that signifies much more than you think. Even when you're not uttering a word you make me want to laugh. I felt I knew you from the word go, but I'm not going to get to know you any further or in any other way.'

When he did not answer but continued to stare at her, she closed her eyes and her body slumped until she appeared to lose inches, and her voice sounded as tired as she looked when she said, 'You don't understand a word that I've been saying or why I've had to say it. And how should you? I knew last night I shouldn't stay here. . . . I'll go in the morning.'

'You needn't go because of me.' He could hardly press the words past his tongue, which seemed to be filling his mouth. 'I can keep out of your way.'

'Oh Peter! Peter.' There was a break in her voice, and her words as she went on were mostly unintelligible to him. All he could make out of them was: 'I'll bring you misery . . . tired . . . tired to death. Can't explain anything . . . not a thing. . . .'

She swayed as she stood; her hands were over her face now pressing back her sobs. Last night she had laughed as if she would never stop; now she was crying as if she would never stop.

When his arms went round her and drew her to rest

against him she made no protest but came almost as a weary child and moved her face into his coat as if searching for a place to rest. His hand was on her hair, the loose, wanton yellow hair; his chin could feel the smoothness of her cheek; her body lay close to his, yet it fired no urge. The feelings of the previous moment did not retrace their steps and leap back into him, but as he stood thus in the wood, with night fast closing about them forming a cloak which could be turned into a world to hold them alone, he felt for her only a great tenderness that had its birth in pity, and this tenderness had in it no ingredient for an affair; it brought him no promise of ecstasy, not even a small scrap of comfort, for in some quite inexplicable way he sensed he had linked himself to sorrow. How or why, it was beyond him to explain.

CHAPTER FOUR

The post office was full. Six people were in the shop, four at the stamp counter and two at the grocery. One of the latter was Miss Collins, and when it came her turn to be served, with prim condescension which she would have termed humility, she waived her priority to Mrs Fellows, and after watching the ungodly woman – for Mrs Fellows had never set foot in church and it was her proud boast that she never intended to – being served, and with narrowed eyes having watched her leave the shop, she turned to the waiting Mrs Armstrong and said, 'Ah, well now, what do I want?'

With a robin-like movement Mrs Armstrong put her head to one side, and she smiled and waited.

'I'd better have some biscuits, quarter pound of wholemeal – I'm visiting Grannie West. And yes, of course, I want extra sugar – we picked about twenty pounds of blackberries yesterday.'

'You did?' Mrs Armstrong bustled to the tins lined up with gaping tops behind a glass frame. 'I wish I had time to go picking, the weather's so lovely. The wood must be full.' The lid of the case clicked open. Mrs Armstrong grabbed up a handful of biscuits from a tin, dropped them into the bag, put down the lid again and returned to her position behind the counter before Miss Collins gave an answer to her remark.

'Not so much with blackberries as with people.' Miss Collin's pupils were large.

'Really?' Mrs Armstrong did not look at the scales.

'You haven't heard the latest?'

'No.' The scales bounced gently. Still without looking at them Mrs Armstrong took off the bag, gave it an expert twist and placed it on the counter in front of Miss Collins. Her eyes had never left the minister's sister, and she endeavoured to keep from her expression any sign of the malicious amusement she was feeling, for whatever the latest Miss Collins was about to impart it would certainly not be the same latest that she herself had already heard. The vicar's sister, she imagined, wouldn't be looking so smarmy if she knew that her lamb of a brother walked two solid miles along the main road yesterday afternoon with the piece from the Hart and was so taken up with her that he forgot to make his usual weekly call on old Mr Taplow, and there was Mrs Taplow waiting at the window when she saw him stalk by, stepping out like a spring gobbler – that had been Ray Sutton's expression. Ray had seen them from the byres in the farmyard, across the way from the Taplows. No, whatever she was going to hear from Miss Collins, it wouldn't be this.

'You wouldn't believe it, you really wouldn't.'

'No?' Mrs Armstrong's eyebrows moved up expectantly.

'The major.'

'The major! No, Miss Collins.' Mrs Armstrong's chin came in and Miss Collins's chin went up.

'It's a fact, and what do you think?' Miss Collins leaned across the counter, bringing her head down to Mrs Armstrong's, and her whisper was heavy with the insignia of

95

sin, 'They were lying on the grass together –' there was a considerable pause – 'sporting!'

The result of this information on the postmistress, who was steeped in tattle, was most gratifying. Her upper plate jerked loose in her gaping mouth and she saved it from bouncing on to the counter only by some expert lip contortion. With a final flick of her tongue, Mrs Armstrong got her teeth into place.

'You don't mean to say, Miss Collins!'

'I do. Mavis saw them with her own eyes. And something else, too. . . . Peter Puddleton, he was in the wood looking for her . . . the . . . the woman, not her, not Mavis. And what do you think? He was drunk again! Oh, that poor girl, she was so upset. I happened to be in the vicarage garden as she was passing and I had to bring her in and console her. And that's not all.'

Mrs Armstrong was beyond speech; nor could her eyes stretch any wider. She waited for Miss Collins to continue; and Miss Collins continued, her whisper getting deeper and more ominous.

'What do you think we saw on the road? This was later when I was escorting Mavis home.'

Mrs Armstrong did not move a muscle.

'Mr Puddleton, Mr Harry Puddleton –' she emphasised the Harry – 'and Mr Fountain creeping furtively into the wood. We saw them jump the ditch by the cottage, and with them the old man, Joe. He couldn't jump the ditch but went scurrying round by the gate, hoping to avoid being seen. And they couldn't say they were going fishing for there wasn't a line between them. Can you believe it?'

Mrs Armstrong's head moved very slowly from side to side; then contradicting her reaction she said hastily in an undertone, 'Yes, yes I can. That type drives men mad. Me mother here –' Mrs Armstrong jerked out her chin and thrust her head back towards a half-glassed, thinly curtained door behind which could be faintly discerned the figure of an old woman sitting in an armchair – 'me mother saw her go up the street yesterday, and you know she's not much interested in things now at her age but she was when she

96

saw the Hart piece. Stared after her she did for a long time, and then she said a funny thing.' Mrs Armstrong turned towards the glass door as if to make sure it was closed, then leant across the counter towards Miss Collins and her voice was a whisper now as she went on, ' "Who's she?" she said, "Don't see many like her knockin' about. I know that sort – had some dealing with 'em – always cause upsets, that sort." Then you know what she said? She said, "Puts me in mind of somebody she does." "Who?" I asked. "Can't say right off," she said, "but it'll come. But I remember this much, she was no good." '

The two women looked at each other. 'And then,' concluded Mrs Armstrong, 'have you heard what they're calling her?'

'No.'

'Slinky Jane.'

Mrs Armstrong's round face was an expanse of glee, but the joke found no response in Miss Collins. Her mouth was drawn to a button, bringing her lined face into furrows as she emitted, 'Slinky Jane! Well, whoever named her that knew what they were talking about, I've never heard of a name that suited anyone better. A Slinky Jane . . . she certainly is that!'

Mrs Armstrong's head was nodding and her smile broadening when, as if pulled by a string, it slid suddenly away, and with her eyes directed over Miss Collin's shoulder she said in a clipped undertone, 'Mrs Carrington-Barrett. She's just stopped across the way. She's talking to Mr Johnston.'

Miss Collins did not turn round to ascertain where Mrs Carrington-Barrett actually was, but her eyes did a swift circular exercise. Then in a voice loud enough to proclaim the legitimacy of the excuse for her hurry she patted the biscuits and said, 'I'll settle for these later when I call for the sugar, I don't want to carry it round with me. Grannie West looks forward to her little tit-bit.' She shook the bag and smiled. Then, bestowing a parting and somewhat detached nod on Mrs Armstrong, she turned with an air of casualness and left the shop.

Mrs Armstrong remained still while she watched the vicar's sister make a bee-line for the major's wife. If she wasn't mistaken there was going to be a lid blown off this morning. Miss Collins had been looking for some dynamite to throw at Mrs Carrington-Barrett for years, and now she had it. Mrs Armstrong suddenly hugged herself and waited and watched. And she did neither in vain, for within less than three minutes she saw that Miss Collins had struck.

It was about an hour later when Miss Collins passed the garage. She had no need to pass the garage but she was drunk with the battle of righteousness. During the past hour she had not only paid a sick visit but achieved two victories over the pride of her neighbours, for after having seen Mrs Carrington-Barrett's blood being drained from her face to leave it a sickly grey and the lady's vocabulary momentarily paralysed, she had encountered Amelia Fountain. Now Mrs Fountain was a fluctuating Christian, sometimes she was Church, less Church than Chapel, and because of this she was a source of irritation to Miss Collins. Moreover, there was something else Miss Collins held against Mrs Fountain. During the war and after, gratis choice cuts had now and again found their way to the rectory table; in fact, these little kindnesses of Bill's had continued up to two years ago, when they had ceased, and such was the situation that nothing could be said about the matter. Miss Collins, in her mind, had put the blame wholly upon Mrs Fountain and had only been waiting an opportunity to pay the butcher's wife out for her meanness.

Amelia Fountain was a thin, sharp-faced little woman, the complete antithesis of her husband in everything, including temper, but such was the shock she had received that morning on hearing the vicar's sister hint more than broadly that her Bill was one of the infatuated males who were chasing through the woods after the piece from the Hart that her retaliation almost choked her; it had left her, like Mrs Carrington-Barrett, speechless. Amelia had experienced an almost overpowering desire to jump on the long, thin piece of skin and misery that was Miss Collins, but her thoughts, leaping back to the middle of the night, had further paralysed her, for she could feel the great whale-like proportions of her husband tossing to and fro as he muttered over and over again, 'Ee! she's lovely . . . beautiful . . .' and a word which she couldn't catch. She had dug him with her elbow and he had woken up puffing and blowing as he always did. Then from Miss Collins's lips Amelia was supplied with the missing word – it was Jane! She recognised it immediately, and without even a word in her husband's defence she had left Miss Collins in the middle of further information and made straight for the shop.

After victory number two one might have thought that Miss Collins would have rested. But no, she wasn't done yet – there were the prime movers in this affair to be brought to book, the Puddletons. Yet she was wise enough, following on the events of yesterday afternoon, not to visit Rosie and inform her that her husband, too, had been running loose in the wood – that could wait, she would get that over to Rosie later – but to finish this morning's work there remained Peter and the vindication of Mavis. What she would say to that young man he wouldn't forget in a hurry.

Miss Collins was happy, very happy, and it could be said to be unfortunate for her that she should encounter the twins playing a game to which they resorted only when bored – they were, like their Grandpop, spitting to pass the time. Lying in the ditch bordering the road of the spare piece of land, they were whiling away the time until Peter should return and they could pass on the message that 'the Miss' had given them. The time seemed to hang less heavy when they played this game of attempting to register hits on passing vehicles. Tony's efforts they did not count as he was always in command of an unlimited supply of saliva. As traffic could not be called heavy they lay and sucked the long hollow stems of the grasses between bouts, but would return to the job in hand with enthusiasm on the sound of wheels coming from around the bend. Being unable to see what type of vehicle was actually approaching until it was almost on top of them made the game all the more exciting.

They could, however, distinguish between farm machinery and cars, and the awaited victim now was undoubtedly of the farm variety, as was denoted by its loud rattling and the slowness of its approach.

Flat on their bellies, they got ready, jaws working in anticipation. There it came, its mighty wheels shaking the earth, the noise deafening them . . . splatch! splatch! splatch! Jimmy got in one direct hit, Johnny none. Tony a number he couldn't count. The tractor rumbled past, its driver ignorant of the assault, and the twins, collapsing from their efforts, rubbed their faces down into the warm grass again. But not Tony. Tony continued, at short intervals, to spit at a point in the road, and it was more than unfortunate that Miss Collin's light and sprightly step should bring her around the corner to that point and afford a direct hit for Tony, low it must be admitted, but nevertheless direct.

The squawk emitted by Miss Collins had the power to shoot the twins out of the ditch. They had no need to wait and enquire what had happened, their flying legs, followed by those of Tony, showed without doubt how well informed they were.

Miss Collins, after rubbing at her thick lisle stockings with a handkerchief which she then threw away in disgust, stormed up the drive to the garage and into it, to be confronted by Old Pop sitting on the box with his paper and his pipe.

Old Pop did not look at Miss Collins; he appeared deeply engrossed in the paper which, he realised, was upside down but which he couldn't right without giving himself away. From the garage door he'd had a view of the bend of the road hidden to the twins, and had not only witnessed the whole affair but had anticipated it, and now he was shaking with suppressed laughter.

'Where . . . where's Peter?'

'Eh?' Now Old Pop lowered the paper, folding it as he did so. 'Oh! Mornin', Miss. You want Peter?'

'Yes. You heard me.' Miss Collins looked around the garage with a really ferocious glare.

'Ain't here, Miss.'

'Well, where is he?'

'Farm . . . mending tractor. You want petrol, or summat?'

As the vicarage ran to neither a car nor a motor-mower this was obviously a stupid remark, and was met with compressed lips by Miss Collins, until she sprang them apart to declare, 'I'll put a stop to this.'

'What, Miss?' Old Pop had risen solicitously.

'This.' Miss Collins pointed to the wet stain on her stocking, 'Though it's no good talking to you, you're as bad as they are, and . . . and, that dirty old –' now she was spluttering in her anger – 'your father, who eggs them on. But I'll put a stop to it once and for all, I'll see Constable Pollard, I'll get the police to deal with this, I will. I will.'

'I wouldn't do that, Miss, t'ain't Christian.'

Miss Collins swallowed, drew herself up to her full height, and looked for the moment as if she were about to demonstrate on Old Pop the complaint in question. Then swallowing twice more she turned about and seemed to leave the ground and fly, so quick was her departure.

The happenings in the village during the day were usually reiterated in the Hart at night, and there had certainly been enough events in the past few hours to keep the conversation at a high pitch of stimulation. For had not Miss Collins bearded the major's wife in the street. Major, so it was rumoured, had been larking on the quiet with the guest at the Hart. What was more, 'Melia Fountain had gone for Bill for not keeping his eyes at home, and then the 'Pudd' twins had spat on Miss Collins and she had gone to Pollard and reported them. But the best piece of all concerned Peter Puddleton, for he had been seen coming out of the wood at eleven o'clock last night with the lady who was setting the village on fire. Mrs Booth said she'd had to come downstairs and let her in and had given her the length of her tongue. That was a funny one that, as the Booths were known never to get upstairs afore twelve at the earliest. Ma Booth apparently didn't cotton on to her guest. And now the guest had gone to Newcastle. Everybody knew she had gone to Newcastle for she left a message with the Puddleton twins to tell Peter, and they had told him in front of Dan Wilkins, but they hadn't said when she was coming back.

The question that was covertly going round the room now was: Who was really getting her favours – Harry Puddleton? Bill Fountain? Major? or Peter? it was a big laugh when you came to think of it. But the laughter subsided when Peter made his appearance, yet the greetings thrown to him were even heartier than usual.

His father, Peter saw, was not in the bar, nor was Bill. But as he took a seat on the broad window-ledge Bill came in, and, after nodding briefly here and there and calling for a drink, he came and joined Peter. And it was plain to see that he was not in his usual form; there was no grin fastened on his face tonight.

After taking the top off his beer he nodded and remarked, somewhat dolefully, 'Hallo, lad.'

'Hallo,' said Peter, and as a conversational rejoinder he added, 'been a grand day.'

Bill, lifting his drink again, took another draught and said, 'For some, likely.' And on this simple, yet significant, statement he rested for a moment; then moving nearer to Peter and in a really subdued tone for him he went on 'Been a hell of a day for me, all through that damned eel.'

Peter, his face crumpling with enquiry, said, 'The eel?'

'Aye, seems like I shouted out her name in me sleep, then that old bitch, parson's sister, collared the wife this mornin' and told her I was off last night sneakin' through the wood. And who to see?' He leaned nearer. 'You won't believe it, but the wife's got a bee in her bonnet. She thinks that it was Miss here I was after.' He raised desperate eyes to the ceiling. 'Talk I've done this day till I've been near blue in the face tellin' her 'twas the eel that took me through the wood and that it was her name that was Slinky Jane. "Eel, be damned for a tale!" she says, and if I told that to a cat it would scratch my eyes out; and I was a clever dyed-in-the-wool so-and-so to think up such a thing: "Go and see for yersel," I says, "'tis in the lake." And you know what, Peter?'

Peter shook his head just the slightest, and Bill wiped his

entire face with his hand before resuming, 'She went and came back as mad as Downey's bull. You know what?' Bill's face looked pitiable now. 'The twins were there and they swore there was no eel in the lake. They played at the lake all the time they said, and they'd never seen no eel. Can you believe it?' After staring at Peter with popping eyes Bill wiped the sweat again from his face. 'And that's not all, no, not by a long chalk. You know what those limbs of Satan told her when she asked them if young lady came to the lake? "Aye," they said. "And who else?" she asks. "Sometimes our Peter or me Da," they says, "and sometimes the major, and sometimes – and sometimes Mr Fountain." "And what do they do?" she asks.' Bill paused and stared at Peter over the handkerchief that half covered his face, and his voice dropped to a groaning whisper as he said, ' "They just laugh and lark a bit," they said. My God!' – Bill's face was lost for a moment behind his handkerchief – 'I could kill the pair of them.'

It was in Peter now to laugh, to throw back his head and bellow, but he could see that Bill was in a stew and was seeing no funny side to the affair.

'Wednesday night, an' all,' Bill began again. 'Always take her into a show, Hexham, Wednesday night, but she wouldn't budge.' He drew in a deep breath. 'One thing I do know, I'll never put me foot inside that wood again as long as I live.'

Bill took a long drink, and Peter, looking at the mountain of flesh, wondered just how far a woman could become self-deluded. Love, in this case, had not a thousand eyes, he thought, but must be stone-blind. A woman who could imagine that Bill could be found attractive to anyone like Leo must be both blind and daft. Yet he had always thought Mrs Fountain a very sensible woman. Looking at Bill, he wanted to laugh again and he was pleased that he could feel like this. It was good to find something to laugh about in this business. The whole thing should be funny, an eel and a girl, and a village getting them all mixed up. But somehow it hadn't turned out like that.

Last night he had held her in his arms; he had felt her

103

body almost melting into his; he had buried his lips in her hair; and what had he felt? Only a sadness. She had seemed to inject him with the sadness that was filling herself. Where had she gone today? Newcastle, the message had said. Why hadn't she come and told him herself? She could have done so. And no word of when she was coming back. What if she didn't come back?

This thought brought him to his feet, and Bill, looking up at him, quickly asked, 'What! off already?'

'Aye. Think I'll take a trip into Allendale.'

'Do.' Bill nodded warningly. 'Any place is better than the wood. But,' he added, 'that's not your worry. You're free to go into the wood if you like, but it won't see me again, eel or no eel. Oh, no!'

Peter grinned down on to the worried butcher and said, 'So long, Bill.'

'S'long, Peter.'

Under the covert gaze of the regulars, and of Mrs Booth in particular, he made his way out of the inn, and down past the yard to the bus stop.

There was one other person waiting for the bus, it was Miss Tallow, and she greeted him in her perky fashion as usual.

'Good evening, Peter, good evening.'

'Good evening, Miss Tallow.'

No one ever called Miss Tallow anything but Miss Tallow.

'Been a beautiful day, hasn't it?'

'Yes, it has, Miss Tallow.'

Miss Tallow coughed, pulled her white cotton gloves farther up her wrists, then said, without any preamble, 'I do like your client, Peter. The young lady. She came in for coffee yesterday. Oh, it is nice to talk to someone other than the villagers. Not that I am saying anything against the villagers, you know what I mean, Peter.'

Peter stared down at the tiny little woman and nodded his understanding.

'A most intelligent girl. Remarkable looking, too. Of course, other people may not think so. You can stay too long in one place and your ideas of the world become very narrow, but I found her most exhilarating. We talked of poetry. She knows such a lot of poetry.'

Miss Tallow stared up at Peter, waiting for some retort, and all he could find to say was, 'Does she?'

'Yes, very well versed. It's a pity she's only staying a fortnight. If there were one or two more like her here – I mean of her mind –' Miss Tallow made the distinction soberly – 'we could start a literary group. You know, Peter –' Miss Tallow's voice sank down to her small depths – 'there's very little culture in the village. Mrs Carrington-Barrett does her best, and, of course, there are one or two others, but the rest, dear! dear!' Miss Tallow shook her head, then asked brightly, 'Are you going into Allendale, Peter?'

'Yes, I was thinking of going there, Miss Tallow.'

'Ah, here's the bus.'

The bus rumbled to a stop, Peter put out one hand to help Miss Tallow up, and automatically his other hand went out in surprise and excitement to help Leo down.

Miss Tallow cooed words of recognition, while from the platform the conductor demanded tersely whether Peter was coming or going. And Peter, as if coming out of a dream, exclaimed hastily, 'No, no. I'm not getting on.'

The bell tinkled sharply; Miss Tallow's perky face looked through the window and she raised her hand in a little fluttering salute which Leo answered.

They were left standing looking at each other.

'So you've got back?'

'Yes.' Her voice sounded gay, and he noticed that her eyes were bright, laughing bright. She looked altogether happier, and he wondered where she had been and what had happened to cause the change.

'Were you going into Allendale?'

He smiled shyly. 'Yes, I was.'

'And I changed your mind?'

'That's about it.'

He could not help but notice that she seemed excited, and somehow this depressed him. And then she said, 'Would you wait until I put my case inside?' She nodded back towards the inn and, her voice dropping very low, she added, 'I've got something I want to ask you.'

'Ask me?'

She nodded slowly. 'We'll go to the pool, eh?'

'As you like.'

She held his gaze before turning away, and his neck became hot under her eyes. He watched her moving without hurry towards the inn, and he knew that she would not make her entry unnoticed, nor yet her exit, nor would it go unnoticed that they were making for the wood. Well, what of it; he didn't care a damn what they thought. And in this frame of mind he did not walk up the road so that their meeting would go unobserved, but he waited for her where she had left him. There was a recklessness in him that he was beginning to enjoy. But when she did rejoin him his recklessness did not move him to words; he could find nothing to say to her. He could only smile at her and suit his long strides to hers.

He should have felt uneasy walking in silence the length of the road with her but he didn't, and not until they entered the wood did either of them speak. And then it was he who asked, 'Had a nice day?'

'Yes, very.'

'Somehow I didn't expect you back the night.'

'Didn't you?' She glanced up at him. 'It's odd, but I didn't expect to come back either.'

'No?' Their eyes held, then again they walked on in silence, which lasted until they came to the lake.

As if by common consent they made straight for the edge of the bank and looked down into the water. There was no sign of the eel, and they did not mention her, but after some moments Peter, being unable to restrain his curiosity any longer said, 'Well?'

'Yes? Well?'

Her eyes were cocked sideways at him, and he turned full to her now and said, 'You wanted to ask me something.'

For a second her gaze flickered over the water, then turning swiftly to him she thrust out her hands impulsively towards him, saying softly, 'Oh, Peter.'

His nerves were jangling. He held her hands tightly for a moment, then he lifted them and pressed the palms to his cheeks, so drawing her nearer to him, and when her face was beneath his, he said again softly, 'Well?'

Staring at him, she swallowed then asked, 'Could you enter into a game for the next fortnight, Peter?' Her voice was small.

'A game?' His brows contracted slightly but he was still smiling. 'It would all depend upon what the game was.'

'Loving me.' It was an even smaller whisper.

The colour that flooded over his face seemed to sweep the happiness from it. He could feel it rushing down to the soles of his feet, then up again to form a film over his eyes that blotted her from his sight.

This is what he had wanted on Monday night, an affair; and now it was being offered to him and nothing in him welcomed it. To love her, yes. But the time limit which gave it the stamp of the thing he had first desired aroused in him a feeling of revulsion. He was, to say the least, embarrassed at such an approach. In cases of this nature it was the man who suggested the rules, dictated the pace – took, then moved on – and that, to put it in a nutshell, was what she was proposing to do.

'Peter.'

He saw her face again. Not joyous now, and the apprehension she was feeling came over in her voice as she said, 'Oh, Peter! you think me awful, don't you? Fast as they come – a real tart in fact.'

'No! No, I don't.' He was strong in his protest – all his qualms and his ideas as to the fitness of things were brushed aside. 'I – I think you're the most wonderful creature on earth. That's what I think, and it's true. I've never come across anybody like you. I love you Leo.' His arms went about her and his thoughts took wings in words and rolled off his tongue: 'I do love you, and it's no use saying I haven't had time yet to get to know you. But I don't want just a fortnight of you, I want a lifetime.'

She moved within his hold, and his tone changed and he entreated, wistfully now, 'Leo, listen to me. I know we never clapped eyes on each other until Monday but you know and I know something has happened. And it's no light thing, nothing you can docket in days. Look at me, Leo –' he pulled her face round to him – 'you must feel this . . . you must. Look, tell me.' He was holding her chin none too gently now. 'Is there another man? I can't get the idea of that fellow out of me head. Is there? Don't lie to me, whatever there is, tell me.'

Her eyes, as she looked back at him now, held a dead expression. 'I give you my word there's nobody. Nobody,' she repeated.

'But there has been?' He made himself ask this.

Her gaze did not flicker from his and her voice was cool and steady as she said, 'Yes, there has been.'

He stared at her, refusing to let his mind dwell on this but knowing that later the thought would eat through him. 'Do you love me?' he asked.

He felt the uneasy movement of her body again, and now it spoke to him of impatience. And this was verified when she lifted her chin from his hand and said, 'I asked you to love me, doesn't that answer you?'

'No.'

With another movement she indicated that she wanted to be free, but his arms still held her and she looked up into his face again and said, 'What you mean by love may not be the same as what I mean – I like you –' she brought her eyes from his and looked over the lake – 'I like you a lot, enough to want to make you happy. I cannot promise you a lifetime of happiness which you seem to expect – that would be silly in any case – but I'm offering you something that is sure . . . a few days. There!' She looked back into his face again, and her tone had a flippant air. 'If you don't want it that way there is no harm done . . . none.'

Looking at her he knew he should be thinking, 'She is hard-boiled. This isn't the first time by a long chalk that she has done this'; but the face before him set up a defence for itself. In spite of the look of age or knowledge that the eyes possessed, the face below his was young – there were no lines of calculation, the mouth was generous, and it spoke silently to him now telling him to delude himself no further for whatever his opinion of her might be his answer to her was inevitable.

His lips fell to hers, hard, tight, demanding, and hers yielded hungrily. Their bodies pressed fast, they swayed together oblivious of time, and when at last they drew apart their eyes held the bond they had sealed.

His arm about her, they moved to the bank, and when they sat down it was in a single movement so close were they.

For a long while they said nothing but sat, their cheeks together, staring across the water; then of one accord they turned their heads and gazed at each other. At first their faces showed only the light of their happiness, until Leo, dropping her cheek against his again, began to chuckle. It was soft at first and Peter's smile widened with it, then with a sudden burst she laughed outright, as she had done the first evening, and between gasps she cried, 'Oh, Peter! Peter –' She pressed against him, and his arms held her tightly and he did not try to check her mirth as he had done on Monday night, but he joined his laughter to hers, and it spread through the wood until its echo reached a pop-eyed Miss Collins in the vicarage garden; and Mavis, too, as she patrolled the main road. But Florrie, where she stood within listening distance a short way along the bank, it hit with its full impact and caused her to bite her lip until the blood came. And when the laughter died away each had her own mental picture of what was happening now and was urged to put a stop to it.

CHAPTER FIVE

While subjects varying from politics to the Church can raise hot blood in a town, the village verdict as a whole, excluding the Women's Institute, would be, 'Let they get on with it,' but the contrary happens when the fundamental urge of life is touched upon. Whereas sex can be indulged in without undue comment in a town, in the village it stirs up a strange and strong reaction . . . let it be admitted, mostly in the women. But even in them, passions come under a certain control if the offender be one of themselves, but should she not be of the village or thereabouts their feelings are liable to rise and flood over. Virtue is outraged where virtue never was, enemies are for a time linked together, and life before the particular event appears to have been good, almost holy. And this feeling touches the mildest of women.

To the extent it had touched Rosie can be guessed at, for she was no mild woman, and it had brought her on this Saturday morning to a stand behind the curtains in her bedroom, waiting to see 'her' come out of the Hart, and where she would make for when she did come out. But after half an hour, owing to the pressure of her house duties, Rosie was forced to give up her watch, but going downstairs and into her front room she approached Grandpop aggressively and without any prelude whatever ordered, 'Keep your eye on the Hart and if you see that – that Miss Carter come out, let me know.'

'What for?' Grandpop turned sharply and in doing so set the screws in his legs working, which caused him to explode with a 'Damn and blast them!' And then he added in much the same tone, 'What you want to know for?'

'Never you mind, just you call.'

Rosie, stalking into the kitchen, decided flatly that if 'she'

110

was going to the garage she wouldn't get there alone. She wasn't going to stand by and see her lad made a fool of; she knew that type, unsettle him for life that one would. There had certainly been something in the wood business. Eel! Really! What did he take her for? He must think she was simple. Which just showed how simple he was and how easily he could be caught.

Grandpop watched Rosie out of the room, and then he thrust his head out of the window and called, 'Joe! . . . here! D'you hear? Joe!'

But not until Grandpop's third bellow had filled the square did Joe appear, and Grandpop, almost foaming at the mouth, bawled, 'You stone deaf?'

'No,' said Old Pop testily. 'Who could be with you around? Can't you see I'm busy?'

'Aye, if I'd eyes that went round corners I might. Here!' He beckoned his son nearer to him, and when Old Pop stepped over the flower bed and brought his head close to his father's, Grandpop, his voice now as near as he could get it to a whisper, said, 'Feel owt?'

Old Pop's eyes narrowed and his face screwed up into folds.

'Feel owt?' he repeated. 'What do you mean? About it being sports day?'

'Sports day! Don't be so pluddy gormless,' admonished his father. 'You know as well as me, summat's up.'

'You mean with the lad?'

'Aye, and with 'ole village. Look at yesterday, Miss Florrie going past and never a "Hallo there" – made on horse was mettlesome, didn't turn her eye, she didn't. First time in her life. Then old Ma Andrews comin' sittin' outside the shop.' Grandpop nodded in the direction of the post office. 'Never done that for years, she hasn't six or more. Then Pluddy Bridget goes in twice in afternoon again. And who else waddles in but Katie Booth? What Harry ever saw in that old sow. Flabby, fat – '

'Shut up man!' said Old Pop sharply.

'She's in kitchen – ' Grandpop jerked his head backwards – 'she'd have to hoick her ears out to hear me.'

'She could be as far gone as Hexham but she'd hear summat like that, so let it drop.'

Reluctantly Grandpop let it drop and reverted to the condition of his feelings. 'I tell ee summat's up . . . feel it . . . all this week I feel it.'

'It's yer screws.'

'Screws, be damned!' Grandpop reared and made an effort to straighten out his rheumaticky joints. 'And don't start talkin' pappy. Ain't no screws inside here,' he tapped the top of his cap, 'nor here,' he nudged the centre of his waistcoat. 'Couldn't sleep last night, thinkin'. Mind went right back years. Funny it was, as if it was yesterda'.'

' 'Twill do at your time,' said Old Pop, aiming to soothe, 'it's what to expect.'

For a moment if looked as if Grandpop was going to lift his arm and land a backhander on his son, but he changed his mind and bawled at him instead, 'I ain't dead yet.'

'Who's a-sayin' you are?'

'Then don't talk as if I'd been screwed down. Pay some in this village if they'd a head clear as mine.'

'Yes, 'twould that.' Old Pop agreed readily now for he could see that his father was on his high-horse. And there was no doubt that he was right about summat funny being up in the village, and he knew who was the cause of it. Yet she was a civil-spoken Miss, as pleasant as you could hope to find in a day's march – she made you feel young, she did. There was no denying that she had that queer something that made an old 'un feel young and a young 'un feel old – old enough to matter at any rate. And that's how the lad now felt.

Old Pop suddenly rubbed his hand over his eyes as if trying to shut out all he knew. Who would have thought it? The apple of Rosie's eye – him that was so far removed from the rest of her menfolk. It would serve her right in a way and level things out a bit if she was to know that her lamb was the fastest worker of them all and he'd like to bet that included the old 'un himself.

'Get your head out of the way.' Grandpop suddenly pushed at Joe to get a view of the Hart, then exclaimed in excited tones, ' 'Tis the Miss comin' out and makin' for this way. That's another thing, she – ' he jerked his head towards the kitchen again – 'she's been on the look-out for her. Spent God knows how long upstairs she did at window, heard her creakin' on boards. Then down she come. "Tell me when Miss comes out Hart," she says. She didn't say, "Tell me if she makes for garage," but that's what she meant all right.'

Old Pop looked narrowly at his father. 'You gonna tell her?'

'Not damn likely – whãt d'you take me for? What'll she do if I tell her, eh? Skip down garage and say to Miss to leave him alone, as if he was Wee Willie Winkie. No; lad's to have his fling . . . 'bout time he started. She's had him lashed to her back for years. If he don't make a move he'll end up with that sick cow – ' he head moved violently now in the direction of the Mackenzies' house – 'and what she'd give him wouldn't tint the white innards of a black beetle.'

With a chortle of laughter in his throat Old Pop was about to make for the gate to watch the approach of Leo when Grandpop said angrily, 'You make off round back, you ain't got the sense you were born with. What if she stops for a word? Rosie'd be on her like a wasp on jam.'

Ignoring the insult to his intelligence, Old Pop turned away muttering, 'Aye, aye. Perhaps you're right,' and with some reluctance went round the back, leaving Grandpop apparently immersed in the scraping and filling of his pipe. His good eye appeared to be in attendance on this occupation while the one with the cast seemed to be roving at will. Whether this was an illusion or not, Grandpop was able to discern the miss as she looked towards him and at almost the same time he followed the approach towards the post office of both Miss Collins and Mrs Booth, walking side by side. And the excited rumble in his stomach, translated, would have said, 'Never happened afore in my time, Church and pub together; summat's up somehow or I'm a Dutchman.'

It is true that Mrs Booth and Miss Collins had come through the village together, but that was five minutes ago. Now within the cramped space of the post office they were standing as wide apart as they could possibly get, and Miss Collins was endeavouring to widen the distance even farther. But only at the risk of stepping into a box of oranges could she do this, and so she turned her outraged expression down on to the fruit, then back to Mrs Booth, and that lady, her fat moving gently with satisfaction, said, 'Well, I was only pointing out that she doesn't even leave a minister of God alone, I wasn't suggesting anything. But Mrs Armstrong here can tell you it's all over the place. Isn't it, Mrs Armstrong?' She appealed to the red face of the post-mistress. 'Aren't they saying that the Reverend forgot to call on old Taplow all through him talking to her? Walked right past the door he did, so they're saying. And as I was saying, I wasn't looking for it nor yet thinking about her – I've better things to do with me time – but I just slipped down the bottom of the garden for a bit parsley and there I saw them. There's no mistaking the minister, is there, Miss Collins?' Mrs Booth smiled a little smile before torturing the minister's sister still further. 'There he was, like any gallant, and as perky as you like, helping her over the stile bottom of Reed's cottage, and held her arm right to the wood he did. As jaunty as a cricket he looked. But that's over an hour gone, and now she's just gone up to Peter Puddleton. Allots her time seemingly. You should hear what they say in the bar.'

Mrs Booth stopped for want of breath, but Miss Collins did not nip in as might have been expected and deny the implications being levelled against her brother, and a very uneasy silence fell on the shop. When it could be borne no longer, Mrs Armstrong busily rearranged some of her merchandise on the counter, and remarked in a sad voice, 'It's getting awful, it really is . . . even Tony Boyle. All the years I've been in the village I've never known anything like it.'

The eyes of the two women turned now on Mrs Armstrong, those of Miss Collins somewhat reluctantly, as she appeared to have to drag her attention away from the turmoil of her mind.

'Tony Boyle?' said Mrs Booth, her face screwed up.

'Yes, Tony Boyle. It's right. Stan Dolton saw her yesterday, nearly at the crossroads they were, walking hand-in-hand.'

The faces of the women now all showed a tinge of horror and disgust.

'With Tony Boyle?' repeated Mrs Booth again.

'With Tony Boyle,' said Mrs Armstrong in sad, awe-laden tones. After nodding significantly she continued, 'And Stan stopped the car and spoke to them, for, as he said, he thought he'd better. He said perhaps she didn't know about Tony. He even offered them a lift, but she said no, they were looking for the twins. The twins that far, huh! And he said Tony was laughing his head off. I told Mrs Boyle when she was in not long since. I told her "If you don't want no trouble you look out." Say he turns on her, she'll have you up, her kind would.'

'You did quite right. What did she say?' asked Mrs Booth.

'She said she'd give him his hammers, and she will an' all, she'll lather him.'

At this point the glass door leading to the living-room opened and old Mrs Andrews, with the aid of two sticks, made her appearance. But her daughter did not look over-joyed at this interruption and she called loudly to her mother, 'Now, Ma, what you about?'

Ma, hobbling round the counter, grunted, 'Gonna sit out front.'

When the old woman came to Mrs Booth's side she tried to straighten her back and look up into her face, but this being too great an effort her words were directed floorwards as she said, 'Nice folks you're housin'.'

Apparently Mrs Booth had not to ponder to find out what the old lady meant, for she answered immediately, 'We've no choice, we're an inn.'

The old woman gave a long significant sniff, then asked, 'Where's she this mornin'?'

Mrs Booth now bent down to her and jovially shouted, 'Gone up to garage. What do you make of her, Gran?'

'Whore.'

Mrs Booth's body jerked up and her head went back and her laugh rang out, but Miss Collins did not laugh, for the word, besides shocking her, conveyed to her the complete seduction of her brother, and she looked for the moment as if she would collapse.

The old woman, conscious of all eyes on her, now said with authority, 'Wondered who she minded me of, an' it just come up in me mind not five minutes gone.' She turned her eyes towards her daughter. 'Connie, her that caused riot. Afore your time it was . . . same type as this 'un. They ducked her they did. Had no more bother with her after that. Saw it meself, I did.' She chuckled.

'Who ducked who?'

They all turned towards the open doorway and there stood Florrie, sombre and haughty-looking this morning, with the steely light of battle in her eyes.

'Oh! Good morning, Miss,' said Mrs Armstrong, with just a touch of obsequiousness.

'Good morning, Mrs Armstrong.'

'Good morning.' The greeting moved around the shop as Florrie came in, and Mrs Booth, with a wiggle of her body preluding the slightest narrowing of her eyes, said, 'We was just talking of a certain lady, and Gran here says she reminds her of somebody that was like her . . . Connie Fitzpatrick. Perhaps you've never heard of her though?' The suggestion was malicious, to say the least, for it had been Florrie's great-grandfather who had built the cottage for the same Connie.

'Why should you imagine I haven't heard of her?' Florrie did not like Mrs Booth. She looked down on her for various reasons and her feeling came over in her tone.

As usual, it was not lost on Mrs Booth, and her quick reply held her retaliation, 'Oh, well, if you've heard of her that's all right then, you've nothing to learn. Only Gran here says my visitor's another like her and 'twould seem she's right, with Peter Puddleton at the head of her calling list.'

Florrie stared at the big woman for a moment and her slim body seemed visibly to lengthen, then with a small drawing together of her brows she went towards the grille that denoted the post office section, and with her head slightly turned she threw a question over her shoulder: 'Do you know where your husband is this morning, Mrs Booth?'

In spite of the polite way in which the question was asked Mrs Booth was not unaware that this was an attack, and she thrust out her bust and advanced a step towards Florrie's back, snapping, 'In bar, getting ready for opening. That's where my husband is, Miss!'

'There you are mistaken, Mrs Booth.' Florrie's eyes flicked round and met those of Mrs Booth before turning to the grid again.

'What you meaning, miss?'

'Do you know where Miss Carter is?'

'She's up in garage with Peter Puddleton by now. I told you.'

'She's not, you know, Mrs Booth.' There was a vicious snap in Florrie's words. 'She didn't go to the garage, she turned up Wilkins' cut, and there I saw her meet and speak to your husband. It seemed as if he were waiting for her. And you know where Wilkins' cut leads to; it leads to the wood, Mrs Booth.'

It looked as if Mrs Booth might explode, but for once she could find nothing to say, mischievous or otherwise, and old Mrs Andrews who could not have heard all that was being said but who judged the substance, from the expressions of those about her, gave Mrs Booth one long look before moving towards the shop door, and there she cast her eyes towards the clear, hot sky and stated, 'Rain – smell it. Always rains sports day, an' it'll rain the day. And more besides water it strikes me. Aye, it will that.'

Back in the shop, Mrs Armstrong, with feverish haste, was trying to attend to her customers all at once. She had an urge to be rid of them, for, as she told herself, she liked a bit of gossip as well as the next but Katie Booth was looking as if she might get rough with Miss Florrie at any minute, and she didn't want that, not in her shop she didn't. Let her do what she liked outside, and good luck to her. 'Twas as her mother said, it would rain more besides water afore the day was out.

CHAPTER SIX

Peter tried desperately to hold on to his temper as he looked from the older to the younger Mackenzie. Taking yet another deep breath he said for the countless time during the last half hour, 'I'm not selling.' Then in staccato tones he added, 'I've told you I'm not selling; nor am I letting out any shares, do you hear?' He thrust out his chin. 'I'm not selling, and I don't want to hear any more of it. And you needn't worry about the agent if that's any solace to you. I'm not selling to him, an' I'm not selling to you. I'm not selling at all, I've told you. Why should I? Would you? I'm not a damn fool altogether, you know.'

'No, no, lad,' said Mr Mackenzie soothingly, 'we know you're not, but as we see it you need money to expand. This – ' he waved his hand round the old blacksmith's shop – 'this won't do for the future, it'll have to be rebuilt, and where are you goin' to get the money from?'

'That's my business.'

'Yes, yes, we know that, an' all.' Mr Mackenzie's voice was as smooth as butter. 'As you say, lad, it's your business. So all right, we'll leave it for the time being. You never know what changes a man's mind – never. Ah, well, we'll away, but we'll be seeing you, lad.'

As they departed Peter's voice hissed out at their backs, 'I won't sell a stone, so you needn't bank on me changing me mind.'

'We heard you.' Davy's reply, thrown over his shoulder, was not as smooth as his father's, and turning at the garage door he added, 'There's one thing I will ask, and that is if you do change your mind you'll let us have the first refusal – you won't go and do another dirty trick on us.'

Before Peter could make any retort to this, Mr Mackenzie

reprimanded his son with a loud, 'Come on, come on, enough of that.'

Peter almost sprang to the garage door, the urge strong in him to get at Davy, but he was forced to restrain himself on the sight of his mother coming out of their gate, sails all out. Even at this distance he could detect the signs, and when he saw her heading up the street he returned hastily into the garage and began busying himself.

Rosie swept upon him. Nothing else could describe her entry, and without any lead-up she began where she had left off at breakfast time. 'If you think I'm putting up with this, you're mistaken.'

Peter said nothing. He went on greasing the steel rod in his hands.

'The place is on fire, everybody's talkin' . . . are you mad?'

There was still no retort from Peter.

'If you don't think of yourself, you should think of me. Three of 'em I've had to put up with in this way. All me life I've had it, and now you start. God in Heaven! It's unbearable. And with a hussy like that.'

'Shut up!'

The bark almost lifted Rosie from the ground. It lifted her hand to her mouth and she gasped, 'Don't you dare speak to me like that!'

'Well, be careful what you say.' He was looking at her in a way that he had never done in his life before, as if he hated her.

But Rosie, refusing to recognise any change in her son, went dauntlessly on. 'Well, don't think I'm going to stand by and let you make a fool of yourself, as big as you are. I've still got some say in this family, and you'll find that out. And mind you – ' she raised her finger to him – 'if you take her to the sports the day you won't see me there, and there'll be summat to do.'

'Well, there'll be summat to do, because she's going.'

For a moment Rosie was silent and startled; then through tightly drawn lips she brought out, 'You can't be serious, lad, not with her. I think I'd rather see you take up with

119

Mavis after all. Better the devil you know. At least she doesn't look like a – '

'Shut up, will you!'

Rosie stared at her son. He hadn't barked this time, in fact she could only just make out what he said, but it was the way he had said it. It wasn't her lad speaking. For the first time she began to doubt her power over him, and it made her afraid, but she showed none of her fear as she cried, 'You can't do it, you can't! You'd be worse than any of them. The ones that they took at least looked decent.'

He swung round on her, his face ablaze and his anger choking him, and they glared at each other until she wrenched herself about and went out, her body shaking with unintelligible sounds.

Slowly he passed his forearm over his wet brow. He would never have believed that this could have happened between his mother and him – never. He put out his hand and gripped the doorpost to steady the trembling of his body. Oh, this business was damnable, damnable. If he knew where he stood he could have said firmly, 'There's nothing you can do about it, I'm going to marry her,' but he didn't know where he stood. He couldn't think that he was to have Leo for only another week, yet he knew without doubt that when the car was put together again she would go. For a moment he wished that he had never set eyes on her. Then he refuted this thought sharply. She was the most wonderful thing that had happened to him in his life. He also felt now that there hadn't been a moment in his life when he hadn't known her. Yet what did he know about her? Nothing. He could only keep guessing. He was tortured by the thought of the men in her life. He had the constant desire to find out just what this last one had meant to her, but he had not the courage to bring up the subject boldly.

In the space of a few days his life had become a sort of sweet hell dominated by her. And on the outskirts stood his mother and the villagers watching his every move . . . and there were the sports this afternoon. God! He groaned aloud.

Since he was sixteen, apart from the two years he was away on National Service, Peter had on sports day run in the race over the fells; he had also manned one end of the tug-o'-war, had a shot at climbing the greasy pole, and had been successful on three occasions in getting the goose from the top, and yearly he had attempted to beat the record at mending a puncture. Also he invariably had his fortune told by Miss Tallow, who wore a mask and a gipsy costume, and the reading of his fate had always been accompanied by guffaws and side-chat from the listeners outside the tent. And finally he had danced on the uneven grass to Ned Poole's fiddle and Harold Casey's melodeon, and altogether always thoroughly enjoyed himself. How much of this enjoyment had been derived from popular acclaim and from knowing that, the Mackenzie men excepted, he was without an enemy in the place, he never questioned. He only knew he liked the sports. But today was different, he was afraid of the sports. He did not want Leo to go to the fete at all, and there be the focal point of sly interest on the men's part and something not so pleasant on the women's, for he, like his great-grandfather, was feeling that all was not as it should be, even outside his own home. To some extent he could understand his mother's attitude, but not that of the other women. What is it? he asked himself. Why don't they like her? And to this question he gave himself the answer: Well would they now, with she as she is and they as they are?

The race over the fells did not start until two o'clock. But shortly after one Peter left the house. Rosie was in a silent-martyr mood, which was worse than her yelling, and unbearable to him.

Grandpop looking somewhat soberly from the window, said, 'Early off, aren't you?'

'Aye,' replied Peter briefly.

'Gonna be rain.'

'Yes, it seems like it.' He looked up at the grey-tinted sky. 'Could be a storm.'

'Aye, it will be, an' be a bad 'un, I can tell yer.'

'So long.'

'So long, lad. Take care of yersel'.'

Peter turned at the gate and paused for a moment and looked across the garden at the old man. He did not feel annoyed at the caution inferred, rather did he feel a tenderness rise in him towards this querulous and still sensual individual, and he smiled across at him and nodded, saying, 'Never fear, old un, I will.'

He was going to the lake, and the nearest way from the house was up Wilkins' cut. There were several people on the street but he made no effort to hide his destination. Let them talk; they would talk in any case. But in spite of this bold way of thinking he was thrown into some confusion when turning sharply into the cut he almost fell on Mavis and Florrie. His colour went soaring, but without a word or nod of recognition he passed them both; and was acutely aware that their eyes remained hard on him until he cleared the stile.

It was common knowledge that only one thing existed between Mavis and Florrie and this was condescension which one bestowed and the other refused to recognise, but now seemingly they were one, and Peter had not the slightest doubt who was the cause of this affinity. It said much for the change that had come about within him that this meeting, apart from making him blush, did not worry him. Three days earlier he would have been in a stew, with his tow technique in action. But that was three days ago, the only thing that now remained of the old Peter Puddleton was, he knew, his name.

When he stepped into the clearing Leo was lying on her back on the grass, a book by her side, and she didn't rise but turned her head lazily towards him and held out her hand. In a moment he was down beside her, his arms about her and his lips tight on hers, and when he released her she gasped for breath, then laughed gently and touched his cheek saying, 'No one will convince me but that you had your training in the big city.'

He took her hand from his cheek and rubbed her fingers across his lips, and as he looked down into her eyes he said, 'The big city came to me.'

After allowing him to hold her gaze for a moment she

eased herself up into a sitting position, and with a small laugh she said quietly, 'I couldn't make you or anyone else believe that I'm not big city, could I, Peter?' She was looking across the water as she said this, and in spite of the smile that was still on her face he thought he detected a sadness in her question and a drooping in her whole attitude. It reminded him of the night when she had cried, that night that now seemed so very far away in the past, and he checked the retort of, 'No, you couldn't,' and replaced it with, 'Big city or small town, you came and that's all that matters to me.'

She put out her hand gropingly for him, and he pivoted himself round to her side. 'You're nice, Peter.' She squeezed his fingers. 'Do you know –' she turned her face to his – 'now don't contradict me when I say this, for it's true – that you can love someone without liking them, but if you like them and love them, too, then you have the world . . . I like you, Peter.'

'And love me?'

She dropped her head towards his shoulder and rubbed her cheek against his coat. 'First things first.'

Such a reply could have plunged into mute silence the man he had once been, and that individual would have thought, 'There can be no half measures, you either do or you don't.' But into this association had come so many shades of feeling that now he just clutched at whatever she gave and tried to bank down the fire that was demanding more fuel.

As she lay against him she nodded towards the water and said, 'I haven't seen her today, nor have the boys – I felt sure I'd see her again, and if the storm breaks she will certainly go. Somehow I feel she knew me. I'll miss her.'

'I'll bring my line and you can sit and fish.'

'That's an idea.'

'You like fishing, don't you? I never imagined I'd ever meet a girl who liked fishing.'

'I like sitting.' She laughed, and the thought intruded into his mind that she was right there, she liked sitting. She was as indolent as a sun-drenched native, only there was no

123

evidence of the sun on her – she was the palest thing he'd ever seen. This thought swung open the door that was never really closed, and Mrs Booth walked through it again, and although he banged it shut in her face she managed, as always, to shout at him. 'Well, where has she been this last year? She doesn't say, does she? And you're afraid to ask her. You haven't the spunk.'

In an effort to get away from his thoughts, he said, 'I must go.' But he made no effort to rise, instead he reached for the book that was lying at her other side and asked, 'What are you reading?'

'Oh, just a book. I liked the title.'

With his free hand he turned it over and read 'Words of a Woman in Love', then looking down at her he asked, with a twist to his lips, 'Had it long?'

There was some laughter in her eyes as she replied, 'Since Wednesday,' and his eyes, betraying a leaping hope, held hers a moment before he began to scan the pages. When he stopped flicking them and began to read she eased herself away from him, and putting her arms around her knees she looked about her at the lowering sky now seeming to rest on the tops of the trees on the far side of the lake; and after a time, during which he had made no comment, she asked, 'What are you reading?'

He gave her no answer, and there followed another pause. Then somewhat self-consciously and without having looked at her, he began to read aloud, his voice low and thick and halting:

'Would I like woods without you?
And bird-song and pollen-laden bees,
And trees;
And the night sky, and dawn,
And young things just born;
And eating out of doors,
And a hundred and one chores;
And autumn with its flame of dying
And wood to chop and leaves to burn,
And coals to lug and the fire to hug
And lights ablaze about the house

124

And steaming water in the bath;
Thick snow on the winding path;
And bed, and sleep, and dreams . . .?
What are they without you?'

As he finished the last line he brought his gaze to hers.
And she turned and looked at him, and he repeated, 'What
are they without you?' There was so much compressed
passion in his voice that when he cried, 'Leo!' and made to
pull her towards him she shook her head quickly and, sliding
with an unusually swift motion to her feet, said, 'Now,
Peter, don't let's get involved. Not like this – not in this
way.'

She took the book from him, and holding her other hand
down to him said, in a matter-of-fact way, 'Come on . . . up!
What about the sports? Listen to that noise over there.'

'Leo.' He stood before her, his face set now, his laughing
facade ripped away. 'Leo, I've got to know where I stand.'

'You've got to know nothing.' Her voice was suddenly
harsh. Even the semblance of the drawl had gone, and her
words came tumbling out rapidly as she went on, 'It was a
bargain, wasn't it? So let us leave it at that. Why can't you
be satisfied? You're like them all –'

'All?' His face looked grey, and suddenly old, and his
voice had a rusty sound.

'Oh, I didn't mean that.' Her head rocked. 'I meant all
men in general, honest I did. Oh, Peter! Why can't you leave
things as they are?'

There was no vestige of fond light in his eyes now. His
look constituted a glare as he ground out, 'Leave things as
they are! What do you think I am? Have you like this for
a week . . . two at the most, then off you go and I forget
about you? I must have been daft.'

'But it's what we agreed on, remember. Or would you
rather things hadn't been like this at all?'

He did not answer, and with a weary gesture she put her
hand to her hair and pushed it back from her brow, saying,
'Oh, why must you start on an afternoon like this, so heavy
and close! And we're fighting!' This statement seemed to

surprise even herself and she closed her eyes. When she opened them it was to stare up into his tense face, and her voice was weary and flat-sounding as she said, 'I'll tell you something, Peter. Perhaps this might make you see. I never expected to have an affair in my life again. Yes, I know you can raise your brows, you don't believe me. But I can tell you honestly I wanted this no more than you did, it was just one of those things. And I tell you again it's not for good. I'm being brutal, I know, but it's best that way. I know it's best that way.' She stood back from him and said gently now as she surveyed the anger mixed with pain on his] face, 'Do you want it to go on, or would you rather not? Whatever you like, I'll fit in. You've just got to say.'

He stood staring at her, fascinated, bewitched by her. He seemed to suck into his body everything that came from her, pleasure and pain. What had she done to him? Her last words appeared to him to be as hard-boiled as anything he had heard, yet, as always, her face, her eyes, belied them. With an intake of breath he turned from her towards the gap, but as he did so he thrust his hand out behind him and drew her after him.

Peter came sixth in the race he had won for two successive years, and was greeted with such laughing remarks as 'Losing yer grip, lad?' and 'Eeh! love always plays havoc with the legs.'

As he stood wiping the sweat from his neck, his eyes searched for Leo, but he could not see her anywhere in the crowd. After leaving the clearing she had gone back to the inn with the promise to be on the field around four o'clock, at which time he was likely to return from the race, and now it was nearer five. It wasn't until after he had joined his half-hearted effort to the tug-o'-war and made an attempt at the greasy pole that he saw her. He had, in fact, just finished cleaning himself up at the tap that fed the cattle trough when he glimpsed her coming in the gate. A quick dive behind the hedge and he got his trousers and made his re-appearance in a matter of seconds. Tucking in his shirt, his coat under his arm and without any hesitation, he wended his way towards her.

When he came up to her she was still standing by the gate, there was a look of uncertainty about her that was unusual, and her greeting suggested relief at seeing him. 'So you're back. Did you break any records?'

'What do you think?' He paused. 'In my condition?' He smiled as he said this, his eyes looking into hers, and she answered his smile and shook her head. Then together they walked on to the field.

As they moved through the groups, heads were turned here and there, and here and there voices called, 'Hello, Peter,' as if they had not seen him before. And eyes moved from him to Leo. He was not unaware of the nudging, winking and bobbing heads, but he took no notice, and it would seem that Leo was oblivious to anything that was going on around her.

Coming to the children's races he saw Florrie. Her face was red, almost purple. The heat was now oppressive, but her colour was not caused by the heat alone, for as she raised her eyes to his he was conscious of her sending out to him a blaze of hate. And when the twins, galloping at him, complained to him of her unfairness in handicapping them in the races, he found he could not laugh at their discomfiture. He had not expected Florrie's reaction to take this form towards himself and spite to the twins, to whom she had on all óther occasions shown prejudiced favours. If he had considered what her attitude would likely be, he would have expected her to adopt her mother's manner and treat him and the whole business with cool condescension.

To get away from the vicinity of Florrie and incidentally to soothe the twins he took them to the White Elephant stall, where after picking ticket No. 13 he was presented with 'The Monarch of the Glen'. This picture was the village joke, for it went the rounds every year. It was after this incident that Peter seemed to sense a change in the atmosphere about them, for they were now greeted with loud hilarity wherever they went, a hilarity that he found it difficult to join his easy laugh to. For instance, when Dan

Wilkins stood on a box and yelled out about a mystery raffle, drawing a crowd around him, and then to the consternation of the twins produced a half-smothered squawking Penelope. The laughter became hilarious, but it was mostly, Peter noticed, coming from the men. If it hadn't been too silly to consider he would have sworn that the fellows were showing off, and all for Leo's benefit. It would seem too that for the moment they had lost the fear of their women-folk, for even Bill came up and greeted Leo. But it must be said that his Amelia was nowhere to be seen. Rosie too had kept her word, and this saddened him more than he would admit.

But Leo seemed happy. She had entered into the spirit of the sports; though not partaking in anything she seemed to be enjoying everything. And then she said, 'I'd love a cup of tea.'

There was a tea stall close at hand, and he looked towards it, but she had already turned her gaze towards the marquee. And she asked, 'What about it?'

To take her into the marquee would constitute an act of bravery. Teas in the marquee were reserved for the cream of the parish, none of the lads ever went into the marquee. But now, walking by her side, he went towards the tent.

Teas in the marquee and all they entailed came under the supervision of Mrs Carrington-Barrett, and her second-in-command, as in the Women's Institute, was Miss Collins. From a vantage point inside the marquee Mrs Carrington-Barrett was now keeping a trained eye on the proceedings while Miss Collins was keeping a trained eye on the trays of cakes, making sure that the two-pennies did not get intermingled with the three-pennies and that a solicitous mother, as most of the waitresses were, did not slip a plate of cakes under the upturned brails to a young member of her family – it had been done.

With the exception of a table for four which was, at present, seating only the major – here today under protest – and the vicar – here as a duty and part of his cross – the rest of the twelve tables were occupied. And this was instantly

128

evident to Peter when, Leo going before him, he entered the marquee.

Whereas the reactions to them on the field had been somewhat covert, now they became definitely visible. Interest could be seen running like a swelling wave around the tent, and the crest hit the major and the vicar with seeming force.

The vicar's reaction was writ large on his face, for the poor man was still shaking with the implications levelled at him by his sister a few hours earlier. The major was of sterner stuff, though a battle raged in his drawing-room only yesterday when, admitting he had lain on the grass with the lady now sailing straight towards him, he had at the same time stoutly denied any monkey-business but had bravely threatened it should he hear another word of such nonsense, by God! And then at lunchtime today Florrie, who had always been his ally, had had to lean across the table and ask him out of the blue, 'Do you remember the tale of Connie Fitzpatrick?' Connie Fitzpatrick! Had they all gone mad?

Now the major rose and smiled a greeting, and Leo, returning the smile, said with a familiarity that was seldom used towards the village autocrat, 'Hello there, Major,' and the major, inclining his head into a bow which as a rule he reserved for high occasions only, replied, 'How d'you do?' Then reaching forward he pulled out a chair, adding 'Hello there, Peter.'

'Hallo, sir.'

Try as he might, Peter could not prevent some nervousness from coming over in his voice. And who wouldn't be nervous with Mrs C-B. and Miss Collins looking at her like that . . . he had been stark raving mad to let her come in here.

'You have met our vicar?' The major levelled his gaze on the obviously writhing and wilting man, and Leo, sitting down while at the same time with a swansdown tap touching the vicar's sleeve, said, 'Oh yes, we have met – and talked.' She stressed the last word, then added with a bubble to her voice, 'And not of pews and steeples and the cash that goes therewith either.'

On this quip the major let out a staccato and bullet-cracking roar that filled the marquee and brought a sweat to Peter's brow while seeming to cast a spell on all the other occupants, and in the stillness the major's voice sounded as if he were speaking into a tunnel as he boisterously finished the quotation: "But the souls of Christian peoples. Chuck it, Smith!" Good old Chesterton! Well put, Miss.'

The major was now fully aware of his wife's eyes beating a tattoo of signals towards him, and he took a gleeful delight in ignoring them. All the years he had been married to her she had never been able to cap a damn line of his, nor understand one of his quotations, yet she played the learned lady to those who knew no better, and it served them damned well right for being taken in – they didn't read, nobody read these days – but this girl here, she might look like a Floosie but, by damn, she had a mind. Look at the other day when he had come upon her in the wood and said, 'You all alone?' and she had quoted Dickens as pat as pat: ' "Lo the city is dead. I've seen but an eel." ' It was odd but she seemed to know he had a weakness for quotations. Ah, he had enjoyed that hour. But would he have done so had he known he was being watched? Watched! The thought infuriated him still. Blast their eyes, for sneaking, brainless busy-bodies.

'What d'you say?' There was a bark in the major's voice as his attention was brought to the Reverend again.

'Nothing . . . nothing. I wasn't speaking.' And Mr Collins wasn't speaking, he was choking. His sister was not more than three yards away and the look she was fastening on him was causing him to experience a most odd feeling, as if he had been caught committing an indecency, like in a dream.

He coughed into his handkerchief, and the major said, 'Take a drink of tea, man. It's that cake, it's dry. Well now –' he looked at Leo again – 'you'd like a cup of tea, wouldn't you? Where's everybody?' As he raised his hand to beckon one of the tea-bearers, Peter said hastily, 'I'll get it, sir.'

'Oh, all right. And bring me another one, too, will you, Peter? What about you?'

This simple question seemed to startle the vicar still further and he stammered, 'No . . . no thanks. I was j-j-just about to go . . . prizes.'

'Let them wait, man, they won't run away. Well, what do you think of our sports?' Once again the major gave Leo all his attention, and she smiled widely at him as she said, 'I think they're excellent. It's very well organised.'

'Hm! Nothing like it used to be. Real races at one time . . . horses, from here to Blanchland, round Bannock Fell Farm and back. Grand day! Fine do it used to be! They came from all over the county, and beyond, to compete. Now folks are too busy – or no money. Or if they have they do show jumping – nothing for the sport of the thing. Have us put down the hunt they would. . . . Don't be cruel to the foxes – bah! What d'you say, Vicar?' There had come into the major's eyes a deep, humorous glimmer.

'Well – well –' the vicar stretched his neck in an attempt to assert himself and to make a show of his principles even under these very trying circumstances, 'you know what I think of racing . . . of – of any kind, Major.'

'Now, now, what about it?' The major pointed to the open end of the marquee where could be seen the races in progress, and when the vicar shook his head, dismissing such a trumpery comparison, the major leaned towards Leo and said, 'What about one to fit racing, eh?'

Returning his twinkle and entering into his mood, Leo put her head back and looked up thoughtfully towards the apex of the tent; then after a moment of consideration, she shook her head saying 'No, I can't think of one. No.' Her head still back she turned it to the side as if still thinking, and from this position she watched Peter threading his way back towards them with a tray of tea, and over the distance she sent him a look that caused the blood to flood up into his face, and as he neared the table she called playfully to him, 'Do you know a quotation for racing, Peter?'

'Quotation for racing? No, I don't.' He wished she wouldn't act like this. She was doing it on purpose, a sort of teasing. Something had got into her. She looked as if she was in love with him, and the major, and the vicar and all mankind. Why was she doing it? There seemed to be a kind of devil in her, an egging-on, teasing devil. He'd had glimpses of it before, in the bar when Mrs Booth was behind the counter.

The women were furious. He was thankful his mother wasn't here after all. It was bad enough to see Mrs C.-B. She looked as if she was going to take off through the roof at any minute – it was evident that Mavis had talked. As for Miss Collins he wouldn't be surprised to see her have a fit, or pass out. And there, near the door, was Mrs Fountain, with Mrs Booth of all people. Like thunder they both looked.

'It's a lovely cup of tea.' Leo sipped at the tea, pushed the damp hair back from her forehead, then said musingly, 'Races. You know, I can't think of one to fit races.' She bit on her lip, her eyes laughing into the major's over the cup brim. Then putting the cup down, she exclaimed excitedly, 'Only that one about the human race.' She leant across the table towards him:

> ' "I wish I loved the human race,
> I wished I loved its silly face." '

'You know that one?'

The major, placing both his hands on the table, bounced his head to each word as he joined it to hers now:

> ' "I wish . . . I liked . . . the way . . . it walks,
> I wish I liked the way it talks,
> And when I'm introduced to one
> I wish I thought what – jolly fun." '

They emphasised the last two words, and, but for their joint merriment and the buzz of noise from outside, for the second time within a few minutes there was absolute silence in the marquee, a shocked silence. It even enveloped Peter. Why had she to do it? And the major acting like that . . . he'd never imagined the major could go on like that . . . like his father or Bill Fountain when they were tight. He could well imagine him getting drunk, roaring drunk, or going mad on a horse, or raising hell in the house, but to act this way . . . silly, daft like a bairn. But she was egging him on. Why was she doing it? This would really set the place on fire.

It certainly brought the vicar to his feet, but not for the reason that Peter and the rest of the gathering imagined – they could not know that the Reverend Collins was not shocked at this unseemly display between the first gentleman of the village and this unusual-looking girl from the Hart. He was shocked at himself: first because it had taken him all his time not to join in and show them, particularly the major, that he wasn't the only one who knew Sir Walter Raleigh's rhyme and, secondly, the discovery had been thrust upon him that he was jealous because the major was finding so much favour in her eyes. Really! really! He wiped his brow, and with a brief nod which included them all and singled none of them out and vindicated himself somewhat in the eyes of his sister, he left the tent.

In the hushed murmuring that crept gently into the silence following the vicar's exit, the major, seemingly oblivious of anything unusual in the atmosphere, took a long drink of his tea. And as he did so there came the first rumble of thunder. 'Ah! been waiting for that.' The major nodded at Peter. 'It'll be some storm when it breaks . . . swamp everywhere. I'd best be getting back – horses don't like it you know. Will you excuse me?'

He inclined his head towards Leo, who smiled at him fondly as he stood up and came round the table. Then bending over her he whispered, 'What d'you say Slinky makes her getaway tonight?' And Leo, as if playing a game with a child, strained her face up to his and whispered back, 'Almost certain.'

In an attempt to do the right thing Peter had risen to his feet with the major, and he now stood looking gloweringly uncomfortable. Yet it was nothing to what he was feeling, for he was now as mad at her as he had been at the major for acting the goat. She had, he felt sure, gone out of her way to encourage the old fellow.

'Pity.' The major's smile lingered on her as he straightened his waistcoat. 'Fine sight. Well, goodbye. Bye Peter.'

'Goodbye, sir.'

He sat down again opposite her, his face straight and Leo, ignoring his look said, 'I like him. I think he's grand. I can understand your father swearing by him, can't you?'

When he made no reply her face lost its laughter and she said softly, 'I'm a wicked woman, a hussy, because I laughed with him?'

His answer came from deep in his throat: 'It's not that.'

'It is that.' Her voice was as low as his. 'And I did it on purpose. I admit it. Do you think I am blind and insensitive to the feeling about me?'

She swallowed painfully as she stared at him. Then dropping her eyes to her cup she went on, 'I'm sorry if I've upset you, but I want to laugh – I must laugh. I told you, and you can't laugh with women, they won't let you. . . . I shouldn't have come here, you shouldn't have asked me to, I see that now. It was like flaunting me under their noses, and they won't forgive you.'

He pushed his shoulders back as he said, 'What I do is my business. As for me bringing you here, where I go, you go.' He leaned towards her now as he added, 'You know that.'

He had almost become oblivious of the eyes upon them. But she hadn't, and softer still she warned, 'Be careful.'

What answer he would have made to this was checked by a rumbling of thunder following on a flash of lightning, and within seconds it became so dark as to seem almost like night.

There was a lively stir all about them now, and getting to his feet, he said, 'You'd better be getting back. You haven't got a coat, you'll get drenched.'

She glanced about her before saying, 'Let them get out and then we'll go.'

Another flash of lightning, followed immediately by a deep roar of thunder, acted like a spring and gave speed to everybody's legs, and in a few moments the marquee was empty but for the helpers, feverishly packing up.

'Come on.' Peter took her firmly by the arm and led her to the door of the marquee, where a blinding streak seeming to cut the heavens checked their steps and caused her to turn her face towards him for a moment before moving on.

Outside, as far as the sports field was concerned, they

stepped into a changed world. Stalls were already stripped bare and their goods were being borne by willing helpers to the big tent adjoining the marquee. In the far distance the last of the spectators could only just be discerned crowding through the gate before making a dash to the village and home.

Another flash of lightning and an ear-splitting burst of thunder caused Peter to exclaim in some anxiety, 'This is going to break any minute; we'd better run for it while we can. Come on.'

'I'd rather walk.'

'Walk?' He hesitated for a second and looked at her. 'But you'll get drenched.'

'It doesn't matter. I don't want to run.'

Her tone was one he had not heard before. It was utterly flat-sounding and had about it a stiff finality which tended both to puzzle and irritate him. He was tempted at this precise moment to treat her as he would do one of the twins if they were being unnecessarily trying under such similar circumstances – clout her ear, grab her by the hand and gallop her over the field. She was, he told himself, just being contrary, and as far as he could see there was nothing he could do about it. Not trusting himself to speak, he moved in silence to the gate, and there the first drops of rain came, large, slow drops, spaced wide apart. Then one minute there was only the darkened sky and the heavy stillness in the atmosphere about them and the drops of softly falling rain; the next the wind was sweeping the field with the intensity of a gale, and Peter, having to shout now, looked down on Leo in some bewilderment, and demanded, 'You still want to dander?'

'Yes.'

He could not hear her voice but the movement of her head accompanying the words made her meaning clear to him.

'All right –' he made himself smile grimly as he yelled 'we dander!'

Buffeted by the wind they walked on, Peter suiting his pace to hers, while past them now most of the helpers were running madly for shelter. This was crazy – daft. When the storm really broke God alone knew what it would be like, and they had to go through the fields yet.

Then as if the lock gates of heaven had been opened a deluge of water seemed to fall in a complete sheet and envelope them, and in as short a time as it takes to say, they were both drenched to the skin. As she huddled against him he decided grimly that he was having no more of this damn nonsense, and so putting his arm about her, he began to run. Bringing her feet almost off the ground he propelled her forward, and he had managed to get her some way before he took any notice of her hands clawing him, but even then his determination to get out of the storm made him ignore them, and it was not until they had covered quite some distance and her hands had ceased their clawing that he looked at her. And then he was brought to a dead stop.

'Leo!' His voice was carried away from him. 'Leo!' He tried to raise her rain-drenched face, but her chin was dug into her chest and her shoulders were heaving as if she were swimming, and he shouted now in panic. 'Leo! Leo, what is it?'

Firmly he pulled her face upwards. Her hair was plastered across it, her eyes were closed, and but for the rise and fall of her breast she could have been dead. Her face had the alabaster look of death, and he cried out in real fear, 'Leo! Leo! What's the matter? For God's sake tell me! Look ... Leo! Leo!'

He stood braced with his back to the wind, sheltering her. The water was pouring down his neck as if from a spout but he was not conscious of it.

'Leo!' He shook her gently. 'Say something, for God's sake. Do you hear?'

When she made no effort to answer he looked wildly about him. They were on the main road just clear of the fields, but so dense was the downpour of rain that he could barely make out the banks on either side. He held her to him, and at that moment a car, turning from the field path, moved slowly past them. It was, he saw, packed to capacity. Naturally it did not stop. After one more moment of hesitation he stooped and, picking her up bodily in his arms, stumbled along the road.

The wind, really at gale force now, drove him into the ditch, and it took him all his time to save them both from falling headlong. Fortunately the ditch was shallow, and propping one leg on the bank he rested for a moment, holding her inert form tightly to him. He was frightened, filled with panic. He couldn't ever remember feeling like this. He peered down into her face. But there was no movement from her, even her breast wasn't rising as it had done, so hitching her up to him again he went on.

He was now nearing the vicarage gates when another car coming from behind rounded slowly in front of him and turned into the drive. It, too, was packed, and through the opaque windscreen he could just make out Florrie at the wheel. He knew, too, that she had recognised him, but he had ceased to care what she or anyone else might think. He yelled out to her, but if she heard she took no notice, and the car within a moment was lost in the gloom.

He had covered another few yards or so when Leo moved and spoke. Although her lips were against his ear he could not make out what she said, but the movement of her body indicated that she wished to be put down.

Almost faint with the feeling of relief he gently eased her on to her feet, and his arms still about her he mouthed the words, 'Are you all right?'

There was no change for the better in her face, and she made no effort to speak but inclined her head once slowly, then dropped it against him.

'Can you walk, or shall I –?' He made a motion to carry her again, but she put out her hand to check him, and leaning heavily on him she moved forward.

He wasn't conscious that his own shirt was clinging to his back and his trousers sticking to his legs, but he was very much aware of her wet body beneath her soaked clothes, he could even feel the squelch of the water as he moved his hand at her waist. A terrible crash of thunder rending the heavens brought her round to him, and he stood pressing her face into his neck. They were within sight of the Hart now and after a moment he urged her gently on again, and at last brought her to the side porch. Once under its shelter, and prey now only to the slant of the driving rain, she stood leaning against the wall gasping for breath, but she made no immediate effort to go in through the side door and up the stairs. It seemed as if she were fighting, besides for breath, for composure before entering the inn.

He took her hand and, holding it between his own pressed it gently to his chest. 'Are you ill, Leo?'

She made a small movement with her free hand, and he said, 'Look, go straight up to bed.' It took some effort for him to offer this advice which would send her to her room, for once she was there how could he know just what was happening to her.

She dragged her eyes up to his face, then murmured, 'I'll . . . have . . . a bath.' There was a considerable pause before she added, 'I'll try . . . to come down . . . later.'

He released her hand, and she touched his arm, saying, 'Don't worry . . . I'll – I'll be all right.' He could say nothing, so full now was his heart of an odd fear, but he pushed open the door for her and helped her into the passage, then watched her go slowly up the stairs. And not until he heard her door close overhead did he turn away and make for home.

Free now to run or gallop as he wished, he did not tear along the street towards the house but walked through the deluge at much the same rate as that which had brought him to the inn.

At the house, Grandpop, opening the window just the slightest, yelled, 'You aiming to become a duck?' And when Peter passed him without as much as a look in his direction the old man blinked, banged the window and said over his shoulder, 'I wouldn't stand there with me mouth wide open, I'd get a tub of hot water ready. Strikes me he's in for summat.'

For once Rosie did not retort in her usual vein to the old man's orders, but turned away and went into the living-room. He was in for something all right! For the past few minutes she had been standing at the window behind

Grandpop watching his coming. The twins' account of the sports, and their Peter and the Miss, had worked her up to fever-pitch. She'd had enough and was going to put a stop to this business or else she'd know the reason why.

The light was on in the living-room, and on one side of the flower-filled hearth sat Old Pop reading, and on the other side was Harry. He too was reading, but evidently just to while away the time until the storm should ease and he could go out, for he was fully dressed even to his cap which lay on his knee. As Rosie bustled through the room towards the kitchen, the two men lowered their papers and glanced in her direction, then looked at each other before resuming their reading again.

Rosie reached the kitchen as Peter entered from the back door and she looked at him as he stood on the mat, while the water ran down him and made a pool at his feet. He returned her look and saw that she was in a fury of a temper such as, at times, he had seen his father arouse in her. And strangely enough it hardly disturbed him, for his mind was full to overflowing with a feeling of anxiety that was utterly new to him – something was the matter with Leo; what, he didn't know. She was young and she didn't run, and when he had forced her to, it looked for the time as if he had killed her. He was worried, puzzled – and frightened, and so his mother's reactions at this moment touched him hardly at all. And she sensed this in his tone when he said, 'Will you bring me some dry things down?'

Rosie's bust swelled and she answered meaningly, 'Yes, I'll bring you some dry things down.'

As she stalked again through the living-room, Harry lowered his paper and followed her to the foot of the stairs, and there, standing with his palm covering the knob of the banister, he said under his breath, 'If you take my advice you'll keep your tongue quiet.'

'I don't want your advice, thank you.'

Harry punched at the paper as he watched her mount the stairs, then returned to his seat in the living-room, and after giving his father one significant look he punched at the paper again. Then they both raised their eyes ceilingwards to where could be heard her voice going at the twins, ordering them to stay up in the attic and play. When, within a few minutes, she again passed through the living-room they were both deeply engrossed in their reading.

In the scullery Rosie placed the clothes slowly on a chair and said with deep emphasis, 'Now!' Then joining her hands tightly at her waist she waited.

Peter, already stripped of his coat and shirt, was rubbing himself with a towel. He did not stop, and Rosie, keyed up to bursting point, cried, 'It's no use you stalling. I want to know what's going on.'

'I thought you knew . . . everybody else does.'

Did Rosie hear a chuckle from the living-room? Her eyes flashed in that direction for a second, and she said as if she were still speaking to her lad and chastising him for back-chat, 'Now I'll not have any of that.'

'Look here, Mam, leave me alone.'

The words crisp and cutting, so unlike Peter's and so like her husband's, left Rosie with her mouth wide, and when she saw him grab up his dry clothes and go swiftly past her she could say nothing; she just gaped at him, seeing, she felt, the death of the only joy in her life.

Slowly she walked to the window and stood staring out at the driving rain. And ten minutes later she was still standing there when Peter, in mac and cap, came through the kitchen and went out without a word to her. The lump that came into her throat threatened to choke her, and when Harry, following almost on Peter's heels, stood behind her and said quietly, 'I told you, you'll never learn', she rounded on him, her expression teeming with words. But all she could bring out was, 'Damn you! Harry Puddleton.' Then diving past him she ran through the living-room and up the stairs, leaving Harry standing, turning his cap in his hands, his face showing a concern that would have surprised her had she seen it. He wanted to go and tell her to have patience, that this business was only a bit of fun, an affair if you like but one that would fizzle out. These things always did. No man took a girl like the Hart miss seriously. She and her like were to Harry's mind the type that gave a man

140

that . . . that lift that was so necessary to his self-esteem, but as for getting serious about them, no fellow would – well, certainly not country-reared blokes who had inbred in them a sense of the fitness of things, and by that he meant the choosing of a mate for life. If he had dared he would have said to Rosie, 'She's the type I meself liked to have a lark with. But lark was the limit. And it's the same with the lad.' But he knew it would be no use. Rosie saw indecency in a laugh if there was another woman present. And if she went on in this way at the lad she would, as she had done with himself, make him give her something to worry over.

Harry looked down at the cap; he turned it over and examined it without seeing it. He was himself worried, but he would not admit that there was really anything to worry over. He told himself he was as bad as her, yet he was not at all happy in his mind about the business and the way it was going. Slowly putting his cap on to his head, he pulled the peak well down and went out.

CHAPTER SEVEN

Peter did not go straight into the Hart but stood looking at one of the two cars parked in front of the inn, and as he stared at it more confusion was added to his already over-burdened feelings. He had seen the car before . . . twice. It was – the car. That meant . . . What it meant he did not explain to himself but entered the bar, his eyes flicking about him, and almost immediately they found what they sought. The man was standing at the bar counter with his back to it and holding a glass of spirits in his hand, and although everyone in the packed room seemed to be immersed in conversation he was neither talking nor listening to anyone in particular but rather was he taking in all that was going on around him. And he took in Peter immediately and whereas he had appeared somewhat bored, his manner now showed a spurt of interest, for as Peter made his way to the counter he purposely pushed to one side to make room for him, and over a number of heads he nodded and called, 'Hello, there.'

When Peter, not taking advantage of the offer of space, merely nodded in answer to this greeting, the man jerked his head and said, 'Here a minute, will you?'

Skirting a little group, Peter joined him at the corner and looking levelly at him asked pointedly, 'What is it?'

'What'll you have?'

'Nothing thanks, I'm joining . . .' His vague indication could have been meant for anyone in the room behind them.

'Well have one with me first.' The man threw off his whisky and calling to Mrs Booth, who was serving along the counter, said, 'A whisky and . . .' He glanced at Peter, and reluctantly Peter added, 'A beer – small.'

'A small beer. There now.' The man leant his elbows on the counter and nodding backwards towards the window said, 'Hell of a storm, this.'

'Yes, pretty bad.'

As Mrs Booth placed the drinks before them she looked at Peter with a look that was more in the nature of a glare, and it did not go unnoticed by the man, who dropped his gaze to his drink, which he picked up. Then turning his back on the counter, he muttered, 'That's what's commonly known as a cow, and udder no circumstances to be trusted.' He gave a silly sounding giggle at his own joke.

Peter made no comment. But when the man went on, 'The Sunday Rags aren't in it – thinks she knows the lot,' he knew that Mrs Booth had been talking, and about him and Leo. And this was immediately verified when the man in a soft, insinuating tone, added, 'You both got wet?'

Peter, in the act of taking a drink, stopped. 'Anything wrong in that?' It was a challenge.

But the man did not take it up; his voice was even conciliatory, as he said, 'No . . . no, but not very wise of her. But then –' he sipped at his whisky – 'Anna was never very wise. She might give you that impression – oh, yes, she

142

would – but she never was, and never will be.' He shook his head sadly.

'What are you getting at?'

'Me? Nothing.' He half turned away and looked about him as far as he could see; then almost eagerly he exclaimed, 'Look there's two seats in the window. Those people are just off. Must want to get home badly to go out in this, but that's their look-out. Come and sit down.' And not waiting for any answer, for or against, he pushed through the throng and Peter, determined now that he had got this far to know all there was to know, followed him.

When they were seated on the broad sill the man said, 'There now, what were you saying, son?'

'I wasn't saying anything, you were doing the talking. And I'm not your son.' The last sounded petty and childish but he could not restrain himself from, as he put it, getting at this fellow.

The man, after looking steadily at him, gave a short laugh and said, 'Only a saying, no harm meant, and as you said I was doing the talking . . . you were quite right. Well now –' he leant forward until his face was near to Peter's – 'you won't believe it but I'm going to try to do you a good turn. Oh, I knew you wouldn't believe it, nobody would – I wouldn't meself in your place – but nevertheless I am, and it's this advice I'm going to give you.' His voice dropped. 'Keep away from Anna.'

Although Leo had already said that this man was not her husband Peter found he was doubting the truth of it now, so much so that had the man claimed to be her husband he would unreservedly have believed him. As if sieved through his teeth, he brought out the questions, 'Why should I? What's it got to do with you? Who are you anyway – her husband?'

The man's eyebrows seemed to move up into a point before he said, 'No, I'm not her husband . . . well –' he wiped his trim, short moustache with the tips of his fingers and his eyes slid sideways to Peter – 'not in name. Now! now! look here.' His manner underwent a lightning change and he put out a restraining hand and said under his breath,

'Don't get on your high-horse, lad, for let me warn you I can shoot as straight a left as anyone for my age. Don't let this deceive you.' He patted his flabby paunch. 'What I'm saying to you is for your own good. You asked a question and I gave you a straight answer. I was her husband of sorts, but that's over. Even so, she's not for you, and if you'll take my advice you'll cut loose and save yourself some heartache.'

'And leave the field to you?'

The man drew in his breath. 'I don't want the field, as you call it, but I happen to know it better than you. Anyway –' he threw off his whisky with a touch of impatience – 'why the hell am I bothering! I'm just wasting my breath and –' His words were cut short by the screeching of brakes as a car was brought to a standstill almost in the porch itself, and swiftly turning his attention to the rain-smeared window, he cleared his vision somewhat by rubbing vigorously at the misted pane, then exclaimed, with definite anger now, 'Blasted fools! ripping her guts out.' He kept his eyes on the blurred outline of the car as it backed from the porch and disappeared into the yard. He seemed to have forgotten Peter and the very personal topic in hand, for he turned his eyes towards the door and waited, the look on his face much darker now. And when four internally soaked young men came into view, debating loudly in the passage-way whether to go into the bar or the saloon, he muttered, 'Bloody young fools!'

'In here, fellows.'

'No, in here.'

'No, come on in the bar – beer, skittles, girls and victuals.'

So hilarious was their laughter, so loud their shouting that in one after the other of the groups around the bar the talking died down and smiling and interested faces were turned towards the young men.

The newcomers seemed to be between the ages of twenty-five and thirty-five, and all except one were far advanced in their cups. This one happened to be the smallest among them, and although he was apparently in the merry stage he was still in command of himself, and also, it seemed, of his companions, for he hustled them now bodily into the bar and to the counter, but not regardless of the human obstacles in the way, for the people who moved aside he thanked with courteous and even elaborate thanks.

Peter's angry mind was momentarily drawn from the man at his side to the tallest member of the party, who stood well over six feet. He was blond and big-boned and could, when sober, have represented a travel advertisement for Sweden, and it soon became evident, not only to Peter but to the entire room, that this young man's name was Tiffy.

'Come on, Tiffy, sing,' the other two urged, while their apparent leader between giving the orders for drinks, added his plea, 'Yes, Tiffy, you show 'em. You show 'em.'

Tiffy, his body swaying and his face one great beam, appealed to the entire company, 'You want a song?' And when there were a few restrained murmurs and nods from one or two quarters, Tiffy received these as wild acclaim and cried, 'All right! all right! What d'you want, eh? Come on tell us. Rock 'an Roll to Rigoletto – come on, what's it to be?'

But there seemed a reluctance on the part of the company to put forward their requests, and one of the men, addressed as Max, turned to the bar, saying, 'Aw, let's drink. They wouldn't recognise good music if you injected it inta them – let's drink.'

Whereupon, with much laughter and embracing of shoulders, they turned to the bar and drank. And over on the window seat the man, too, drank, throwing off his drink as if in disgust. It was evident that he had no use at all for the types at the bar, and he said so, taking Peter into his confidence as if they were buddies: 'That kind makes me sick. Ah, don't I know them. Meet 'em every day in life, without a penny to rub against the other. Get to colleges on grants. My money, and your money. Then look down their bloody noses.' He snorted. 'Ah well, the quicker they get out of here the better I'll like it.' He turned his attention fully to Peter again, and, pulling his neck out of his collar and squaring his shoulders as if to regain his poise, he said. 'Well where were we, son? Oh! sorry, I'd better say lad, eh?'

Ignoring this latter remark, Peter answered his question,

'You had decided against giving me any more advice.'

The man gave a short laugh and through narrowing eyes said, 'You're not such a fool as one might think. You sound as if you'd been around yourself, country boy or no country boy.'

Peter's lips fell into a tight line, and he kept them there for a moment before saying, 'Your kind always underestimate the other fellow. There's no country boys, as you call them, left. There was a war on, remember? But if there were any they'd still be able to show you a thing or two. You don't like that lot over there –' he nodded at the merry group at the bar – 'because they see through you, because they won't stand for you and your sharp-shooting car deals or, given the chance, they can outshoot you any day in the week. And they're young.'

This last remark seemed to sting the man more than anything else Peter had said. His eyes narrowed considerably as he got to his feet, and it was evident to Peter that he was going to make a parting shot, one which wasn't going to be softened by any pseudo-paternal feeling. Knowing it would surely be connected with Leo he braced himself for its impact by getting to his feet, too, but as he did so a loud command came from the leader of the group at the bar, and such was its tone that it had the power to draw their attention.

'Order! Order! You are now about to hear the golden voice of Brother Tiffy.' The small fellow endeavoured to hold the blond young man's hand up as far as his reach would allow, which seemed to convulse Tiffy.

'Order! for Brother Tiffy, the star of the theatre – Steven's Theatre.'

On this last remark the other two men, now known respectively as Max and Shaggy, turned to each other in a paroxysm of laughter. Their arms hanging around each other's necks they roared, until the small man cried, 'Stow it! you two, you're holding up proceedings. This is to be a major operation. Brother Tiffy is about to show his larynx as never before.' He turned to his widely grinning and befuddled friend, and after crying once more, 'Order! Now

146

order!' he said, 'All right, Tiffy, off you go, it's all yours. Take it away.'

The room became still. Max and Shaggy broke away from each other and stood supporting themselves quietly against the counter. The only noise was the background din from the saloon; all faces in the room were turned on the great blond man as he straightened himself, took a deep breath and soared without prelude into 'Samson and Delilah.'

'Softly awakes my heart, as the flowers awaken
To Aurora's tender zephyr.
But say, O well-belov'd, no more I'll be forsaken.
Speak again, O speak for ever!

O say that from Delilah, you will never part!
Your burning vows repeat; vows so dear to my heart!
vows so dear to my heart!'

At this point Peter forgot about the man at his side; he even forgot himself and his churned-up feelings long enough to think, My God! what a voice.

'Ah! once again, do I implore thee!
Ah! once again, then say you adore me!
Ah! I here implore thee,
See, I implore thee.'

And it could have been Samson, the giant himself, singing to his Delilah, and in a voice so pure and strong that his love was forced into the ears of his hearers. A power was filling the room, and without exception it had caught the attention of everyone present; every face was focused on the singer. So fine was the voice and so unusual the range of tone that even movement was captured and held enthralled, for not a hand went towards a glass. And within a few minutes even the noise from the saloon was stilled. And it seemed to the onlookers that the singer's voice had enraptured even himself, for although he would turn his head here and there his eyes looked unseeing, or were seeing beyond the walls, as on and on he sang:

'So sways my trembling heart, consoling all its pain,
To thy voice so dear, so loving.
The arrow in its flight is not swifter than I,

147

When, leaving all behind, to your arms I fly!
Unto your arms I fly.'

Mr Booth, content for the moment to stop adding to his till, stood behind the bar, his hands characteristically touching the edge of the counter. A little way to the left of him Mrs Booth had allowed her buttocks to rest against a barrel and her face had taken on an almost tender look, and who knew what thoughts were ranging through her mind as she gazed at the Adonis-like profile of the entertainer. He looked to her too good to be true, and she sighed.

Oddly enough, Peter was thinking much the same thing. The blond man seemed to be possessed of everything – looks, voice, and charm, but most of all, a voice. He was likely some big actor – a star, and this was just a lark, they were all out on the spree. His eyes were riveted on the mobile face. One minute he saw the singer's mouth wide open, sending passionate words out on golden notes, but the next moment, the mouth still open, the song had abruptly ceased and the expression on the singer's face was not far away and lost in the realms of love but was showing wildly delighted surprise. He was looking over the heads of the others towards the door leading into the passage, and as Peter's eyes flashed in that direction the blond fellow's arm shot out and he cried, 'God Almighty! See what I see, fellows – look!'

Standing in the doorway was Leo. She looked fearfully white and slightly spellbound, but when, as if recovering herself, she turned to make a hasty retreat her escape was cut off by those behind her, and with a loud scuffling and whooping she was immediately surrounded by the four men.

So unusual was the scene that the other occupants of the room and those in the passage remained quiet as if witnessing another part of the entertainment set up by these strangers. Nor did Peter move, he seemed fixed by his unblinking stare.

'Leo! Why, Leo! Well, who would have expected to see you here.' The small man's voice could be picked out now from above the rest. He was holding one of her hands, her other being lost in the two great paws of the singer, who was

148

crying in an emotional voice, which was undoubtedly aided by the load he was carrying, 'Aw Leo! Leo, my love. Aw Leo!'

A pain, like a thin blade piercing his chest, struck Peter as he watched Tiffy, with his arm about her now, draw her to the counter. He was still effusing maudlinly for all to hear, 'My day is complete, my life is complete. Leo of all people! Leo!' He looked around his companions for confirmation of his pleasure, and Max, walking backwards in front of her, cried, 'What are you doing here, Leo?' But before she could answer, Tiffy cried, 'Breaking hearts, I bet. What do you say, aren't you?'

'You're drunk, Tiffy.' Her voice was low, but it seemed to be caught up by everyone in the room.

'Yes, I'm drunk, Leo. I've been drunk all day – we've all been drunk. Come on, you have a drink, anything you like, it's an occasion. . . . Let me look at you.'

The silence fell heavy on the room as Tiffy, holding her at arm's length, stared down into her face. Then in an even louder voice, he cried, 'You're looking grand – grand.'

On the face of her appearance this seemed rather a strange remark to make.

'Quiet, Tiffy. Let her have a drink. Is it grapefruit, Leo?'

It was the small man again, and Leo turned to him and said, 'Still keeping order, Roger?' And he, smiling somewhat soberly back at her, answered, 'Someone's got to do it in this outfit, Leo. How are you really?' This last question was hardly audible to Peter, even in the silence.

'All right.'

'That's it.'

Peter watched the little fellow as his eyes lingered on her. Then Roger, his voice louder now, asked, 'You passing through?'

'No. I'm staying here for a time.'

There came a quiet uneasiness among the four men following this statement. Max and Shaggy drank; Tiffy, his eyes on her all the while, took occasional sips from his glass and made occasional unbelieving movements with his head while repeating her name from time to time, as if he still couldn't believe his eyes.

As the room came slowly back to normal Peter, his gaze riveted on Leo, willed with all his might that she should look at him, and when turning with her grapefruit from the counter to answer a remark of one of the group her eyes came to rest, not on him, but on the man standing at his side, he saw that she was startled and he watched her turn quickly to the counter again.

His companion's face, he now noted, looked grey, and he, too, was holding her with his eyes. In spite of Peter's concern for her, a sudden revulsion of feeling against her came over him. She could handle drunks that was evident. Four of them, all milling round her! And how many men had she known like this fellow here beside him? The question did not shout in his mind but probed him with deadly insistence, more powerful than flashing anger. It was like a slow injection of blood, proving itself as it ran through his veins, gradually giving him strength to reject this mania that had come upon him. Perhaps he wasn't a blasted fool altogether. . . . Perhaps they were right. He forgot that just a short while ago he was worried sick because he thought that she was ill.

People were beginning to drink and talk again in a somewhat desultory fashion. Remarks could be heard about the rain, and when another crash of thunder came some weather sage propounded, 'Travelled ten miles, the storm has, since that last crack.'

It was just when people were seemingly falling back into the tempo of the room as it had been before the appearance of the group at the bar that Tiffy's voice ringing clearly out aroused their interest more so than before as it cried, 'Aw, come on, Leo. Come on, sing. Remember Christmas Eve? That was a do. Come on. The duet? Come on, love.'

At this moment Peter's view of the bar was suddenly blocked out by the bulk of his father and Bill. They were standing dead in front of him, and Harry's voice said quietly, 'Let's go, lad. We could get the bus into Allendale, or go Blanchland way – it'll be passing in a minute.'

'Aye, do that Peter,' urged Bill. 'This place is too crowded

150

the night by half – no enjoyment in it. Come on, lad.'

'Kiss me – come on, give me a kiss.' This demand, shutting off the chatter like a sound-proof door, caused all eyes to turn in the direction of the counter again, and Mr Booth, thinking it time to assert his authority, cried, 'Now, gentlemen! gentlemen!'

'Come on, Leo . . . my love.'

It was a slow, drawn-out plea, and although it sounded laughable no one laughed, there was not even a snigger.

The little man, Roger, intervened quickly now, his voice no longer merry. 'Don't act the goat, Tiffy. Stop it! D'you hear?' He pulled at his friend's arm, but was pushed laughingly aside, and Tiffy, encircling Leo with his arms pleaded again, his voice filling the stillness as he lisped, this time in baby talk, 'Just a leetle peck – just a weeny, teeny little peck. Ah! kiss Tiffy, Leo.'

Tiffy was apparently unaware of the scuffle going on near the window, and not until he was dragged round from Leo did he show any surprise, and then he was still full of good humour.

'What's up? Who are you?'

'You'll know in a minute. Get out!'

'Oooh!' Tiffy's face seemed to brighten with knowledge as he blinked heavily at Peter. 'You a friend of Leo's?' He nodded his head in great bounces, denoting his understanding. 'Well, I'm a friend of Leo's an' all! We're all friends of Leo's, aren't we, ducks?' He looked towards Leo, where he held her at arm's length now with his big white hand. 'But me, I'm a special friend, aren't I? You see – ' he leant forward and with his free hand thumbed Peter in the chest – 'I know Leo as you don't know her, nor nobody else. . . . Oh! you would, would you!'

In spite of the drink Tiffy knew when he was going to be hit, and ducked, and as Harry, grabbing at Peter's raised arm, cried, 'Give over, lad,' Tiffy's smile vanished completely. His brows darkening, the whole expression of his face altered and he said thickly, 'It's like that, is it? It's a fight you want. Well, I'm game – game for anything. Stand back!' He pushed his friends aside.

'Stop it! Do you hear! Stop it!' It was Leo's voice high and pleading, but it was not directed towards Tiffy but to Peter. And to it was now added the man's. He was standing by her side and he cried in anger, 'Yes, stop it! I should damn well think so. You're taking too much on yourself, you are, far too damn much. I'm the one to deal with this.'

'Oh! you are, are you!' Peter's furious glance swung from Tiffy to the man, but Harry, tightening his grip on his son, urged sternly, 'Come on out of it. Come on, lad.'

The man, with his hand on Leo's arm as if to protect her, now set the spark to Peter's fury when he addressed himself pointedly to Harry, saying, 'That's it. Get him off home before he gets ideas about himself and his capabilities.'

In that moment no one could have stopped Peter – his father, nor Bill, nor yet the combined efforts of three of the four merry-makers, not Mr Booth, who with the agility of a gazelle had leapt the counter – for his arm swung up and out, and under the blow the man was flung back among the tables. Immediately, there was pandemonium. Two women sitting nearby screamed, and to their screaming was added more from the passage; there were cries from Mrs Booth, who, as she saw the man righting himself preparatory to making a dive for Peter, yelled, 'Get outside! Outside, the lot of you!'

She was herself unable to get into the room for the crush of men blocking the let, and this infuriated her further. Her eyes searched out Leo where she stood with her back pressed against the counter, and rushing towards her she grabbed at the back of her shoulders, twisted her round and screamed into her terrified face, 'You! This is you! Get out! Go on, before I knock your bloody jailbird face in for you, you dirty – !'

Mrs Booth's elucidating epitaph was lost in the fury of her voice as with a ferocious shove across the counter she pushed Leo almost into the melee of shouting, swearing, struggling men. It was only Harry, separated for the moment from Peter where he was now being held by Bill and Roger, that saved her from falling to the floor. Grabbing at her, Harry steadied her against him, and she clung to him, gasping.

The room now seemed to be divided into two groups those around Peter and the rest hanging on to the man; only Mr Booth seemed separate and only his voice could be heard crying repeatedly, 'Get on outside with you. Outside! Outside! I'll call the police, mind. Outside! Get them outside!'

There was no escape for the girl, Harry saw, through the passageway. But his mind, as confused as anyone's at that moment, was clear about one thing: he knew he must not leave her with Katie Booth or else there'd be trouble of perhaps a more serious nature. The girl looked scared, almost petrified. She no longer looked the miss he had got a kick out of knowing, she looked as if she would collapse at his feet.

'Come on.' He drew her round the outskirts of the shifting shouting mass and to the window, where just a few minutes before Peter had been seated. Thrusting up the sash he assisted her over the low sill and out into the rain-swept porch. Then a quick glance back into the room showed him that Mr Booth, with the use of his own brawn and the help of the locals, was persuading the combatants into the passage. So he followed Leo through the window.

The shouting and yelling filled the street as the men came struggling out of both the main and saloon bars and milled about under the porchway, reluctant to be pushed into the downpour. And Peter's voice came clearly above the din when in a roar that would have done credit to Grandpop, he yelled, 'Leave go of me! Leave go, do you hear!'

Shaking himself like an enraged bull, he flung himself clear of the hands holding him. It was unfortunate that in doing so one of his thrashing fists should contact Bill. In a twinkling Bill was measuring his full length in the road.

The sight of the momentarily prostrate figure with the rain beating down on him seemed to inflame still further the tempers of those directly concerned, for Tiffy, taking up the cudgels of the man lying on his back, now pushed his way to Peter, and lifting his huge fist, aimed a blow at him. It was as well that the direction of the blow was drink-controlled or Peter, too, would have joined Bill, But the blow, skidding past him, incensed him as much as if he had met its full force, and he struck back with such ferocity that within a second Tiffy and he were in the road bashing it out, blinded with rain and rage.

Harry had left Leo against the wall at the far end of the porch to rush to the aid of Bill, and he had just managed to get him to his feet when two things attracted him simultaneously: his lad was fighting in the middle of the road with the singing fellow, and the man, who, in Harry's mind, had started all this, had broken away from those who were trying to deter him and was making for the combatants, not, Harry knew, to assist Peter.

'No you don't!' Harry left the dazed and rocking Bill and practically threw himself at the man, and in a second he, too, was engulfed and hitting out in desperate self-defence.

The road outside the Hart now showed a scene that had never before been witnessed in Battenbun, and every door and window that could look upon the inn was filled with its shocked spectators, and it seemed to them that their village had suddenly gone mad. For the peacemakers who had been endeavouring to separate the combatants were themselves drawn into the melee, and blows, whether used for attack or defence, are hardly distinguishable to the lookers on.

It was only after a great deal of yelling, tugging, pulling and shoving, that the parties were separated. But the noise covering the green was like that of a cup final and one that had not pleased the majority of the crowd. Even with the two contesting groups spread apart the noise still went on.

It was with some element of surprise that Peter found himself neither giving nor receiving blows, but standing round the corner in the inn yard with his back against the wall, gasping for breath, and with blood running into his eyes and almost blinding him. He knew there was someone on each side of him, and dimly he recognised the little fellow's voice as he said, 'Take it easy. Sit down here.'

Dazed and still panting as if his lungs would burst, he allowed himself to be drawn forward and down to a seat which, experience told him, was the step of a car.

'I'll put that right for you. Max, get me the kit. And you,

Tiffy, get inside and keep your mouth shut. See to him Shaggy, I won't be a minute.'

'There!' Peter felt a painful sting that hurt more than the blow that had cut open his eyebrow. Then slowly his vision cleared, and close above him he saw the master of ceremonies. The little man's dark thin face seemed to have changed entirely in the past moments, and his voice had a commanding ring as he said, 'Rest easy now till I stick something on it.' There was a pause while his fingers moved round the cut; then he muttered rapidly, 'That'll stop the bleeding . . . it won't need stitching.' Another pause and then he went on, 'I'm sorry this has happened. Tiffy's a fool but he meant no harm. You know when all's said and done you asked for what you got . . . we're all fond of Leo, Tiffy particularly. He did a great deal for her, it made a difference – he got to know her rather well.'

The mention of Leo's name seemed to have as astringent an effect on Peter as the stuff that had been applied to the cut for it brought him lumbering to his feet. He stood swaying slightly as he rubbed his hand roughly over his face; then he said thickly, and not without sarcasm, 'I can believe that.' Then, try as he might, he could not resist asking, 'And what did he do for her that was so different from all the others?' His tone, like his lips, was curled in a sneer.

The small man blinked, then in a somewhat off-hand manner, he said, 'Oh, well, he was in the theatre and attended her for months afterwards. She was an interesting case besides being a damn fine girl.'

It was painful to screw up his eyes but Peter's bewilderment slowly puckered his face as he exclaimed thickly, 'You're not actors then, you're . . .?'

'Actors? What gave you the impression we were actors? – we're doctors.' There was a crispness about the reply.

'Doctors?' In amazement he repeated the word, yet it was as if he were giving himself a long-awaited reply.

'Yes, doctors.' Roger gave a small laugh now. 'I don't suppose we appear quite the accepted idea but you've got to let your hair down sometimes in this business or you'd blow your top. Don't you know about Leo?'

Peter was standing quite still, looking down at the smaller man but not seeing him.

'She's ill, you know that?'

Peter's lips moved without emitting any sound, and when finally he did speak he could scarcely hear his own words. 'Ill? How?'

'Come on, let's get out of this blasted dump.'

Roger turned to where Max was leaning out of the car window and said curtly, 'Calm down, I won't be a minute.' Then putting his hand on Peter's elbow he guided him away, and when they reached the comparative quietness of the corner of the yard he looked up at him and made a statement, followed by a question: 'You're in love with her. Seriously? Now don't –' he raised one finger sharply – 'now don't say that's your business. Give me a straight answer.'

Here was no merry drunk. Looking at the man now it was hard to believe that he had touched a drop that day, and Peter did as he ordered and his reply came firmly as he said, 'Yes.'

'And you hadn't guessed she was ill?'

He shook his head in a pathetic fashion. 'No – not really. Only this evening she couldn't run out of the rain and. . . .'

'Well.' The doctor bit on his lip, stretching it down behind his teeth. 'Well.' He moved uneasily. 'There should be time to tell you this. Not in this fashion and here – ' his eyes flicked around him – 'and after this set-up. Still, you'd better know for I think you're in earnest about her – I'm coming!' He turned an angry face towards Max who was once again calling from the car window. Then resuming slowly, he said, 'When she left the hospital, four months ago, she had, at the outset, a year to live. She was supposed to report back at regular intervals, but once she was out she never came again. From something she let drop to Shaggy he got the idea that she was going to drive that old car of hers until she could go on no longer, then finish it. Of course, we could do nothing as it was just a surmise of his, and then when she didn't turn up and we didn't know where she was, we felt it had been no surmise and perhaps, after all, she knew what she was doing. Now and again her name would crop up because she was one of the gamest creatures we'd had through our hands. And then to come across her like this. . . .'

The urge to punch and bash, fear of what he didn't know, fear of what he did know, even his blind jealousy of the man whom he knew definitely had been part of her life, were swept away, driven before a flood of compassion and love – and weakness. The weakness made him want to put his head in his hands and cry, cry with loud pain-easing sobs. Almost conquered by this feeling, he turned away and looked down towards the bar garden, and saw beyond it, in his mind's eye, the wood and the lake and the eel. She had been content to sit and watch the eel and wait for its going, and what had she thought as she sat there all alone? Of dying? Of the quick end she was going to make of it? Always in her mind must have been that thought.

Sweat suddenly enveloped him, outdoing the rain that was streaking his face. Then the doctor's voice, brisk but full of sympathy, put an end to his weakness: 'If you love her you'll stand by her. Not that that'll be easy, for unlike most women of my experience she rears from pity like an unbroken colt, but that's merely because she thinks it's her role. She's always been taken lightly, she's the type that's always good for a laugh and a lark, but she's got another side. We found that out during her long stay in hospital.'

Peter was forced round. 'What is it? What's wrong with her?'

'Growth . . . malignant. Here.' The doctor pointed to his chest.

Peter's mouth was bone dry and he rubbed at his swollen lips before saying, 'But there are cases where they –'

'There are miracles. You could pray for one, but as things stand I've told you what to expect. Still, as you say, there are cases, and pharmacy has no medicine that I know of to come up to the stimulant of love – a good love.'

'Hi there, Peter!'

Peter turned to the entrance of the yard where his father and Bill, now joined by Old Pop, were standing.

'Come on.' Harry did not advance any farther. His voice

was harsh and he looked very much the worse for wear. But his face had escaped lightly, whereas Bill, besides a cut lip, was already showing signs of a beautiful black eye.

'We'll be off now.' The doctor turned towards his car, adding as he did so, 'This has been a strange half-hour to say the least. Goodbye. Tell Leo I'm sorry for all this, will you? Tell her I'll write to her here.'

From where he stood Peter watched the doctor get into the driving seat, and as the door banged behind him he moved hastily forward and, bending to the window, he brought out somewhat haltingly, 'I'm sorry . . . I'm sorry this happened. It was my fault.' Then turning his gaze on to the back seat to meet the scowling face of Tiffy, he repeated, 'Sorry about it.' Whereupon, as if an oiled rag had wiped it away, Tiffy's bad temper cleared and he shuffled his huge body saying, 'Oh, it's all in a day's work. We'll call in again sometime.' He even laughed, and to the astonished gaze of Harry, Bill and Old Pop, and equally to a number of men still standing under the porch, the occupants of the car waved to Peter as it moved out of the yard, and, more astonished still, they watched Peter answer with one self-conscious lift of his hand.

'Well, I'll be damned!' Harry squeezed the wet out of his hair, then again repeated, 'Well, I'll be damned!' And turning on Peter as he slowly advanced towards them, he demanded, 'What d'you mean by waving after such a bloody do, all pals together like?'

Peter, ignoring the remark and the blame attached, asked, in an oddly quiet tone, 'Where is she?'

Harry held on to his temper and said, 'Round the corner, drenched and scared.'

'And the other bloke?'

'Oh, he's gone. Thought it best . . . got a bit too hot for him.'

Peter moved past them now and past the lingering men, and as he reached the front of the inn, Mrs Booth, pushing her way out of the door, confronted him and, her face convulsed with fury, cried, 'You'll pay for this. You'll see. You and your cheap street –!'

'Shut your mouth!'

For a moment it looked as if he might hit her, and she, too, must have thought this for she recoiled a step, then screamed, 'You would, would you! You try it on and see what you'll get. You're a disgrace. A disgrace to the place, you and her, and don't you show your face in here again, ever – ever!'

After giving her one long, contemptuous look that spewed her words into an unintelligible gabble he moved past her and went through the men and to Leo, where she stood against the wall, her face turned away, like a child in trouble. And when, without a word he took her arm and led her slowly into the street in the direction of home she made no show of resistance but walked by his side with her head lowered.

Peter's intention of taking her home hit Harry like a brick in the neck and brought him, in a spurt, to his side. Yet any protest he was about to make was stilled, not only by the look on his son's face but by the awful look of the girl, and so with a helpless gesture he dropped behind them and joined Bill and Old Pop as they came up. The lad was mad, stark, staring mad; this could only lead to trouble – Harry drew in his breath through his teeth – and some!

Although there were only five of them on the green, the village had never seemed so full of people, for the doors and windows were crowded, and when Bill, paring off from the cortege, went towards his own door his wife's tirade swept into the street and caused Harry to wince.

Not only was the Mackenzies' doorway blocked by Mrs Mackenzie and a now even more virtuously indignant Mavis, but the men were braving the rain to stand at the gate. But whether it was Peter's look or Harry's or Old Pop's, or the combined looks of all three, they were allowed to pass in silence to their own garden gate, and to Grandpop.

For once the old man was not seated at the window but was standing just inside the front door. He had his back to them and was brandishing his stick and yelling.

Before reaching the gate Harry had taken in the situation, so stepping briskly to the front he pushed by the old man and confronted Rosie, who was blocking the passage, to be greeted with a stammering ferocious protest of rage, 'How dare you! How dare you! She's – she's not coming in here.'

Following a movement from her husband that could be defined as a violent push, Rosie found herself in the living-room with an equally ferocious Harry bending over her and hissing into her face, 'Not a word out of you, d'you hear! It'll keep.'

'Don't you think you're –'

'Shut yer gob!'

'Shut me gob, d'you say? You'll see whether I'll shut –'

Rosie stepped back from Harry, and as she did so her eyes swung to the doorway where now stood her son and . . . the woman. For a moment she was afraid, not of her husband's threats, but at the sudden wild leaping feeling inside of her, for she had an almost unconquerable desire to spring on the girl and tear her to pieces, And when she saw her lad gently lead her towards a chair she had to turn away in case the feeling should get the better of her, and as she pressed her hand over her mouth to still the moaning sound that was rising from her stomach there fell on the room a dreadful quietness, which not even Grandpop's garrulousness could break.

The men's eyes were meeting and questioning. What next? Then they all, with the exception of Peter, looked towards Rosie. Peter had turned his eyes again to Leo, but she, too, was looking at his mother. He saw her fighting for words. Then, her voice breathless and cracking in her throat, she brought out, 'I'm sorry for this, Mrs Puddleton but I won't stay long – just until I can get my things from the Hart.'

Her words made no apparent impression on Rosie, other than to stiffen her back still more, but to Peter, through his new knowledge of her, they spoke of her utter solitariness and twisted his feelings into knots. And he bent over her saying, with a gentleness the sound of which was unbearable to his mother, 'Come on and lie down for a while until we get things straightened out.'

Lie down? Lie down, indeed! Furious indignation reared in Rosie. Not if she knew it. The only place she could lie would be in his room and she wasn't having any of that. No, she wasn't!

She swung round, her mouth already open, but it seemed that Grandpop had been waiting for exactly this reaction, for he pelted his own words into it as he endorsed what Peter had said, 'Aye, aye – shut up, you!' He glared at her. 'Best place bed. Best place, strikes me. You go on, miss, and nobody'll say you nay in this house. No, they won't, not as long as I'm alive and kicking. Don't stand there, you lad. Go on up with you. Take her up.'

Even while giving this last daring order Grandpop still kept his eyes on Rosie. Harry and Old Pop said nothing; as strong as they might be they would not have had the nerve to do this.

Once again Leo looked up at Rosie and there was pleading in her eyes, but Rosie's answered it with what almost amounted to a blaze of hate. And when Peter, his face stiff and hardening, assisted Leo to her feet and felt her trembling under his hands, he turned a look on his mother that matched her own and sent a weakness through her limbs. It made her feel physically sick and caused her to moan inwardly, 'All through that piece. Oh, God in Heaven!'

She watched him showing such tenderness to the girl as he led her out of the room that she became embarrassed by the sight of him. Her big, casual, easy-going son had in the course of a few days shown her so many new sides that she was bewildered by them, but this one, this soppy goofiness, as she put it, was unbelievable and – and unbearable.

When she heard the click of the bedroom door she raised her eyes to the ceiling, then brought them flashing down to her menfolk and demanded, 'Well! nice, isn't it! Suits you, doesn't it, the three of you? It's a wonder you didn't think of starting it years ago yourselves.'

'Now look here.' Harry moved towards her, at the same time pressing his hand back on his father to still his retort, and standing facing her he said, quietly but with hard emphasis, 'He's always been the apple of your eye, hasn't he?' There was a covert accusation in this. 'You've given him a long apron string, but you've kept it fast about his

161

ankle. Well now, he's snapped it and whether you like it or not you've got to face it. He's on his own and for good or bad he's done his own pickin'.'

'You're glad, aren't you? You're glad it's happened.'

The words came brokenly from Rosie now, and Harry, shaking his head, said, 'Lass, have some sense. You may not believe it but I don't think he's even glad himself the way things have turned out. And I know better than you what he's going through at this minute.'

'Yes, I'd believe that all right.' Her voice was strident once more. 'You can tell all right, you've had experience. You and your affairs! And now you've got him like you, the lot of you.' She brought the two old men into her distracted glance. 'Now you're all satisfied.'

Harry's face darkened and he drew in his breath, but instead of making the biting retort that this last merited he let his breath slowly hiss out as was his way and was turning sharply about with the intention of going from the room when the sound of a door closing above checked his steps, and he waited. They all waited. Grandpop eased himself into a chair and Old Pop followed suit, but they all kept their eyes turned in one direction. And when Peter came into the room he did not, as they expected, face their glances angrily but went slowly to the table and sat down, and after a second he rested his head on one hand while they all looked at him.

The sight of him thus, wet and blood-stained, brought the mother-love sweeping back into Rosie – his poor face all cut and knocked about and that gash above the eye, it should be stitched – but when he raised his head and said with quiet firmness, 'I've got to talk to you all,' she stiffened again.

'Go on, lad. You have your say.' Grandpop drew himself to the edge of his seat and bounced his head, and Harry swung a chair round, to sit on it without a word but in a way that proved his willingness, even his eagerness, to listen to his son.

As Peter looked from one to the other the words crowded in his throat, cutting off his breath. He passed his hands over his eyes; then getting swiftly to his feet he brought out in a mumble, 'She's ill . . . very ill. She's . . . she's dying.' And with this he moved with blind steps into the scullery, leaving them all motionless.

The men, with shocked, darkened glances, looked at each other, but Rosie looked towards the scullery.

Dying! Huh! that was the best bit yet. It was a cheap trick of hers to catch him, and he had fallen for it . . . dying! The bigger they were the softer they were. Dying! Huh! Then Rosie's cyncism faltered, just the slightest, urged in that direction by unashamed hope. When she came to think of it there was something wrong with her – that look. But what? Anyway if she was dying there wasn't much future, was there? Slowly, as if she were being drawn there step by step, she moved towards the scullery.

He was standing by the window, and he did not show that he knew she was there, but his head dropped to his chest and she knew he was crying. As she watched him she seemed drained of all emotion, good, bad or indifferent. When a man cried over a woman. . . .

After a moment or two she watched his head lift, and he turned to her, unashamed of his tears, and with a deep sense of shock and renewed loss she saw that her lad had gone from her for ever. Not even figuratively would she be able to apply the name to him again for here, before her, stood a man, stronger in spite of his tears than the three back in the room, stronger even than Grandpop. Dead or alive, the girl had done her work, and when he said thickly, 'I must talk to you, Mam – I'm leaving,' she made no protest, but sat down in case the rapid beating of her heart should cause her to collapse.

CHAPTER EIGHT

It was just sixty minutes later, but to Peter it could have been sixty years, so much had happened, so much decided. Yet on the other hand he knew that it hadn't taken any length of time to establish his plan, for from the moment the doctor had spoken to him in the bar-yard everything he was going to do was already in his mind, it only needed formulating, and that had taken place when he'd said to his mother, 'I'm leaving.'

When he had stood at the other side of the table and added, 'I want to sell up, straightaway,' Rosie had made no protest whatever, and in her very silence he was made to realise the depth of the hurt he was dealing her. Yet, in this moment, he had no compassion to spare for her.

After a seemingly long time and in a voice he hardly recognised Rosie had said, 'If she's bad, why go?' and he had answered, 'Even if she would stay it wouldn't work. And, anyway, this place has suddenly become –' he had stopped and glanced in bewilderment about the room, but his look had embraced the entire village, yet he did not finish what he had been going to say – 'too small for me.'

But Rosie knew what he meant, as she also knew that if she didn't agree to selling the garage he would go in any case and with bitterness which might prevent him from ever coming back, whereas if the girl died. . . . She had not let her thinking go any farther at the moment but had said, 'Selling's not going to be easy. Although they've got nothing to do with it –' she inclined her head towards the kitchen – 'they'll be up in arms, they'll go mad.'

And Rosie's statement turned out to be correct. Although Harry, Old Pop and Grandpop had been touched to the heart by Peter's words, for the girl upstairs was fundament-

164

ally their kind of woman, yet from the moment Peter and Rosie had come back into the kitchen and Peter had thrown his news with the effect of a hand grenade into their midst, the girl was thrust aside by the disaster facing them, for it would be a disaster for all of them. The loss of the garage just at this time would mean the loss of money and prestige. With each of them the prestige came first, but things being what they were they knew they couldn't have the second without the first; to have a strong financial footing in the village was power, and power was prestige. Each in his own way needed power and each had suffered when watching power growing in, to his own way of thinking, the wrong hands. It was no solace to any of the three men that their neighbours were held in little respect for, say what you liked, in one way or another money talked and always would.

The mere thought of selling the garage was bad, in fact it seemed that nothing worse could happen; then came the greatest blow of all. Peter had almost stupefied them with it when he said, 'I'm going to sell to the Mackenzies.' Even Rosie had gaped, then balked at this. But Peter, the surprising possessor now of cool reasoning, had explained that three hundred pounds was three hundred and he could run them up to that amount over and above what the estate agent was now offering.

From this point had started a non-stop battle of bitter words, which, but for the brief break when Peter went upstairs carrying a hot drink he had himself made, had not stopped. And now Harry, holding the floor, was resorting to compromise.

'Look, what's going to happen when the money's gone? It's only half yours, you know. You'll have to start from scratch again and you'll never have the cash to buy another place. You'll come back here and tear your hair out when you see them sitting pretty on what they're making out of the garage alone. Look, if you must do this bloody mad thing, let them have a share, and they can take over for the time being. But even that makes me want to vomit.'

'I want no shares with Davy Mackenzie – it's sell or

nothing!' Peter's face was grim, but he continued to speak quietly.

Old Pop's voice joined in the fray but he addressed himself pointedly to Rosie now and said, 'Mad! Clean, stark, staring mad! Summat should be done – he just can't do it. An' you standin' there and lettin' him get on with it! You've made your mouth go for years 'bout other things, now when it should be snapping like a trap you're standing there like. . . .'

'Me!' All the blame for the inner fires which were consuming Peter and directing him along this mad course was transferred with the inflection of her voice back to the accuser, and his father, and his son.

'Me?' she repeated again on a higher note. 'Who's he following in this, and everything else, I'd like to know? Blaming me! For as many years as this village can remember the name Puddleton has been a byword connected with loose –'

'Shut up!' Harry barked angrily, while at the same time pushing his enraged father back into his chair.

'Be quiet! all of you. Listen!' The command brought their eyes to Peter, where his were directed towards the door, and Grandpop muttered, ''Tis only the lads,'

But it wasn't the lads. As Peter reached the door and pulled it open Leo stepped slowly into the passage from the stairs. She had his coat about her and her face looked more ashen even than when she entered the house, and her eyes seemed to have sunk deep into the back of her head.

'Why did you get up? I was coming . . . go on back.' In a flurry of anxiety he took hold of her hands, and she left them unresisting in his, but she shook her head saying, 'No. No, I can't go back. If my dress is dry I'd like it. And – and I'd like to see your mother.'

He moved his head in perplexity, then guiding her towards the front-room, he coaxed, 'Come in here, there's no one in here. You shouldn't have got up.'

When she was seated she did not look at him but kept her eyes directed towards Grandpop's empty seat on the dais before the window, and then she said quietly, 'I must see your mother. All this trouble over me, will it never cease?'

'It isn't over you,' he lied firmly. 'Come back to bed. Come on. You can see her in the morning.'

'No, it must be now.'

'But Leo. . . .'

'It's no good.' She moved her head with a weary motion. 'If you don't let me see her I'll walk out this minute and go back to the Hart. They can't forbid me entry. I must get my things anyway, and Miss Tallow might put me up for the night.'

'Look at me, Leo.' He had dropped on to his hunkers before her, and there was no indecision in his tone, or in his manner, as he brought her face round to him 'Whatever you've got to say to me mother makes no difference. I'm leaving here . . . we are going together. It might take a day or two for me to get things settled up but I'll make it as quick as possible.'

'No.' She jerked hastily at her hands, trying to force them. 'Oh, no You're not coming with me, now or at any time. You don't understand – you understand nothing. I tell you, you're not coming.'

'Be quiet.' He patted her hands as if she were a child. 'Nothing you can say will stop me. Nothing. I love you and that's just that.'

It was a casual sounding comment, and he made to rise on it but she grabbed at him, staring into his face in a puzzled fashion. Then she said, 'You're different. Why – why aren't you pelting me with questions? Asking about Tiffy and Roger and them all . . . why?'

After a prolonged stare she said in a whisper, 'You know already, you know who they are. You know about . . .'

Quickly he pulled her hands to his lips, and pressing them to his mouth he spoke through her fingers, passionately and urgently, in a way he had never imagined himself capable of: 'I only know I love you . . . I worship you. I never want to be away from you . . . not for the rest of me life.'

Slowly she pressed herself back in the chair and turned her face away from his gaze, and repeated in an agonised whisper, 'A moment of your life!' Then bringing her eyes to his again she said, 'You know that's all it will be, a moment of your life. Oh! –' she seemed to regain some of her energy, for she tossed her head and moved as if searching for a way of escape – 'why had this to happen? Why had they to come? They, of all people.'

'Well, they did,' he said gently. 'It seemed as if it was all planned. I've a feeling now that I've been marking time for years, just waiting for this. And I know this much, at least: if I was to see you no more after tonight these few days with you would be equal to a lifetime of happiness with somebody else. So –' he smiled gravely at her – 'in the next few months I'm going to live a number of lifetimes. There is only one thing I'd like to know, and then you needn't tell me that if you don't want to . . . do you love me a bit? It – it wasn't only a passing fancy?'

As her fingers tightened on his, the tears spilled from her eyes and her words were almost lost in her throat. 'Love you? Oh, Peter!'

In a moment he was kneeling by her side and holding her close and marvelling that the emotions of sadness and joy could at one and the same time flood his mind and body and make themselves equally felt by him. He stroked her hair as he said, 'Don't, darling, don't cry like that. Come on.'

'Peter.'

'Yes?' He waited.

'I feel so tired I can't fight any more.'

'Well, that's one good thing, anyway.'

'You may as well know – I've . . . I've loved you from the word go. And so much, so very much.'

She lay against him quiet and relaxed, and over her head he looked about the room. There was Grandpop's seat. There was the sideboard with the dish of artificial fruit situated dead centre. Arranged at angles so that you could move round them were the couch and the other chair belonging to the three-piece suite. There were knick-knacks on the mantelpiece and pictures on the walls. He should know these things – he had lived amongst them for twenty-eight years – they should be familiar, unconsciously loved or hated things. But now they were neither, they were strange to him, and the walls that housed them were surroundings that had held a man who no longer existed. In this moment if he had thought of the niggling worry occasioned by Mavis and Florrie he would have believed that they had never existed either. Never again would there be the path of least resistance for him. That road was closed.

He moved his lips to her hair when she said, 'What'll I say to your mother now? I was so sure a few minutes ago, I had all the words ready. "I'm not taking your son away, so don't worry," I was going to say to her, but now, how can I start?'

'Don't worry, she knows.'

'Everything?' It was a whisper.

'Yes, everything.'

'Oh, Peter!' Then in a voice even lower now she said his name again, 'Peter?'

'Yes?'

'I must tell you about Arthur.'

Arthur. There was no need to question, he knew whom she meant. 'I don't want to know about him,' he said.

He lifted a strand of her hair, and she reached up and caught his hand and brought it between their faces so that she could look at him. 'I want you to know.'

'You can tell me later.'

'No, now. It might be too hard to tell later.'

'All right. But it makes no difference.' He rose from his knees and, pulling a chair close to hers, sat down and took hold of her hands again.

'I lived with him for a year as his wife.'

Involuntarily his fingers stiffened and the joy was pressed temporarily out of him, but he kept his eyes steady and their expression unchanged until hers dropped away and she began slowly and haltingly to talk.

'It happened after I had finished a year touring the provinces. I had saved up a little and I wanted a car. I knew a lot about cars. There was one of the Company, a Mr Fuller. He was getting elderly and had a mania for collecting car brochures and catalogues. On long, boring journeys he would talk cars, and I became bitten with the bug, and it was . . . it was when I went to a second-hand car mart that I met him – Arthur. He tried to sell me one car after another, but I took a fancy to the old Alvis. He was called away at one point and I continued to look round, and I was examining a car when a man came up to me and asked my opinion of it. Perhaps it was because I was hatless and in jeans that he took me for one of the staff. And it tickled me so that I kept it up. And when he got his eye on the Alvis I remembered all Mr Fuller had told me about that particular make, her being a grand car but very spirited on the brakes, and so on, and I was ladling this sort of thing out when I became aware that he – Arthur – was standing listening to me. But instead of being wild he winked encouragement. Well –' her voice became weary – 'to cut a long story short I sold that man a car, and Arthur said that if I'd work for a month in the showrooms he'd give me the Alvis, sales or no sales, he would take a chance.'

She looked up at Peter. 'That's how it started. He was married and soon I got the Misunderstood Husband story. But when I met his wife I could well believe a little of it, for when there was nothing more between us than the business of selling cars she suspected the worst. After eighteen months he asked her for a divorce. She wouldn't give it, so he left her and we lived together.'

She paused here and wetted her lips, and drawing her hands from his she rubbed the palms together. 'I had a baby.'

Her words caused something to jerk within him, as if he had received a blow in the ribs from inside, but he still kept his eyes, unwavering, on her face. And she kept hers fixed on her hands.

'It was born too soon – it died. I never felt the same after. Not ill, but not well.' Her hands parted and she turned one palm upwards and examined it as if it were new to her, before continuing. 'Then one day I found myself in hospital. And that was that. From then he suddenly developed a conscience, he remembered he had a lawful wife and he hadn't played fair by her.' Her voice trailed off. 'There was never anyone else. Doctor Patterson – that was the short one, Roger – and the blond one, Tiffy, they helped to keep me sane. Tiffy did – did the. . . .'

Not swiftly, not slowly, but with a steady sureness he gathered her hands together again and their eyes met as he said, 'It's all past. Forget it, forget everything but you and me.' He smiled, and had he analysed that smile he would have discovered it was, in a way, a smile of relief. There was no one else, she had said. Somehow, deep down, knowing how she reacted on men he had imagined a train of them.

'Listen, beloved.' He paused at the sound of his own voice softly speaking the endearment, for it was the first time in his life he had used it. Then, his smile growing more tender, he went on, 'You're not to worry about a thing, not a thing. From now on I'll do that. Think for you and –' he nodded – 'talk for you. Just you lie back there while I see about your dress.' He would have liked to add to this. 'My mother'll bring it.' But on this point he could not even let himself hope, so after holding her face for a moment close to his he left.

In the kitchen all was quiet. Old Pop and Grandpop were seated, but taut, in their chairs. Harry was standing, his arm resting on the mantelpiece. No one spoke when he entered the room, but they all looked at him. And when he saw that his mother wasn't there he just returned their glances for a brief second, then went into the scullery without saying a word.

Rosie was at the table making an effort to prepare the supper, and she did not move or raise her head when he asked, 'Is the dress dry?' but replied curtly, 'You'd better find out.'

With his face now set stiffly he went to the airing rack and taking off the dress felt it, then moved to the table. And there he stood looking at her, watching her hands moving swiftly and fumbling over the dishes.

'Mam.'

She did not look up.

'Do one thing for me, will you?'

'I didn't think you needed me to do anything for you.' The moving of the dishes went on.

'Take this in to her. Talk to her. She needs you . . . someone like you, more than me.'

Rosie's answer was to draw in a deep breath and turn from him to the sink. After a moment of watching her clattering with the dishes, he moved towards the door, and then her voice, gruff and biting, halted him. 'Put it down,' she said.

It was enough. Putting the dress on a chair he went out of the scullery and through the kitchen again and into the passage.

He was lifting his old mack off the rack when Harry appeared at the kitchen door. 'Where you off to?' he asked, unable to keep the acid note from his voice.

'Mackenzies'.'

'My God!' Harry's chest swelled. 'Can't you leave it for a day or two?'

'No, I can't.' Peter spoke below his breath and drew his father back into the room again by pushing past him. Then he turned and closed the door so that their voices would at least be muted as Harry cried indignantly, 'If you want to act Sir Galahad isn't this as good a place as any for it? If she's in the condition you say, you're mad to move about.'

The quip of Sir Galahad touched Peter to a flashing retort, but he bit on it and said with somewhat heavy sarcasm 'And enjoy the nice, quiet village life? It's no good talking, you might as well save your breath.' And on this remark, which was in no way calculated to soothe, he turned abruptly and swung out, while Harry, after a number of quick movements which appeared as though they might be a prelude to his wrecking the room, strode into the passage after him, and he, too, went out, but down the back garden and over the fence into the sodden fields.

Grimly the two old men sat looking each into his own particular patch of space, and when Rosie passed through the room, carrying the girl's frock on her arm, they turned to look at her. But even Grandpop was deterred from comment, and not until he heard her enter what he termed 'his room' did he speak. Looking at his son, he commented sadly, 'End of summat, somehow, here.'

CHAPTER NINE

The village street was deserted. There were no longer faces at the windows and doors, for who could have guessed that as a climax to that remarkable day Peter Puddleton would be going to the Mackenzies' to do a deal about the garage.

For the lack of spectators Peter was indeed grateful, for in spite of his high resolve it was requiring all his new-found courage to carry him to his neighbours' front door. He was no longer afraid of confronting Mavis – she had virtually ceased to exist for him – and he certainly wasn't afraid of either of the Mackenzie men, but his fear was that when it came to the final issue he would not be able to tolerate the thought of them having his garage and that this attitude might decide him to wait and see the estate agent. The two things against the latter were time and less money.

He knocked once, a sharp rap, indicative of his feelings to get it over. And when the door opened and Mavis stood before him he could have laughed, had a laugh been left in him, so large was the amazement written all over her. After one gasp, and the usual struggle of her lips to meet, she gave a loud 'Huh!' and went to bang the door in his face for Mavis was no fool; whatever she might imagine was the business of his visit there was one thing certain in her mind now, it had nothing to do with her.

With his foot firmly placed against the door, Peter said, 'Hold your hand a minute, I want to see your father.' His voice was loud and brittle and it penetrated the house, and

Mr Mackenzie, coming from the kitchen, said, 'What is it? Who is it?' Then the door was pulled out of Mavis's hand. Mr Mackenzie stared at Peter. His astonishment was no less than his daughter's, and for a moment he did nothing to hide it. Then, his voice almost a splutter, he said, 'Well! well! Talk about surprises. This is one, and no doubt about it. Well, Peter lad, and what can I do for you, eh?'

'I want a word with you.'

'Oh, a word?' Mr Mackenzie's head moved slowly up and down. Then his attitude changing to his usual brisk, business-like manner, he cried to his daughter, 'Get out of the way, girl.' And he pressed back his arm on her, pushing her against the wall as he said, 'Come in. Come in. Well. Well now, come in here. Get by, girl, out of the way. Don't stand there gaping.'

'Davy!' Mr Mackenzie was calling up the stairs. 'Visitor here . . . Peter.'

'Who?'

It was as if Davy had been catapulted out of his room, for almost instantaneously he appeared at the top of the stairs, and in a second he was down them and had followed his father into the sitting-room, where after staring at Peter, he exclaimed, as his father had done, 'Well! well!' then added, 'Hallo again. Some water and blood passed under the bridge since we last met up, eh?'

It took a deliberate effort for Peter to ignore this remark, and forcing his attention round to the father, he said, 'You've got a saying, Mr Mackenzie – "No beating about the bush!" Well I'll use it and come straight to the point. I'm willing to sell the garage and land for fifteen hundred cash, right on the nail. And I want everything settled within the next two or three days.'

Davy's lips had fallen slightly open, but his father's were pressed tightly together, and he nodded while he stared at Peter. Then thrusting his hand within the rim of his trousers, he said, 'Ah, well now, this has got to be talked about. Sit down, sit down. Yes – aye, there's some talking to be done here.'

Peter sat down, and Davy, regaining his breath, said,

'What's bitten you all of a sudden? Oh, I know –' he waved his hand airily – 'it's your own business. But fifteen hundred! Eh, Dad?'

Davy turned to his father, who said, 'Aye, fifteen hundred – we can't do that lad.'

Almost before he'd had time to settle in his chair Peter was on his feet again. 'That's all I want to know. That's the price and I'm not coming down, not a solitary penny, so you can save yourself the effort of bargaining.'

'Now, now, lad.' Mr Mackenzie laid a restraining hand on Peter's arm. 'Don't let us get excited. Business is business and cannot be dealt with in a minute or so, nor yet a day or so. Not a thing like this, anyway.'

'See here –' Peter looked from one to the other – 'you've been pestering me since Monday to sell. Now I'm going to sell, but on my own terms and in my own time. Do you want it or not?'

Neither of them answered, but after a brief pause Mr Mackenzie, his face working and his hands hitching at his trousers, went towards his desk standing in the corner of the room and sat heavily down.

'Give you thirteen hundred.'

It was Davy speaking, and Peter, turning and looking at him steadily, said, 'Funnel will give me my price if I wait a few days. And –' he nodded – 'he's not the only one interested, let me tell you.'

This last remark was merely a piece of wishful thinking, coupled with an effort to play these two at their own game, but Mr Mackenzie, knowing he was on a good thing, would not have been surprised had Peter named half-a-dozen men who were after it, so he pursed his lips and said to his son, 'Leave this to me, lad. Well now –' he stood up – 'you're driving a hard bargain, Peter, for you know, but for the road coming this way you'd be lucky to get a thousand.

Peter did not at this point remind them that their value of the garage had previously not exceeded eight hundred pounds.

'Well now, where are we going to get this amount from pronto?' Mr Mackenzie looked at his son. 'We haven't that much in raw cash, have we?' And Davy, taking the cue from his father, said 'No, that we haven't.'

'We could, with a lot of raking around, let you have half and the rest later on.'

Mr Mackenzie was now fixing Peter with his small bright eyes, and Peter returned his look and said quietly, 'I want it altogether, Mr Mackenzie.'

'Well now, you're setting me a poser, Peter.' Mr Mackenzie scrubbed roughly at his chin with the palm of his hand. 'I'll say you are. You appear set as I've never afore seen you. Changed you are. Looks to me as if you've got the makings of a business man about you.' He let out a chuckle on a long-drawn breath, which took some flavour from the compliment, then exclaimed loudly, 'There then it's a deal. Well I never!' he slapped his thigh – 'and to think after the way. . . . Oh, well now, as you're here and that's settled we'd better have a statement . . . pen to paper, eh? Just to make things right, temporary like.'

As his father busied himself at the desk Davy moved into a position where he could look more fully at Peter, and he gazed at him, frankly bewildered as much at the evident change in him personally as at the reversing of his adamant attitude not to let them have the garage. Inwardly Davy was seething with excitement; the garage and land, as it stood, was worth twelve hundred, but to get it for fifteen hundred with its future prospects was an absolute snip. In a few years' time with a bit of titivating they could ask five thousand and get it. His look was pitying. He knew why Peter was making this lightning decision . . . the sucker. Still, they continued to be born every day, even in this age. He would have liked to do a bit of leg-pulling and get him on the raw, but thought it wiser to wait – that piece of paper he was now signing had in itself no binding value. He watched Peter lay down the pen, and noted the greyness around his mouth that spoke of inward strain. He watched him reluctantly shake hands on the bargain. He was about to offer his own hand but again thought better of it, and he did not, with his father, accompany him to the door, but from the window he watched him move heavily into the street.

The door had hardly closed before Mr Mackenzie was back in the room, and father and son regarded each other. Then their hands gripped and held.

'At last!' said Mr Mackenzie. Then buttoning his waist coat he added, 'Get the car out.'

'What for?'

'We're going to see Tyson.'

'At this time of night? He can't do anything.'

'Can't he? He can. Talking takes time. I've put him on to a good thing recently and he'll do this for me. Anyway, we can get everything settled but the writing. He'll have that agreement all ready by Tuesday at the latest, because, between you and me, I'm as anxious to push things as Peter Puddleton, more if the truth were known for I'll not feel we've got it till it's signed and sealed.' He slapped his son's back and a beam spread over his face. Then his eyes narrowed and his head nodded as he counted his assets. 'The contracting, shares in the mill, and that won't end there either, and now the garage and the land for fifteen hundred! Give us a few years and it'll be a gold mine. He'll want to cut off the hand that signed that paper when he sees what we'll do with his garage.' He thumped Davy in the chest and added finally, 'We'll show 'em who's running what when this village gets on the map.'

Sunday morning came soft and calm. Nature had apparently forgotten her tantrums of the previous evening. That the swelled congregation was not due to the entrancing beauty and the allure of the morning, nor yet to an over-powering desire to hear him speak the word of God, the Rev Collins knew. As he looked down on his flock he knew that those faces he saw only at weddings, christenings, Christmas and Harvest Festivals were present not for the good of their souls but because after the service there would be the one opportunity of the day to gather and gossip, and moreover to do so without censure.

He had heard an account of the fantastic happenings of last night at the inn, and although he had been chivvied for hours by his sister to alter his sermon and deliver a

resounding rebuke on all who drank and had dealing with
. . . loose women, he had steadfastly refused even to consider such a thing. For the vicar was fighting his own battle. He was profoundly disturbed because he could not rid himself of the memory of sunlit water, a grassy bank, two kind eyes, and a voice that could shut from his mind everything but itself.

As he stood in the pulpit, the minister's thoughts made him feel faint and weak, and it was all he could do to read his sermon, let alone deliver it with any semblance of feeling. So it was to be understood that he wasn't the only one who sighed with relief when he stepped down from the pulpit.

Moreover, the service ended, he was finding it unbearable to stand and smile and mutter polite nothings to the departing congregation. So picking Miss Tallow as the one who would likely comment the least on his abrupt departure, he left her after a flabby handshake and in the middle of her views on the weather of yesterday.

The major, coming out on to the gravel path from the porch, turned his eyes to where the minister was hurrying away to the side door of the church. The major's nose twitched, and he thought, 'Queer fellow. Bit unsteady really. And what a sermon! not even worth sleeping to . . . no humour. And look at yesterday. Ran like a rabbit because the girl teased him. Damn bad thing about that girl – Harry said she was ill, dying.' He couldn't believe she was as bad as that. A bit pale, but that was her type and the make-up she stuck on. Suited her though, and gave her that added something. But it made the women hate her. By God! yes. Look at last night. The house raised because he sat with her in the marquee and had a laugh, and young Peter there all the time. Florrie had a bee in her bonnet, too. And bringing up the old family scandal of Connie Fitzpatrick again. What had the girl to do with Connie? You'd think she had started a loose house dead centre of the village to hear Florrie go on. She was worse than her mother where the girl was concerned. Of course, Peter was at the bottom of it. She had always been a little too friendly in that quarter, and that would never do really. No, never. Well, that was settled, and a good thing too. Peter, by all accounts, had gone berserk last night because some fellow had tried to kiss the girl. Really! really! But he wished he had been there. Of course, with her type that sort of thing was sure to happen. Dying? Nonsense! He wished he was younger, by God! he did. He'd give his household something really to worry over.

The major straightened his shoulders, pulled down his coat, thrust his neck out of his tight, stiff collar, and exclaimed to himself, 'Where the hell are they?' He marched down the path that led into the cypress-sheltered graveyard, and there he saw both his wife and daughter the centre of a group of six or more women, and his mouth clamped tightly. They had got their teeth in. Well, in that case, he would leave them to do their tearing and also to find their own way back. With a certain amount of satisfaction he strolled down the path and into his car and drove away.

Both Mrs Carrington-Barrett and Florrie, quite oblivious that their escort had departed, continued to listen to Mrs Booth. Mrs Carrington-Barrett's mouth and eyes mimed her disgust, but Florrie's face showed no emotion other than sullenness as Mrs Booth continued to pour out her venom. 'Four of them larking round her, and she egging them on to kiss her. Talk about disgusting! I've never seen anything like it in all me born days. And the other man, like a vulture, standing there watching them. But as I said afore he hadn't anything on Peter Puddleton! You never in all your born days . . . never. He was like a madman, and him who wouldn't say boo to a goose. Soppy he was, I used to think sometimes . . . nothing in him . . . did what his mother told him. And then, out of the blue, he changes and all in a couple of days. I tell you she turns men crazy. Every man in the village she's been after. Sex, she oozes it!'

'Same as her they ducked.'

'What d'you say, Gran?' Amelia Fountain, who by her sufferings at the hands of the harlot, as she put it, felt entitled to be one of this particular group, even though she was rarely to be seen at church, now bent above Grannie Andrews who was leaning on her daughter's arm, and enquired again, 'What, Gran? What were you saying?'

The wrinkled flesh of Gran ran into patterns as she munched her jaws before repeating, 'I said duckin', that's what she wants. Only way to cool blood like hers. Sent the other one scooting, it did. Cooled her capers.' Gran spoke of 'the other one' as if the incident had happened last week.

Mrs Carrington-Barrett laughed an amused laugh and exclaimed, 'Now, now, Mrs Andrews. We must remember as the saying goes, that "them days are gone". We have to use other methods in these times.'

'What you say?' Gran, detecting a note of censure in the major's wife, suddenly became deaf and exclaimed again, 'What you say?' Whereupon her daughter repeated, in a much higher key, what Mrs Carrington-Barrett had said: 'She says you can't do that now – duck people. She says them days are gone, we've to use other methods.'

All eyes were on Gran, and Gran looked from one to the other, bestowing on each a flash of her eyes before she brought out: 'Aye, you might. Not so 'fective though, by half. Village'll be turned into a land of Soddom and Gomorrah, you'll see. Mark my words. I've seen the havoc her sort can play. No man's safe, nor never will be. Well, I've had me say. Come on.' She jerked at her daughter's arm. 'Can't stand much longer. Had about enough now.'

'Goodbye, Gran.'

'Goodbye, Gran.'

'So nice seeing you out, Gran. You must try to do this more often.'

'Goodbye, Goodbye.'

The varied farewells sent the old woman and her daughter down the drive and left standing, besides the Carrington-Barretts, Mrs Booth and Mrs Fountain, Mavis and Miss Collins who had both remained singularly quiet during the chatter of Mrs Booth and the old woman. But now Miss Collins spoke, and she brought all eyes round to her as she exclaimed, 'I've never before wished that I wasn't a Christian.'

This remark was so potent in its meaning that the group with eyes slightly widened, waited, and Miss Collins's next words caused each one of them to react by some movement

– the scraping of a foot, the shifting of a bag, the lifting of a shoulder – as she said, 'If she settles in this village no man will be safe – no man.'

There was a pause during which no one made any comment, they just waited. And she went on, 'I know it, I feel it. Slinky Jane. Never was anybody more aptly named, for she'll slink under each man's skin. There'll be no peace, not as long as she stays. No woman will know where her man is . . . or perhaps she'll know only too well.'

'Who said she was settling here?' Florrie's voice was thin and vibrating, as if her words were strung on a taut wire.

'Mavis.' Miss Collins nodded to where Mavis stood. 'She says he's going to marry her.'

'Marry her!' The exclamations formed a chorus in which Florrie did not join, but she brought out, sharply, 'Who told you that?' She was confronting Mavis squarely as if the issue lay between their two selves, but Mavis, now the centre of interest, became evasive. 'I don't know who said it exactly, it was something I heard.'

It was evident to the group that Mavis was holding something back. It was also evident to Mrs Carrington-Barrett that her daughter was giving herself away. She wished she would use more control and not bring herself down to the level of the villagers. For more reasons than one she herself would be only too glad if Peter Puddleton did marry the girl. At least, if she was married there'd be no further sporting in the woods – there was never smoke without fire.

'Come, Mavis,' she said. 'You couldn't have forgotten such an important thing as that.'

'Oh, leave me alone. I tell you, I must have made a mistake.'

'Really!' Mrs Carrington-Barrett was definitely offended by Mavis's tone, and she did nothing to hide it. 'Really!' she said again.

Mavis, now red to the ears, struggled valiantly in her embarrassment to cover her teeth. If only her dad hadn't gone on so, she would love to tell everything she knew, but it was more than she dare do to mention a word of the pending business transaction, for, with his eye on her and his finger thrust into her chest, her father had warned her before leaving the house what would happen should she let out anything about the garage affair.

'If anything leaks out,' Mr Mackenzie had said, 'Funnel will likely as not be on the spot first thing in the morning offering him God knows what. So mind, you open your mouth if you dare. You know nothing, you've heard nothing, understand?'

Mavis knew she had been a fool and said too much already, but she hadn't thought Miss Collins would go on like this. She was definitely puzzled at Miss Collins's attitude, for had she herself wanted Peter she couldn't have gone on worse. Her attention was brought from Miss Collins to Mrs Booth as that lady declared, in vibrant tones, 'Well, that settles it, something's got to be done.'

After delivering this statement, Mrs Booth's mouth snapped shut and her eyes rolled upwards; indeed they were turning inwards looking at the situation, for, in her own mind, she was certain that something would have to be done. If that piece stayed in the village the Hart wouldn't see her again nor many of the men; they would go farther afield. After all, the Crown was just a mile as the crow flew, and you could, from Battenbun, follow the crow's flight through the woods and over the fells. And Mrs Booth had a mental picture of Leo, in the guise of the Pied Piper, leading the entire village of men over the fells to the Crown, for, as her husband had put it, that one attracted custom like a strip-tease artist. Something would have to be done.

Away over the gravestones and the sloping grassy bank Mrs Booth caught sight of the heads of Grannie Andrews and her daughter slowly bobbing above the hedge as they made their way back to the village, and she murmured something to herself, which Mrs Carrington-Barrett failed to catch. And so that lady prodded, as was her custom, 'You were saying, Mrs Booth?'

'Aye. Yes.' Mrs Booth seemed to come back from a long way. 'Yes, I was just thinking, it's a pity we don't live a little earlier back. Grannie Andrews was right, rough medicine often proves the best purge.'

Mrs Carrington-Barrett's thin laugh trailed away among the cypress trees. 'Now, now, Mrs Booth. We mustn't resort to that. Dear, dear. Must we, Miss Collins? Not in this day and age.'

Miss Collins did not reply for a moment but remained still, staring away into the distance as Mrs Booth had been doing. Then as if answering her own thoughts she said, 'It's right. Things can't go on as they are. She's affected this village like a plague. I don't have much time for the devil –' her eyes now flicked around the group, giving the evidence of her modern outlook – 'but it seems to me past the bounds of iniquity to concoct a story of an enormous eel in the little lake miles from the river. And it is funny, isn't it, that no woman has seen this eel, except her. She's clever. An eel would attract the men, not the women or children! Why didn't she make up a story of elves and pixies to fetch the children, or a male film star retreating to a cave on the fells to fetch the women? One is as likely as the other. But no, it had to be a simple and subtle attraction for the men, so we have an eel.'

With the exception of Florrie's, there was a ripple on the faces around her as if her audience had a desire to laugh, but Miss Collins's expression forbade laughter. This was a very serious matter to all of them, but to her it was of the most vital importance. She was about to resume, perhaps to answer the sugar-coated urgings of Mrs Carrington-Barrett and the insane ravings of Mrs Booth, when Mr Fraser, the verger, came hurrying round the path, and before reaching the group he called to her, 'Miss – miss. I think you'd better come, vicar's in a bad way.'

'What!' Miss Collins had already sprung away towards Mr Fraser, and Mr Fraser, turning on his heel without stopping, went back the way he had come talking over his shoulder to the vicar's sister, 'Sick he's been, throwing up. My! never seen vicar in this state. Upset he is about something. Talking twenty to the dozen, and how!'

As the voice of the verger faded away the women looked from one to the other. Then Mrs Carrington-Barrett said, 'Poor man, nerves, I suppose. He did seem a little unusual during the sermon, don't you think? Overwork.'

They all looked back at her and in their eyes was the same knowledge. Nerves . . . nothing. Overwork? That was funny in this village. It was her; she had even got the vicar now, it was history repeating itself.

Florrie was the first to break away from the circle, and she summed up all their thoughts as she said, 'Well, that would indeed seem to be that!'

CHAPTER TEN

Rosie's outside world was, through necessity, centred around her family. That it had been rent and thrown into a state of chaos by the events of the last few days was not altogether surprising, but that her inner world, the tower wherein she housed her unbending self, should be brought to the same pass was both surprising and distressing.

She was given to firm opinions: a thing was right or it wasn't; people were right or they weren't. There were no half measures with Rosie, no interwoven patterns of grey. With people, she had thought she could judge them right away. But now, this belief had undergone a severe shaking.

Last night when she had gone into the front-room she had known exactly what she was going to say; it was to be brief and to the point. The girl might be ill; she might or she might not be dying – on this last point Rosie's mind had swung in a very short space of time towards doubt. And then, when she had been confronted by the girl, she had said nothing. It was the girl who had done the talking. And when someone blamed herself for all the worry that had come upon you, what could you say?

Rosie had found herself thinking, 'She doesn't talk like she looks'; and she also found herself thinking, 'I can see what got him.' Yet what it was she couldn't exactly explain, but it was something, and it was there confronting her. She could feel it, that something that the blonde bedraggled hair and Peter's old top coat did nothing to diminish. If Rosie had been capable of clear thinking she would have associated the elusive quality with one still more elusive, which was honesty. Anyway, the result of the meeting had been that she had, somewhat tersely, ordered the girl back to bed and with the promise to bring her something up. And finally she had heard herself suggesting that she stay in bed the following day. This last charitable act had not been without motive though, for no matter how much her feelings had been toned down she still couldn't bear the thought of seeing her lad and this girl together. No matter how much she now appeared to have in her favour, dying and all that, the fact still remained that this time last week he hadn't known her, hadn't even known she existed . . . and now he couldn't exist without her. Everything had been thrust aside on her account, everything, even herself – mostly herself. No, Rosie decided, she couldn't stand to see any carry on. Bed was the best place for her while she was in this house, for what the eye didn't see the heart didn't grieve over. Yet, when Peter had come back from the Mackenzies' and had gone upstairs, she had felt worked up And when she did not hear the drone of his voice her imagination ran wild and presented her with shuddering scenes, so that she wondered if her suggestion had been right after all.

But on Sunday her feelings were again mollified, for Peter scarcely stayed in the house at all. From early morning he had been in the garage, and two short visits upstairs was all the time he had spent with the girl. It was as if he had sensed how she felt about this facet of the matter and was going out of his way not to upset her unduly.

It was late evening now and Peter was still at the garage. This, in a way, was to be expected as he wished to leave everything as straight as possible, from his books to the storeroom, mostly the storeroom. But what was now puzzling and testing Rosie's mental powers to the utmost, and had done since lunch-time, was not the girl, or Peter, but her husband's changed attitude towards the selling of the garage, and not his alone, but that of the other two as well.

Harry's temper had not improved when he returned home last evening, and most of the night he had tossed and turned and muttered. She knew this to be a fact, for she herself had hardly slept. It being his Sunday on at the Manor, a self-imposed task that she had always quibbled at, he had gone out first thing with a face like thunder. She had prophesied to herself that it was going to be a nice day, with one thing and another. Then, knowing her menfolk as she did, she had been immediately openly suspicious when, on Harry's return, his whole attitude towards the affair was changed and he had not only offered to give Peter a hand but had, for all to hear, openly declared to him that perhaps after all he was doing the most sensible thing in selling.

To an outsider it might have looked as if Harry had, after thinking things over, changed his mind about something that was inevitable anyway; it might appear to the same outsider, that he was a sensible man; but Rosie had for a great number of years been on the inside of Harry, and his mellowed attitude put her straight away on her guard and she felt, and naturally, that there was something behind all this. Oh, yes . . . and more so when the other two had by tea-time come to follow his suit. Instinctively she was reminded of the time she had made her bid for liberty.

Eight years ago, when she was forty-four, she had made a stand against the band of Puddletons. She had decided that in future they would look after themselves – all, that was, except Peter. She would supply them with what she called a skeleton service, for she had decided she was going to get out and about and see the world, as far as Hexham each week, like every other woman. And even Durham or Newcastle on a cheap day trip. But she made one mistake. In a glorious row one night she made her plans known to the Puddletons, all three of them, and she could swear to this day that they got together and planned what later developed to crush her revolt; for from the day following her rising her husband began unashamedly to court her all over again. He ceased to dive into the house, swallow his meal and dive out again to the Hart, or fishing, or . . . to them others, as she thought of the women she imagined he was for ever consorting with. Instead, he plied her with his attentions. And she wasn't saying it wasn't nice and refreshing for a time – she blossomed again . . . people noticed it. And then, bang! She woke up one morning to find she was pregnant. She was forty-four and past it, things were safe. But she was to find nothing was safe. She had counted without the exception, and in due course she was presented with twins, and, insult to injury, boys again, each with the hooked nose, Puddleton mouth, and the cast. Aye they had buttered her up then, and now they were buttering Peter, and she was on to them and as suspicious as a newly-made detective.

Although she would have given anything in her world to undo the present state of affairs she was only too well aware that, for good or ill, her lad's life was tied up with that of the girl's upstairs, and that the girl, for a number of reasons, could not stay in this village, so Peter must go, too, and the garage must be sold. That it was sold, and to the long-standing enemy of the house, was what had embittered them all so, particularly Harry. Yet here he was, with his father and grandfather, abetting Peter now, and saying it was likely all for the best. No, no, such an attitude was against all reason. She knew the Puddletons, oh! she knew the Puddletons, only too well did she know the Puddletons. They were up to something again, something to keep him here.

As bad as things were now Rosie saw they could be even worse. For instance, if the selling of the garage fell through Peter would have to stay; if he hadn't any money he would hesitate to take her away, at least until things could be reshuffled. That would mean the girl and herself in this house all day, with the old 'un openly on her side. No, no. God in Heaven! no, she couldn't stand that.

When at last at the end of the longest Sunday she had ever known Peter and his father and Old Pop came in, tired, and, she noticed, somewhat more saddened than they had appeared earlier on in the day, she hurried them over their washing so that, as she said, they could get their supper and she could get cleared away before midnight. And when, with surprising docility, they obeyed her and marched into the room, she tapped Peter on the arm, giving him a nod to indicate he should wait behind. Then closing the door and drawing him away from it towards the sink, she whispered, 'Do you smell a rat?'

He looked at her, his eyes screwed up. 'Smell a rat? What about?'

'Them.' She nodded back to the kitchen. 'What's made your Da change his tune? He could have killed you last night for selling. And when it was the Mackenzies I thought he'd go off his head. You should have heard him in bed, he kept on and on. And now look at him and the other two. I tell you there's something afoot.'

Peter looked away from her and out of the window, his mind moving rapidly now. She was right, they had all changed their tune and he had thought it was because they didn't want to part bad friends. And after the scene of last night he had been only too glad to accept this attitude. But now he could see, as she said, they were up to something. But what?

He looked at his mother again: 'There's no trick in the deeds, they're straightforward?'

'As far as I know.' She was whispering now. 'But there's something. Ask yourself. You're taking away the thing they were all building on and they act like angels. 'Tisn't natural, not with them. Last night was, but not the day. Could he have got at the Mackenzies this morning?'

'What good would that have done him?' said Peter soberly. 'They want the garage as they never wanted anything. Anyway, I saw them both going off around ten o'clock, Hexham way, and if I know them they'll hurry this thing up as fast as a deed can be written out. They know they're on a good thing. Trust the Mackenzies. They wouldn't have agreed to the fifteen hundred else.'

They looked at each other; then Rosie, turning away, sighed and said, 'Well, there's something.' Then, on the sound of a low chortle of laughter from the other room, she looked sharply back at Peter and said, 'See what I mean.

And the old 'un's never barked at me nor nobody else since dinner-time. I'm telling you, you'd better keep your wits about you.'

As his mother bustled out of the scullery Peter remained where he was, considering her words. She was right, but what could they be up to? He racked his brain, but could find nothing that they could do to stop the deal going through.

Whereas last night, for financial reasons alone, it had been necessary that he should sell the garage, the happenings of today had now made it doubly so, for it seemed that the entire population of the village was against him. Previously he had only to walk down the street any number of times in a day to be hailed with a smile, a wave, or a call of 'Hallo, there, lad', from his elders, or, 'Ho! Peter', from his contemporaries. But today he had seen people turn indoors or cut over the green to avoid him. The entire blame of last night's brawl had been put down to him, and if not to him, then to Leo, and that amounted to one and the same thing. Then the scene in the Hart this morning when he had gone to collect her things would take some forgetting.

His mission had at first been delayed by Mr Booth, who had endeavoured to bully him into paying the damage done the previous evening to two chairs, the leg of a table and ten broken glasses. And he was standing in the passage with Leo's cases at his feet, his way obstructed by Mr Booth, who was threatening him with a summons, when Mrs Booth came in. It wasn't clear then, or now, what she had said, but what had impressed itself on him was the almost terrifying force of her vindictiveness, for she had acted like someone possessed. She had gabbled about the vicar being ill and the major forgetting his position and making a fool of himself, of Amelia Fountain going to leave Bill, and others. She kept referring to 'others' with her popping eyes on her husband, until he, with some force, pushed her into the living-room, and in doing so allowed Peter to make his escape.

The slighting by his friends and the scene in the Hart had somehow upset him even more than last night's business. For him the village was finished, as, indeed, apparently was the village finished with him, and although he would not admit it he was hurt by this rejection.

He passed through the kitchen, answering Rosie's look from the table with a murmured, 'I won't be a minute.' and went upstairs.

When he opened his bedroom door Leo's eyes were waiting for him, as if they had not changed their direction since he had left her at tea-time. Without a word he went to the bed and took her into his arms. And she clung to him with a strength that was in contrast to her thinness. Then with his lips against hers he gently pressed her back on to the pillows, and after gazing at her for some moments he asked tenderly, 'Been a long day?'

'No.' She shook her head. 'The boys have been so good, keeping me company.' Her fingers outlined his cheekbones. 'I've been learning all about you and this room. All your life seems to be bound up in this room. Peter – ' her voice became urgent and she clutched at his hand now – 'I feel so guilty. If it wasn't for me you'd still be happy here. This is your place – this house, this village . . .'

'Be quiet.'

'No, I can't.'

'You just will. Look – ' he held her face between his hands – 'let me tell you something. I've just realised these past few days that I've never felt alive before; I was easygoing, even lazy, I was neither happy nor sad. I just wasn't alive, not aware of living, not really.'

As his eyes moved lovingly over her face she said, 'You can talk but I know.' Then she asked, with an eagerness she tried to hide but which did not escape him, 'When do we go, Peter?'

'As soon as I sign that paper.' He rubbed his knuckles gently up and down her cheek.

'Your mother cannot forgive me, she never will.'

'Yes, she will. I know her. She'll come round. She's working that way now.'

Leo shook her head, then said, 'I wouldn't in her place. Where are we going, Peter?' After she had asked this question she gave a little laugh and added, 'See? I don't know where I'm going anymore.'

With a swift movement he slipped his arm under her shoulders and, drawing her up to him again, he said softly, 'That's how things should be, I'll be driving from now on. And I can tell you you'll be safer in our old Austin than ever you were in the Alvis. We'll find a little place somewhere, a cottage or a flat, and I'll start the business of getting you better.'

'Oh, Peter – ' her face took on a look of pain – 'don't hope like that, it'll make things harder. I used to, then I had to – '

He brought one hand to her mouth and placed his fingers gently over it, and smiling down at her, he said with such firmness that he almost believed it himself. 'You'll get better, or your name won't be Mrs Puddleton. Aw there, don't – don't cry. Leo, darling, don't.'

As he dried her eyes, Rosie's voice came from the bottom of the stairs, startling them. 'This supper'll be stone cold.' They looked at each other understandingly, and he whispered, 'Smile . . . come on. Just another day or so and then. . . .'

And when she smiled and kissed his fingers with her wet lips he had to leave her swiftly in case the pain of his love should overwhelm him and he should join his tears to hers.

There was silence at the supper-table when he sat down, and he did nothing to break it. But after some moments Harry spoke, and his question brought all eyes in his direction.

'How're you having your money?' he asked. 'Cash, or in a bank?'

His fork half-way to his mouth, Peter said, 'Cash. Why do you ask?'

'Nothin'. Nothin' . . . I just wondered.'

'Why?' asked Peter again, his fork still poised.

'Now can't I just ask a question?'

'Funny one to ask, strikes me.' Peter bolted his mouthful of food.

'Well, I could say it's funny you having cash, couldn't I?'

'No. Because I don't know where I'm going to settle, I

may want ready cash at any time. But when I know where I'm going to stay I'll open an account.'

In deference to Rosie's feeling he kept to the 'I', omitting the more personal 'we'.

'Lot of money to be carrying around with you,' said Old Pop quietly.

So that was it, they wanted to hang on to his money for him. Rosie's knife clattered to the plate as she cried, 'He's not a child! If he can't look after his own money now he never will.'

'That's right. You're right there, he's not a child.' This stressed agreement coming from her husband took the strong wind out of her sails and left her more puzzled than ever. She was about to resume her supper when Harry, chewing on a piece of sirloin, looked up at her and asked, in a still, quiet, even conversational tone, 'And what are you doing with your share, lass?'

Rosie's chair scraped backwards. So this really was it, she hadn't been mistaken. If they couldn't get his they'd go all out to get hers. So nodding her head at her husband, she cried, 'I'm putting it into the new War savings, the minute I get it. Get that!' Her indignant gaze swept the three men. And when they all, in quite a docile manner looked at her and nodded agreement she felt completely stumped. But when Harry added, 'Good for you, lass,' the situation went beyond her powers of understanding, and she rose from the table and flounced into the scullery, and Peter, glancing at his father tucking heartily into his supper with apparent renewed appetite, thought, 'She's right after all, they are up to something.'

CHAPTER ELEVEN

Grandpop was feeling sad, so sad that he hadn't the list to bellow at the twins and Tony for dashing out and leaving the front gate open. And there it was, swinging wide now, a challenge to all the village dogs looking for pastures new. There'd be pluddy hell to pay when Rosie came back and found any of her flowers trampled. At any other time he would have thought gleefully, 'Let she get on with it'; but today he would, if he could, have so arranged life that Rosie would find no cause for any complaint, at least through him or the delinquency of dogs, for just about this minute she was, he surmised, in Hexham signing away the garage.

Slowly Grandpop turned his eyes up the street. From to-day onwards, he felt, all interest in the street would be gone – he wouldn't want to look at the garage anymore. And yet . . . and yet, if things turned out as they should, perhaps he could sit here and get the laugh of his life. But still, Peter wouldn't be there. His things were all packed up, and hers, too. The morrow they'd both be gone. He'd miss the lad mightily . . . and she. Now why in the name of fortune couldn't things have worked out sensible like, and she could have stayed here. Lay on the couch by the window, she could, and what she couldn't see he would have told her about. And some laughs they'd have had and no mistake, for she had a bright spirit . . . aye, she had. She might be ill, but she wouldn't say die until they shut the lid on her, that 'un. Look at her this mornin' as she had sat just there. Gay she was. That was when Rosie wasn't nigh – she'd made very little headway with Rosie and she knew it, aye, she did. She was sharp. Well, not sharp but wise. Aye, she was wise for her years. Reminded him of someone. His mind started groping. Now who did she remind him of?

'Grandad.'

At the sound of her voice he turned quickly towards the door and automatically adjusted his cap to an angle. 'Hello, lass. I was just this minute thinkin' on you. Come an' sit down, me dear.'

Leo came a step into the room, but said, 'Not now, Grandad, if you don't mind, but when I come back I'd like to. I've got a feeling I'd like to see the lake once more and see if the eel has gone.'

'Oh, she'd be gone after Saturda' . . . all that watter.'

'Yes, perhaps, but it'll be a little walk and it's such a lovely day. I won't be long, Grandad.' She spoke his name gently and her eyes smiled at him.

'Wish I could come along of you, lass.' He returned her smile, wistfully, and the flesh on his cheeks fell into folds. 'Take it easy, mind, and don't be gone ower long. They'll be back soon and that scarecrow of a Peter'll be sayin', "Where she be?"' He cackled softly and knowingly, and now she smiled at him almost lovingly and her eyes lingered on him before she said, 'I'll be back before they are. Bye, bye, Grandad.'

'Bye, bye, lass.'

As he watched her go out her yellow hair seemed to take the light from the room, and when she was half-way down the path something prompted him to call to her.

When she came back to the window, he said, as quietly as his voice would allow, 'Don't go through village, lass, go up street by cut, side of baker's shop. You know –' he nodded at her cautiously – 'best keep clear of 'em, eh?'

She nodded soberly and somewhat sadly back at him as she repeated, 'Yes, best keep clear of them.'

When she had gone through the gate he waved to her, and she answered it with a small salute of her hand that left him with an added sadness, and jerking his cap to the other side of his head, he exclaimed, 'Blast? Damn and blast the pluddy lot of 'em!'

Now that she had gone there seemed to be nothing for him to do but stare, so settling himself in his chair he prepared to doze . . . just a nod, not real asleep. He never slept any place other than in bed, at least so he believed.

It seemed to him only some seconds later, but was actually fifteen minutes, when the sound of the gate being banged back and almost off its hinges brought him out of a deep sleep and upright in his chair, and through his bleared eyes and with fuddled mind he saw the twins galloping up the path and round the side of the house. And before he could collect himself and let forth a bellow they were in the room yelling, 'Grandpop! Grandpop!'

'Name of God! What is it? Shut up yer screamin'. Here! here! You'll have me on the floor.' He thrust away their hands.

'Grandpop.'

'What is it, I say?' He took as firm a hold of Johnny's shoulders as his rheumaticky hands would allow. 'Stop gibbering an' tell us.'

'You tell him.' Johnny turned to his brother, and Jimmy, swallowing and spluttering, gabbled, 'We was playing round back of Institute, spot the tiger with Tony and young Betty and Clara, an' it was our turn for tiger an' we got into the lav at the back. And then the women came round and we couldn't get out cos they would have clouted us, an' they started talking, Miss Collins and Miss Florrie. . . .'

Jimmy paused for breath and Johnny put in, 'Mrs Booth was there an' all. An' Mavis, cos she'd been to the doctor's and she said she'd got nervis bility and was put off for a week.'

'Aye, she did.' Jimmy took up the tale again. 'But it was Mrs Booth what first said "Duck her", and she had seen her going across the fields to the lake, and she called her brazen, Grandpop, and said she was wicked. She's not, is she, Grandpop?'

Grandpop's hands came off the boy's shoulder and on to the arm of his chair and he asked quietly, although he knew the answer, 'Duck who?'

'Miss. Our Peter's miss.'

'Where are they . . . the women?' Grandpop had pulled himself to his feet with the help of his stick.

'They went back in the Hall, cos Miss Florrie said the

more that was in the better, an' Mrs Armstrong would be with them. An' Mavis said, "What if she swims away?" an' Mrs Booth said she couldn't swim, she had told Mr Booth she couldn't. And Mrs Booth said three times under would give her a good chance to try and she'd think twice about staying here. They think she's staying, Grandpop. An' Miss Collins said they should tie her hands.'

'God Almighty!' The old man looked wildly around the room, then his gaze came back to the two youngsters who were looking to him for guidance, and he barked, 'Why the hell didn't you go straight to garage for Old Pop?'

'We did, Grandpop, but he weren't there, an' 'twas shut up.'

'Weren't there? Did you look round back?'

'Aye, an' we couldn't see him nowhere.'

The old man looked down at the legs that would carry him, and then only with great willpower, as far as the lavatory and back, and lifting one foot slightly he attempted to shake it. When it responded with no more than the merest wag he thumped his stick on the floor, then drawing in his mouth until his nose almost touched his chin, he demanded, 'Could you knock down bottom palins?'

'Garden palins, Grandpop?'

'Aye, that's what I said, garden palins.'

Blinking bewilderedly together, they said, 'Aye, Grandpop.'

'All right, go on then . . . But listen –' he stopped their rush to the door – 'once they're down, you Johnny, double back to garage and find Joe. Tell him to come back of lake where elm tree is, he knows the place. Come on, then.'

'You comin', Grandpop?' They halted.

'Course I'm comin'. What you gonna knock palins down for? Use yer napper.'

They blinked at him again, then dashed ahead, through the kitchen and scullery and down the garden, to do a job they'd always longed to do, for you could go almost in a straight line from the bottom of the garden to the wood.

Fencing that has stood for forty years and whose posts have rotted in the ground doesn't take a lot of knocking down, but as the railings were wired together it required the uprooting of quite a number before they could be pushed flat enough on the nettles and brambles in the field beyond to allow Grandpop to slither over them.

With burning impatience he had stood watching what was to him their fumbling and slow progress, and when, finally he was in the field beyond, to his own amazement he found that his legs were moving, if not as they once did, at least as good as they had done two years ago. And with Jimmy darting in front of him to clear the obstructions he made the outskirts of the wood within a few minutes of leaving the garden. But once under the shelter of the trees he stopped, and supporting himself against a broad trunk he took his breath, for he was both gasping and shaking.

After a moment or so he dropped his head to one side in an attitude of listening, and Jimmy said, 'Can you hear owt, Grandpop?'

The old man shook his head.

'Perhaps they'll have their meetin' first?'

Again Grandpop shook his head. 'There'll be no meetin' the day, lad.'

Jimmy stared up at his great-grandfather. Somehow he seemed to have changed; he didn't look old here, like he did when he was in the chair.

It was odd, but at this moment Grandpop did not feel as old as when he was in his chair, for in his mind he had skipped back over seventy years to the time when he had scrambled through this very wood on much the same errand as he was on now. Love had been in his heart that day and curses on his lips, and it was much the same today. On that bygone day he had first called women 'pluddy buggers and bitches', and today they still merited the names.

Although it was now some years since he had been in the wood, he knew, as well as he did his own house, every inch of it. He knew where the best courting bowers were; what had once been the best rabbit runs; the badger sets and the short cut to Top Fell Dyke.

It was of this now that he spoke to Jimmy: 'If we can't see miss afore we get to lake we are going round t'other side, and when we find her you take the road till you come to Top Fell Dyke.'

'But she'll be in the clearing, Grandpop.'

'Well, if she is, all to the good, but it's no use us makin' for there. Once that lot get their eyes on her we couldn't be all that use . . . summat would happen. They'll have to do summat to her to get her out of their systems for she's made of the same stuff as Connie . . . knew she minded me of somebody.'

Jimmy looked puzzled and asked, 'Connie, who, Grandpop?'

And the old man, wiping the question away with a flick of his hand, said, 'It's no matter. What we've got to do is to get her across to t'other side, if she's in clearing.'

Jimmy pulled a brier from the old man's path and let it swing back behind him, then asked, 'But how'll we get her across, Grandpop?'

'Cross treetrunk.'

'Tree trunk?'

'Aye.'

'But you can't get down to tree trunk, Grandpop, it's all tangle in there.'

'We'll get through . . . you'll get through.' Grandpop looked significantly down on Jimmy. 'Badgers still got their run down there?'

'Aye, Grandpop.'

'Then where badgers can go, you can go, eh?' He smiled down at the boy, and Jimmy, without much conviction, said, 'Aye, Grandpop.'

'That's the lad. Move that bit wood.'

Jimmy moved the rotting branch and Grandpop, slithering on again, said, not without pride, 'Legs doing fine, eh?' Then stopping, he raised his hand with a warning gesture. And as Jimmy listened there came to him the faint crackle of feet on undergrowth and he glanced up apprehensively at the old man.

'Come on.'

Not only to Jimmy's, but to Grandpop's further astonishment, his legs began to move faster, with his feet actually clearing the ground, and when Jimmy exclaimed in admiration, 'Grandpop, your legs are going,' his only comment was, 'An' it'll take 'em.'

They were now on the narrow bramble-strewn path that ran round the far side of the lake opposite the clearing, and after traversing some way, with his eyes darting upwards at every step or so, Grandpop pointed to a tall tree whose top was bare of branches and which was kept upright only by the support of the other trees around it and exclaimed, 'That beech tree. It's hereabouts.' He now thrust his stick about on the ground, until it came into contact with a covered stump of a tree. 'There!' he exclaimed 'See that?' He pulled Jimmy to him, and tapping the root with his stick he whispered, 'Right opposite here is where oak's fallen cross pond. Go down one of the runs, but keep to the right – your right hand, see?' He tapped the boy's arm, 'If you don't you'll come high up on the bank, away from tree. When you're through, whistle her softly and wave her over – like this.' He gave a demonstration of silent beckoning. 'But don't shout or they'll hear you.'

Jimmy was far from clear in his mind about what he had to do and he looked his bewilderment and said, 'But what if she won't come, Grandpop?'

'Get along the trunk then and swim over to her. You can swim, can't you? Yell her I'm here. And don't make more noise than you can help. Oh, God Almighty!' The old man's eyes flashed angrily. 'I wish I was young again, I'd be through there. . . .'

'All right, Grandpop, I'll go.' The boy got down on his hands and knees to the questionable comfort of Grandpop's words as he said, 'Go on, push. Don't be feared of a few scratches and bit blood.'

Necessity aiding his wits, Jimmy found that if he lay flat and wriggled on his belly instead of crawling he not only made progress but evaded the brambles. Then, with so much relief that he almost shouted aloud, he found himself within a few seconds clear of the undergrowth and its gloom and forced momentarily to close his eyes against the glare of the sun on the water. He hadn't thought of Grandpop's instructions to keep to the right, but not two yards away was the great upended root of the oak tree, so big that he couldn't see over it. But across its trunk which followed a steep grade down towards the middle of the lake he saw on the other side, standing at the very edge of the clearing the miss, but with her back to the water. . . .

Leo had her eyes riveted on the opening from where, at any minute, one after the other, the women would emerge, and then. . . . The sweat broke out all over her body and she knew fear as she had never done before. That she was dying she knew; there was no doubt about it in her mind. After the first terrifying and sickening shock of this knowledge she had been more upset at its effect on the man with whom she was living than by the fact that at most she could hope for only another few months of life. As day had followed day she had, unconsciously by her attitude towards living, practised letting go of the reins so that at this time last week she would not have cared if the end had been a matter of minutes away. Yet even then she would, she knew, have been afraid of an end precipitated by mad women, and she felt, and truly, that the women behind that screen of undergrowth were, for the moment, mad.

Not five minutes ago she had been sitting on the bank here, praying in her own fashion, giving thanks for the gift and the solace of Peter's love, and her thoughts had been threaded with a wisdom that did not owe itself entirely to experience and which told her she was glad that this love would only live long enough to keep its vitality and freshness, with its essence of giving always to the fore. Nothing, she determined, would mar the numbered days of their life together, and with an eagerness to be gone and start that life she had risen from the bank, and after bidding a voiceless, sentimental farewell by kissing her fingers to the lake and to the eel that could, or could not, still be there, she had gone through the opening, to be brought to an abrupt halt at its farther end.

In front of her, through the boles of the trees and half hidden by an outstretched branch, she had seen a figure standing, not that of a man, although it was in breeches . . .

it was the girl from the Manor. And as she watched she saw her move slowly forward. It was something in the way she walked that had made her turn swiftly, and there, where the path turned into the broad walk, stood Mrs Booth and at her side the vicar's sister. It was the linking of Mrs Booth's eyes with her own that struck instant terror into her, and she had turned swiftly about to make her retreat by the path to the right, only to find standing there more women, three of them. She didn't know them, but one thing she recognised, they had on their faces a reflection of the look in Mrs Booth's eyes, but only a reflection, for if ever she had seen insane hate she had seen it on Mrs Booth's face.

For a moment she had thought, 'Don't panic. Don't run. What can they do? Nothing . . . they daren't do anything. This is . . .' And she had been about to give herself the comfort of this day and age when Mrs Booth moved, just a step, and to her step the others added theirs. She'd had the desire to cry out to them then, to ask them why, why were they acting like it, even to plead with them. But her common sense had told her that talking would be worse than useless; Mrs Booth would act first and talk afterwards because she loathed and hated her.

In undisguised panic she had backed into the clearing again until she came to the edge of the bank, and there she stood, all her small strength draining away from her. She had glanced back once at the lake. Even if she had been able to swim she knew her strength would never have carried her across to the other side. And now it came to her that a casual remark to Mr Booth, in his wife's hearing, that she had never been able to swim had set the seal fixing her death warrant. It was also enabling Mrs Booth to practise the art of suspense.

With her eyes stark wide and her teeth digging into her lip she stood and waited, feeling them every moment moving slowly nearer. As her mind screamed, 'Peter! Oh Peter!' she heard a 'Psst! Psst!' and the low whistle that followed it brought her stiffened head round. She knew that whistle. And when her eyes alighted on Jimmy astraddle the fallen tree, she turned swiftly and waved frantically to him. Then dropping her arms helplessly to her sides she asked herself, what could he do? She could shout to him, she could scream to him and he could run for help. But wouldn't he think it was a game she was having? And if she shouted, 'They're going to kill me,' he would think she had gone mad – her mind used Jimmy's own words for such an occasion, 'up the pole.' And who wouldn't think but that she was up the pole should she shout any such thing – this wasn't the Middle Ages, this was nineteen fifty-nine and people were civilised. They didn't do things like this – it wouldn't be till after she was dead that people would know that they still could and did do things like this. . . . Then through her terrified mind it dawned on her that Jimmy was aware of her plight, for he was alternately thumbing the water and beckoning her with wide sweeps of his arm towards himself and the tree.

The tree lay to her right and, it seemed to her petrified gaze, miles away. She had no idea of how deep the water was a few feet away from the bank. She would likely drown if it became so deep that she could not walk through it. But of the choice that lay before her she thought it better now to drown in an attempt to get away than to be mauled about by them, for that would result in death anyway.

She slipped her feet out of her sandals and grabbed them up, then sitting gingerly on the edge of the bank she slid down into the water. It felt cool, almost cold, as it gently embraced her knees, and she shivered but mostly with her fear. And it was fear which thrust her out from the bank and into the water which reached well up to her thighs. As she moved towards the tree her feet began to sink into the soft ooze and drag her steps. But each step took her away from the clearing, and soon she was past it and there was nothing to her right but a high green wall of undergrowth.

Her heart was beating so fast that she thought it might stop. She was gasping and felt she was going to be sick at any moment. Dragging her eyes from the water she looked towards Jimmy. He seemed much nearer now and he was beckoning her with another wide sweep of his arm which spoke of haste. In her fear of getting out of her depth she moved parallel with the bank, and when she was almost opposite the fallen tree the water had receded from her hips to her knees again. But this was no relief, for in order to reach the tree and Jimmy she would have to move now in a straight line towards the middle of the lake, and this spoke to her, not of safety, but of deep water.

'Come on! Come on, Miss!' It was a hissing whisper from Jimmy, and she nodded to him. Then testing each step for foothold, she moved tentatively towards him. But she had not gone more than a yard or so before she realised that the particular fear of deeper water near the middle was well-founded, for already it was round her waist and rising with each move forward. Her dress was floating like a ballet skirt about her; moreover her feet were stumping against submerged branches that threatened to trip her. Then for a space she suddenly rose out of the water as her feet touched a silted bank, damned likely by trees and mud. Praying that this would hold until she reached the tree she edged her way forward once more. And then, not six feet from the first broken, bleached, outstretched branch of the oak, she felt the bottom going rapidly downwards again, and in a few steps the water had risen to her breasts. Her arms outspread on the surface like stiff wings, she became so rigid with her fear that she could move no farther.

'Come on!'

'I - I can't. Ji - Jimmy.'

'You've got to . . . come on.' Jimmy hitched himself towards a fork in the head of the tree. He was high above her now, almost looking down on her. 'Aw, come on, miss. It's just a little way.'

When he saw her gulp and shake her head he bit on his lip, and his face crumpled as if he might cry.

'Aw, come on. Grandpop's waitin' for you. He's up the bank.'

There was the sound of tears in his voice, and this caused her to put out a foot but when she did so and it found nothing she hastily withdrew it. Again she tried to the other side. And when the same thing happened her breathing almost stopped.

Jimmy, seeing the fear on her face and knowing she wasn't going to make it, said helplessly, 'Aw, miss . . . miss.'

She looked up at him and cried softly between gasps, 'Jimmy – I'm – I'm going back. I'll stay under the bank. Go – go and get Peter.'

'Aw, miss.' He could think of nothing else to say, and as Leo, her eyes tight on the water once more and her arms swivelling to help her to turn, took the first step on her return journey there came a churning of the calm water, and the eel, like submerged lightning, flashed round her, catching her with its tail end as if she had been lassoed. The combination of her struggles and its swift, coiling movements flung her face forward, and whether it was the effect of her terror or the jerk that the eel had given her she found herself with her head above water once more, her feet on a submerged branch and her hands upstretched grasping at another branch just beneath Jimmy's knee.

'Eeh! miss. Oh, miss! Eeh! I thought . . . Oh, come on.' He was pulling at her.

Spitting out the water, she gasped, 'All right – I'm all right. . . . Wait.' She rested a moment, then working her feet along the branch she gradually drew herself out and on to the trunk.

Jimmy now backing swiftly away encouraged, 'That's it, miss. Come on. Come on.' And, like someone hypnotised, she dragged herself along the trunk towards the root.

As Jimmy went to climb down through the roots, he stopped and exclaimed, 'Don't turn round, miss. They've seen you, miss. They're all standin' watchin' . . . Eeh! no they're not, they're goin'. Come on, hurry.'

Spent and gasping for her breath, Leo lay flat on the trunk. 'I can't hurry, Jimmy, I can't. You go on – and – and get Peter.'

After a moment during which he stood and watched her apprehensively she slid down through the roots and sitting with her back against them murmured, 'I – I must rest, Jimmy.'

'But Grandpop's waitin' for us . . . just here, miss.' He pointed up the bank to the bushes.

'Grandpop? Here? You mean – Old Pop?' She raised her drooping head.

'No, miss, Grandpop.'

'Grandpop?' she said again. 'Grandpop?'

'Yes, miss.'

Her heavy lids stretched; she made an incredulous gesture with her hand; then with an effort she turned on her knees and rose to her feet, and looking at the seemingly impregnable wall of undergrowth she asked, 'How – how do we get out?'

'We've got to crawl, miss. But it's only a little way. If you do it on your bell – stomach, it's easy. Up the badger set.'

'Show me.'

She bit on her lip as she followed him in her bare feet over the thorn and bramble strewn bank, and then she lay down behind him and slowly dragged herself the few yards to the top and Grandpop.

When her head appeared almost at his feet Grandpop bent down and clutched at her, pulling her to her feet, muttering in a broken voice, 'Aw! lass. Aw! me dear. Aw! me dear. Aw! the sight of you. . . . For this to happen.' Then in a growl he cried, 'I'll have 'em jailed, so help me, God, every pluddy one of 'em! So help me God, I will!'

'Oh! Grandad.' Leo was leaning within the shelter of his trembling arms and gasping with each breath. 'I'm frightened . . . so . . . so . . .'

'There now.' He patted her shoulder. 'Don't you be frightened of nowt, just do as I say. Go with the lad here. He knows the way to Top Fell Dyke; there's only one road there from this end and it's along this path. Go on now. Aw, your poor feet . . . bleeding.' He looked down at her feet, and she said, 'They're all right. But you – what about you?'

'You leave this to me. Go on now, as quick as you can, lass, and by the time you get there Joe'll be along. Blast him, he should be here now. Never could be where he's wanted, that lad.'

'Listen!' She held her head to one side. 'They're coming. I can hear them.' She looked anxiously up at the old man, and he said calmly, 'Aye, I know. Go on, now.' He turned to Jimmy. 'Go on . . . quick! And when you get clear of the path there's no need to hurry. If those bitches of hell get by me there's three lanes beyond and they won't know which one you've gone, even if they get that far, which they pluddy well won't. Away now.'

Gently he pushed her from him, and Jimmy, holding out his hand, took hers and led her away.

They weren't out of Grandpop's sight before he turned and, moving with doddering steps in the opposite direction, went along the path to where it narrowed and bent sharply at the head of the lake. Here he quickly selected a patch of earth which was bordered by a couple of stakes, remnants of a fence which had once guarded the high and dangerous bank above the lake at this point, and lowering himself very, very cautiously down, he took up his position with his back to the stakes, his legs across the path and his stick firmly gripped in his hand.

Their approach was not heralded by their voices, but by their feet which sounded to him like the pounding of horses' hooves. They came upon him all in a bunch, Mrs Booth and Miss Collins pulling up so rapidly that Mavis and Mrs Fountain were almost knocked backwards.

Miss Collins let out a stifled squeal, for she couldn't believe what she was seeing: Grandfather Puddleton, who couldn't walk more than a few yards, here in the woods! And Mrs Booth's mouth was wider than it had ever been without anything coming out of it. Then snapping it closed, she exclaimed, 'Good God!'

'Aye, good God. And you keep the Almighty's name out of your dirty mouth, Katie Booth, until you're in court and asked to say, "I speak the truth and nowt but, so help me God". And you'll need help, let me tell you, you pluddy mischief-making bitch!'

The taunt lessened somewhat the shock Mrs Booth had received, and she cried, 'What are you up to here? And you be careful what you say. Get up out of that.'

'Can't,' said Grandpop flatly; 'legs is give way.'

'Then move yourself round.'

Mrs Booth was the only one so far who had spoken, for the sight of Grandpop and his implied threat of the police court had, it would seem, returned the others some way to normality. Even Miss Collins backed away a step.

'If you don't move I'll get over you.'

'You try. Just you try it on, you big slobbery bitch. An' you see this stick here?' He brandished the stick up at her, then with not a little glee, he watched her evident wilting and listened to the horrified gasps of her companions as he went into minute details of what explorations he would put his stick to should she attempt her threat.

'You filthy old swine you! You should be locked up.'

'Aye, that's a matter of opinion, Katie Booth. You should have been locked up years gone for what you was up to.' Grandpop brought his back from the staves and raised his chin to her. 'And now tryin' to kill a bit lass cos she has the men about her like flies without raisin' a finger. You've had to do more than raise a finger an' not get as far as she', hevn't you? Go on, you as much as lay a finger on me and I'll crack those big, fat, ugly shanks of yours.' He flourished his stick wildly at her, then cried, 'And you there, 'Melia Fountain, shame on you for being in this. Shame on you! And with her – this village whore here – and she after your man. Aye, aye, you was . . . !' Now he had to brandish his stick wildly to keep Mrs Booth at bay. 'Waylaid him you did, at every turn. Couldn't get rid of you, Bill couldn't. And then you started on Harry. Come on, come on,' he challenged her, as she heaved like some great animal over him. Then flashing his attention to where Mrs Armstrong was trying to hide herself behind Miss Collins, he said, 'And if your man was alive the day Celia Armstrong, he'd tell you a thing or two, an' all. Ask her about the notes she used to leave in orange box near door. Had him petrified, she had, lest you picked 'em up.'

Grandpop suddenly paused for breath and also because his heart was giving him warning. Much more of this, he told himself, and it would be the finish; he'd better steady up. He leant back against the posts again, but as he did so he kept his steely gaze fixed on the purple, suffused face of Mrs Booth, daring her to make a move nearer.

'You! you!' she brought out at last, 'I'll have you up. It's a libel. You dirty . . . you!'

'Aye.' It was a short, sardonical reply which conveyed volumes, and it added to her rage which was so great as to be temporarily suppressing her powers of invective.

Two feet at the back of the group quietly turning round drew Grandpop's eyes to the assortment of legs and to the polished riding boots, and he exclaimed in a voice full of scorn, 'Aye, go off quietly, Miss Florrie, it'll be you what has to face the major. And as long as I'm alive don't look my way agen. Hear that? Nor put a step inside me door. And the rest of you'd better get along with her. And as for you, Miss Collins – ' he paused – 'I told you years ago when you came here you'd better settle in your mind to stick to God, being a little too long in the tooth to harness any lad hereabouts, and place running wild with young heifers at the time. But you wouldn't listen, an' you've gone sour on yersel. Aye, you can rear your skinny neck, but I'd call in me church and go down on me knees if I was you. So I would!'

There was a great tiredness on him now and his words were coming slower, and it was with relief that he saw them, without parting shots of any sort, turn one after the other and glide cautiously away as if afraid now of the sound of their own footsteps. All, that was, except Mrs Booth, and she remained, glaring at him as if she would jump on him and tear his flesh apart.

Grandpop was finding that he hadn't even the strength to outstare her when he heard Joe demanding, 'What's up here?' And never had his son's voice sounded sweet to him before. 'What you up to, Katie Booth, you knocked him down?'

Mrs Booth turned her bloodshot eyes on Old Pop, and her spluttering was near idiot jabbering as she cried, 'Kno – knocked him down! He should be dead . . . dead and buried alive, and you along of him . . . all of you, all the Puddletons, all of you. The – the dirty old swine! The – !' Her lips white with froth, she spluttered in his face. Then like someone drunk she turned and went running along the path, mouthing her venom aloud.

After turning his astonished gaze from the departing figure, Joe exclaimed, 'God Almighty, save us! How you got here?' He looked down on his father straddled across the path, and Grandpop, looking scornfully up at him and with only a little punch left in his voice, gruntled, 'Don't ask pluddy silly questions, I didn't fly. Where you bin? Never about when you're wanted. Same all your life. Here, give me a hand up.'

With some effort on both sides Grandpop was on his feet again, but it was evident, even to himself, that he wasn't the man he had been before he sat down. That do with Katie Booth had took it out of him and no mistake. His legs were like jelly and he was trembling all over, even his voice now. But in spite of this, it still held a ring of authority, and he commanded, 'Come on, let's get movin'. If I don't soon have a drop of hard I'm for it.'

'Where're you going?' asked Joe, as his father turned and moved slowly along the path. 'That ain't the way.'

'I'm going to Dyke. . . . Lass is there.'

'You'll never get to Dyke.'

'Who won't? Got here afore you, didn't I? Lass is near mad. That lot near done for her.'

'They really meant it then?' Old Pop's eyebrows were reaching for his scalp.

'Meant it?' Grandpop turned on his son. 'You stone blind as well as daft? You saw 'em all, and Katie Booth like a witch.'

'Aye. But she always looked like witch when you got at her. Your tongue were never easy on her. But I can't take it in; 'tain't feasible. Johnny says they were gonna duck miss . . . fact?'

'Fact!' Grandpop's voice was withering. 'Why d'you think I'm this far from me chair? Looking for fairies in me dotage? Aw, come on, you helpin' me or is it me helpin' you? Give me yer shoulder.' Slowly, and in silence now, they made their way to where the three paths met.

209

CHAPTER TWELVE

'I'll kill her if I get me hands on her, I'll kill her!'

Peter, holding the sodden body of Leo to him, looked wildly from one member of his family to another as they all stood in a group on the road bordering the dyke. Then lifting Leo's face up to his he begged, 'Are you all right?'

She did not speak but nodded her head.

'We'll get you home and to bed, then – '

'No – no.' To his astonishment she dragged herself from his hold and backed from him. She backed from them all as she cried, 'I'm not going back there – ever – I can't!'

'But, Leo. . . .'

'It's no use – I can't set foot in that village again.'

'But, lass, you're soaked, and you'll catch your death.' It was Rosie speaking, a changed Rosie, for the weird incident had both shocked her and frightened her. In a flash of insight she had seen herself as one of Katie Booth's followers if not in flesh in spirit, and she turned in fear from the picture. And now it was a genuine pity that was filling her, and she said again, 'A day or two in bed, lass – '

'No.' Leo shook her head emphatically and Peter, stepping to her side, said soothingly, 'It'll be as you say, dear. What do a few hours matter anyway. I'll go back and get our things and you can change in the car . . . all right?' He patted her cheek.

'Yes.' Her voice was scarcely audible.

'But you'll catch your death.' Rosie repeated her statement as much now to prolong the departure as because of her concern for the girl, but Harry, who had spoken very little up to now, said firmly, 'It's the best way. Get your things together, lad, and get off.'

Without another word Peter went to the car, and with his

foot hard down on the accelerator he headed back to the village. It may have been just coincidence that the entire street was deserted – in fact, the whole place looked dead; perhaps it was as well that he encountered no one, for the anger in him would have burst over innocent and guilty alike.

It took him only a matter of minutes to gather their belongings up and bundle them into the car before he was once again roaring through the village towards Top Fell Dyke. As he came to a stop opposite the family seated on the grass verge as if on an outing, Grandpop's voice hailed him with, 'Think to bring a drop of hard with you, lad?'

Peter, getting out of the car, drew a flask from his pocket and handed it towards the old 'un, and Grandpop, his eyes sparkling at the sight of the whisky, said, 'Ah, lad, that's the ticket.' But when with trembling hands he filled the lid cup from the flask, he did not gulp it down but handed it to Leo, saying, 'Get that into you, lass.'

Leo hesitated until Peter urged quietly, 'Drink it up, it can't do you any harm.'

As Leo drank the spirit she shivered, and Rosie, as if there had been nothing between her and this girl but affection, said gently, 'That'll keep out the chill . . . come on and get those things off.' And then to the surprise of all the Puddleton men, even the twins, they watched her get into the back of the car and hold the door open for Leo to enter, at the same time shouting in an over-loud voice to Peter, 'I bet you didn't think to bring a towel!'

'I did; there's a couple on the front seat.' He opened the front door of the car and leaning over handed the towels to her to be greeted with, 'All right. Leave them there and get away for a minute. . . . And look, get that bottle off the old 'un, or we'll have a nice game getting him back home. Go on now.'

Rosie was speaking to him as if he were her bit of a lad again, and he knew the reason. Her shouting and bustling was only a way of covering up her embarrassment.

Grandpop no longer had the bottle. It was being passed now from Old Pop to Harry. And when Harry had had his pull he handed it to Peter, but Peter shook his head and stood for a moment voiceless among them, just looking at them. There they were, five of them, the Puddleton men, and as he looked from the youngest to the eldest an odd feeling flooded him. It was as akin to love as ever he had felt for them and he knew that he would miss them, each one of them, more than he cared to admit.

Harry, imbued with the same kind of feeling, put his hand on to his son's shoulder and said softly, 'Well, lad, this is it.' They looked steadily at each other for a moment before he went on. 'There'll be no chance to talk in a minute and I couldn't say this to you then, anyway. But I'd just like to say that when you are . . . alone again, come back, will you? This is your home, lad. This ground, these rocks and hills. And you won't be able to throw them off lightly no matter what you think. And what's more, in a short while folks will have forgotten anything ever happened, and if anybody talks about it later on, it'll just be like another fable, with a smattering of truth in it – or something to laugh at.'

Peter's face hardened immediately and his voice was stiff as he said, 'I'll never laugh at the day's business.'

'No, lad, no. I wasn't meaning that. You know what I mean. But you'll come back, won't you?'

After a long moment, during which he looked from one to the other and saw in their eyes an intensified reflection of the feeling he bore them, he said, slightly non-committal, 'I may do. But it won't be for years – not for years.' His voice was hard with emphasis as he repeated this.

'Aye. Yes, lad. Aye.' It was a chorus joined with shaking of heads. 'We know that. We understand that. But we'll see you . . . perhaps you'll settle not so far off.'

This last was from Old Pop, and Peter said, 'Perhaps. Anyway, I'll let you know.'

'Give us a hand up, one of you.' Grandpop held up his arms and they all went to his assistance. And when he was standing between Harry and Joe he put out his trembling hands to Peter, and, gripping his, said, 'She's a fine lass. Be happy, and later on you can remember the words – ' his voice was shaking and his eyes were full of the unusual

212

moisture of tears as he quoted brokenly – ' "And often glad
no more, we wear a face of joy because we have been glad
of yore".'

The whisky as usual had revived Wordsworth, and Peter
said softly, 'I'll remember, old 'un.'

They stood now, saying nothing but watching the twins
scampering in the hedge, then the car door clicked and Leo
stepped down into the road. The difference in her appearance
that a change of clothes and her hair rubbed near dry had
made brought the first touch of relief to Peter's face.

'That's better.' He touched her hair and said softly, 'You
look yourself again, like a million.'

Leo's smile was wan, and full of disbelief, and still a little
fearful.

Now came the goodbyes. Under ordinary circumstances
Peter hated the business of leave-taking and always avoided
it if possible, and now the urgency to make the break and
be gone caused him to bustle almost as much as Rosie.

'Well, we'd better get a move on,' he said to no one in
particular, 'no use hanging about.' He turned to the car and,
putting his head inside, fiddled with the ignition key. As he
did this Rosie's busy-busying ceased and he said, without
turning his head to look at her, 'All fixed, Mam?'

'Yes, I think so.' Her voice was quiet now and she slipped
out of the car and into the road.

Leo was standing surrounded by the three men and the
twins; the twins were holding on to one of her hands while
with the other she held Grandpop's; Old Pop was patting
her arm and Harry was saying, 'Well, don't forget us, lass.
And don't go too far away, now, will you?' He waited for a
reply, and when her lips moved without sound and she
swallowed, he said hastily, and thickly, 'There now, there
now. . . . Go on, there's that big goof of yours straining to
be off.'

Grandpop's gums were champing up and down, and when
she leant forward and kissed him he looked deep into her
eyes and muttered softly, 'Well meet up again, lass, you'll
see. I've a sort of feeling this isn't the end. God bless you.
Go on now.'

He pushed her as he had done earlier, and she turned away towards the car, and there she was face to face with Rosie – Rosie standing close to her son. It was a testy moment. Slowly she held out her hand and Rosie took it. Then to the further surprise of all the family they heard Rosie mutter, 'Always wanted a daughter.'

Leo gazed at the little dominant woman, then swiftly she bent her head towards her and pressed her lips to her cheek before turning blindly away and into the car.

Now Peter was shaking hands and receiving pats and advice from his elders. Lastly, as he knew it would be, he came to his mother. After a moment of eye holding eye he pulled her awkwardly into his arms and held her close and whispered, so that only she could hear, 'Thanks, Mam.'

'There.' Her voice was shaking and her eyes blind with unshed tears and she stepped back from him. 'Off you go the pair of you.'

When he was in his seat and the engine throbbing she put her head through the window past him and addressed Leo: 'Take care of yourself, lass,' she said, before adding diffidently, 'Perhaps I could come and see you when you settle.'

'Yes. Oh, yes.' Spontaneously Leo's hands went across Peter and touched hers.

'Get him to write.' Rosie nodded at her son. 'He's the world's worst letter-writer.'

'I will, I promise. And soon.'

'Goodbye, lad.'

'Goodbye, lass.'

'Goodbye, miss.'

'Goodbye, Peter . . . Bye.'

'Goodbye. Goodbye.'

The farewells were mixed and toppling over each other; then the car was away and Leo's voice, stronger than it had been yet, could be heard for the last time calling, 'Goodbye Grandad.'

'Goodbye, lass.' Grandpop spoke aloud to himself, for she could no longer hear him. He stood unsupported, the receding car lost in the blur of his eyes. 'Reckon we'll meet up on the road out. Aye, reckon we will, somehow.' His words were clear and firm and brought a quick exchange of glances between Harry and Joe.

The sound of suppressed crying turned them about to see Rosie, their hard-bitten Rosie, her back to them, standing at the side of the road crying her heart out, with the twins, silent and disturbed, one on each side of her.

'Aw, lass. Now, now, don't give way.' Going to her Harry put his arms about her shoulders and turned her towards him adding, 'It's a pity to say this and I wish it wasn't so, but you'll have him back afore long, aye afore very long. So come now.' Then giving a silly laugh, and his voice high, he said, 'You've still got me.' He paused now, and an odd look came over his face and he murmured under his breath, 'Perhaps you'll remember I'm here now, Rosie, eh?'

Rosie, slowly lifting her wet face up to her husband, looked at him, and he held her look, and even through her blurred vision she saw that something had gone from him. Was it the jealousy of their son? For a moment she forgot the presence of the others and a flicker of tenderness passed over her face. Then she turned from him, sniffing and saying, 'It's no use standing here, is it? We've got to get him back.'

'Him', in his wisdom, had called the twins to his side and was engaging their attention, as well as that of Joe, by describing graphically just what he was going to do and say to Katie Booth and the rest of them murdering bitches. He was going to the Hart the night, he was that, and he'd show 'em, every pluddy one of 'em.

'Come on, old 'un.' Harry approached his grandfather, and Rosie rubbing her face quickly with her handkerchief said, with some regret for what appeared like past splendour, 'No garage to send to now for a car, unless we hire one from them. Huh!'

The three men had turned as one and were surveying her, and Harry asked, tentatively, 'You so sorry, lass, that the garage has gone?'

Rosie's head wagged a little as she said, 'Well, if you want to know, I'm sorry that them lot's got it, as sorry as you are. And we'll be more sorry still yet, you mark me.'

'Tell her, lad.' Grandpop's eyes were twinkling, and he chuckled, 'Tell her.'

'In a minute. Here.' Harry called the twins to him and bending over them, said, 'Look, run back home and bring the barrow. We'll take Grandpop home in it.'

. There was a sort of minor explosion from the road. 'Push me in a barrer! No pluddy fear. No you won't, be God! . . . No, be God! I won't be ridden in no barrer.'

'Sh!' Harry laid a restraining hand on his grandfather's jerking and indignant shoulders and whispered, 'Got to get rid of 'em.'

'Ah. Ah, well, that's as may be, but send 'em for summat else, not barrer. No pluddy fear.'

Harry did not change his order but said, 'Go on now and hurry.' And the twins scampered off, glad to be sent on such a pleasant errand with the ultimate prospect of a laugh to see their Grandpop wheeled in a barrow.

'Now,' said Harry slowly nodding his head at Rosie, 'I've news for you.'

' 'Bout garage?'

' 'Bout garage.'

Rosie looked puzzled. The garage was sold, Peter'd had his share and she'd had hers, and Peter was gone with every penny in his pocket, for Harry had not tried to borrow a farthing from him. Yet, as she had felt since Sunday, there was something up. 'Well, let's hear it,' she said.

'How much d'you think you'd have got for it afore the road was going through?'

'Aye, how much?' added Old Pop.

'Eight, perhaps nine hundred. That's what Mackenzie said, but they'd skin a louse for its hide, them skinflints.'

'And how much did you get?'

'That's a silly question, you know what we got – fifteen hundred.'

'Aye.' Harry paused, and the old 'uns nodded. 'That was 'cos road was going through. But there was no mention of that in the deeds, was there? Old Mackenzie didn't make a hullaballoo about it and yell, 'I'm giving you fifteen hundred 'cos road's going through,' did he? No. He knew that when

216

road went through that piece of land and garage would be worth three times what he paid. He felt he was cute not to harp on about it and put it in writing.'

'So what?' said Rosie puzzled. 'Ain't road coming through?'

'Aye, it is. But not through Battenbun, it ain't.' There was a wave of glee connecting the faces of the three men.

'Not coming?' Rosie blinked. 'Not coming? Who said?' 'Major.'

'But 'twere major who said it were.'

'Aye. And he were right then, but apparently committee were divided all along. And then it were found that if they built the road running through Downfell Hurst they could build houses nearly all along its length but not if they built it through Battenbun. You know major, he wouldn't sell an inch and they were stumped. They could run the road by the side of his land but that's all they'd get out of him.'

'But – but won't they come back on us?' said Rosie, looking scared.

'Come back on us? What for?' asked Harry. 'The cat won't be out of the bag for near on two weeks, next committee. Major only told me because he saw I was in a bit of a state about the lad selling, and it was him, hisself mind, who said, "You sing dumb, Harry." He was tickled to death about the whole thing. You know what he thinks of the Mackenzies. And, of course, he's over the moon about the road not touching us. . . . Mackenzie's got a place for his lorries, and that's what he said he wanted, isn't it? But as for the garage, when the road goes through not a damn car will come this way at all. And now he can't do a thing about it, it's all been done in good faith. Them was Mackenzie's own words – good faith.'

'He won't make out our Peter's gone off on purpose and sue him?'

'Let him try.' Harry's face became grim. 'And anybody in the village who doesn't know what's happened the day will by the night, and their lass was one of them who tried it on. Peter took his future wife away because of this village's women's murderous attack on her. 'Twould make good

217

reading in the Sunday papers . . . let 'em start anything.'

Harry drew himself up, and after gazing up at him for a moment a smile spread over Rosie's face and she gave a little hick of a laugh.

'That's it, lass.' Harry slapped her on the back.

'Eh, what a shock!' Rosie's smile was broad now and Grandpop's and Old Pop's chuckles were deepening.

'She – she turned her nose up at me this morning, Winnie Mackenzie.' Rosie put her hand over her mouth to still a chuckle; then she laid her fingers on Harry's arm and tapped it twice saying, 'But it's good job lad's gone, he would have taken it back. The money and the garage.'

'Yes. Aye, that's what were worrying us, weren't it?' Harry looked at his father and grandfather, and nodded and slapped each other. Their laughter mounted, and to it was joined Rosie's. For the first time in her life she was laughing with the combined force of her menfolk, and this knowledge did not escape them and gave further rein to their mirth. Grandpop's sides were cracking with it, his body was rocking. Then one minute he was standing as firmly as any of them and the next he was on the road all of a heap.

'Blast 'em! Damn and blast the pluddy things!'

'Aw, old 'un, your legs?'

'Blast 'em!'

'They give way?'

'Blast . . . blast you!' Grandpop punched at his useless legs. Then glaring up at Harry he cried, 'I ain't goin' in that barrer. Hump me on your back, back through the woods. I ain't gonna be no laughing stock, not at my time, I ain't.'

'I couldn't carry you back all that way, old 'un,' said Harry. 'What d'you take me for – Samson?'

'Well, I ain't pluddy well goin' in barrer.'

'You are so, and here they come with it now. And thank God for it.'

Swearing and protesting loudly, Grandpop was hoisted into the barrow, and, supported on all sides by his family, set off down the road to the village. As they neared it Rosie, with her tongue in her cheek, remarked, 'You won't get to the Hart the night, old 'un, so I would have your say about

218